# *the* Tuscan Sister

BOOKS BY DANIELA SACERDOTI

*The Italian Villa*
*The Lost Village*
*The Italian Island*
*The Bookseller's Daughter*

GLEN AVICH QUARTET
*Watch Over Me*
*Take Me Home*
*Set Me Free*
*Don't Be Afraid*

SEAL ISLAND SERIES
*Keep Me Safe*
*I Will Find You*
*Come Back to Me*

# DANIELA SACERDOTI

## *the* *Tuscan Sister*

bookouture

Published by Bookouture in 2024

An imprint of Storyfire Ltd.
Carmelite House
50 Victoria Embankment
London EC4Y 0DZ

www.bookouture.com

ISBN: 978-1-83525-218-5
eBook ISBN: 978-1-83525-217-8

*For Davide*

# PROLOGUE

LUCREZIA

In all my years of exile I dreamed of Casalta, the villa nestled in the heart of Tuscany, where vineyards and olive groves stretched on the cypress-crested hills.

Casalta had been my haven, before the terrible events that turned my sweet home into a place of fear and loneliness, before I was banished at the age of twelve, like a little Eve out of Eden.

Casalta had nourished me and protected me since I first opened my eyes to the world. Here my mother watched over me, here I shared every moment with my twin, Bianca, and my younger sisters, Eleonora and Maria.

Bianca, Nora, Mia and me, Lulu: this was us, the four Falconeri sisters, the Casalta girls, known in the village as self-contained, aloof and a little uncanny, perhaps little magical...

Our mother had passed on to us the nameless gift that runs in her family, a gift that manifests differently in different generations and different women. Mine is that I can see people's emotions and inner thoughts as halos of colour around their bodies – some call them auras. Bianca can see and hear people long gone – memories and stories imprinted in the stones of our home. As for Nora and Mia, they were too small when I was exiled: their gifts are a mystery to me.

After my banishment, the only way I could go back to Casalta was in my daydreams, cold but indispensable comfort. I made my fantasy so vivid that I could smell each scent, taste each taste. It was more real than reality, and as warm as my mother's hug.

In my dream, I close my eyes and walk the winding dirt road from the village up the hill, the air full of the song of cicadas and of the scent of wild fennel and oregano.

The path is lined with fig trees, elders and hazelnut trees. Every once in a while I stop to eat a fig straight from the branch, examine the shed skin of a grass snake, crumbly and translucent under my fingers, or follow a *Vanessa atalanta*'s black wings fluttering among the flowers – my mother had taught me the names of our native butterflies: *licena, ninfa, icaro...* She loved butterflies, and they represented her perfectly, with their colours, their instinct to fly free. Their vulnerability.

I arrive on the terrace carved out of the hill almost a thousand years before, where Casalta was first built as a small stony fortress for warring peoples. Here, Bianca is waiting for me at the gate, between the two ivy-covered stone dryads that watch us from their pillars. They are like us, identical, specular images of each other. I used to pretend that they came alive at night to wander around the gardens and vineyards, and returned onto their pillars at the first light of dawn.

Bianca opens the gate for me and holds my hand as we make our way into the courtyard. We dip our fingers in the water of the fountain in the middle of it, a little ritual of ours, and slip through the kitchen door.

The kitchen was never cold, never empty. Something was always cooking on the stove or cooling on the marble slab of the table – tomato sauce for the winter, jars of jam, an enormous pot of bean stew or potatoes covered in herbs and olive oil, almond biscuits or bottles of our own wine. I follow Bianca through the living room with its open fireplace, and down the corridor lined with floor-to-ceiling windows. The corridor ended with my father's study: but we never went in there.

In my daydream, that part of the house didn't exist.

Instead, we open the glass door to the rose garden, and make our way to the bench where my mother used to sit and paint. Here I find Mia, sitting on that same bench with a sketchbook in hand, and Nora, playing outside in the sunshine as she always did. Both are frozen in time at seven and eight years old, like the day I last saw them, and they run to me, and hold me tight. Bianca joins our embrace and we're one again, the four Casalta girls. The Falconeri sisters, reunited.

After a while, I climb the stone stairs that lean on the side of the house, and watch my sisters from above – sweet Bianca, headstrong Nora, dreamy Mia, a red head and two brown ones close together to contemplate a rose – and slip through the window across the last step, into Bianca's bedroom. I twirl in the sunny garden painted on Bianca's wall, among the pink roses that decorate the window and the doorframe. Our mother had painted each of our rooms before we were born; she knew, somehow, that she was going to have four daughters, and *who* we were going to be, and she reflected her vision in her frescoes.

I peep into Nora's room, with its yellow roses and the fresco of a beach dotted with running horses, and then enter Mia's, the most spectacular of all. White roses around the windows and the door, and the rest of the space full of galaxies, stars, comets, constellations, in a symphony of blue, black, silver and all shades of purple and pink.

Finally, I step into my childhood room.

It was unfinished, because my mother had gone into labour with me and Bianca while she was still working on it. She'd decorated the walls with red roses, but that was it. She'd told me that she would complete it in years to come, with all the wonderful things I would see and do.

But we never had those years to come, because she died on the hills around our home just before my twelfth birthday, and my room remained unfinished.

My daydream always stopped there, when emotion over-whelmed me and I knew it was time to raise my inner walls again, against the memories, against the longing, against the anger. It was at that point that in my mind's eye, I'd fly out of Casalta, the childhood home I'd been exiled from too fast, too suddenly, to even have the time to say goodbye.

# CHAPTER 1

## PARIS, 12 APRIL 1985

LUCREZIA

I stood in front of the Galeries Lafayette beside a cameraman from Canal Société, holding my blazer, too warm for this beautiful spring morning.

Early spring had always been my favourite time in Paris. Scarves were loosened and coats unbuttoned, people stopped to chat in the streets and slow promenades were taken for pure pleasure again, to soak in the first sun. The city swam in that timid, pale gold light and buildings looked like the petals of new blooms. This city might have never felt like home to my wandering heart, but it was certainly exquisite.

Claude, both my employer and my partner, was ready to turn the bowls full of different ingredients lined in front of him into crepes with strawberries and crème Chantilly, as if by magic. The demonstration was going live in the most popular morning programme of the nation, *Bonjour Avec*, and millions of people would be tuning in. One of the presenters, a slim woman by the name of Amandine, was straightening her skirt, her trademark perma-smile ready to go.

'Ready in three minutes!' someone called out, and the small crowd that had formed in front of the stand swayed in anticipation.

Claude ran to me and tucked a strand of my auburn hair behind my ear. Small flashes of light from the cameras told me that this moment would be portrayed in gossip magazines. Claude belonged to that breed of celebrity chefs whose life seemed to be fascinating to the public, just as much as their cooking. He'd been known to have a new girl on his arm every time he was pictured, until I came on the scene, and then, the consensus was that he could have done better than this unsmiling woman who everyone knew wasn't French, but didn't seem to come from anywhere in particular. All I'd read in my favour – reading what was written about us was part of my job – was that I had a good sense for fashion. Apart from that, I was described as... *thorny*.

Which, to be fair, I was.

'All good, yes?' he whispered in my ear, so close that I could smell his lemon and vanilla cologne. His fair hair was ruffled in that faux-*I just got out of bed* way. And as always in his TV appearances, he wore what he called his civilian clothes, and not chef's attire. Cooking while dressed formally, in pressed shirt and suit trousers, was part of his image.

I was about to answer when something in the crowd caught my attention. Among the women, men and children, the strangers that filled my line of vision, an achingly familiar face made me freeze.

A head of flaming hair, brighter than mine, the curve of a long white neck, a graceful profile and the quick sway of a layered skirt, like a butterfly's wing.

*She can't be here. She's dead.*

But I knew that profile, I knew that body, I knew that *exact* shade of red.

I'd nestled my head against that neck, as a baby, and her hair had covered me and my twin while we slept leaning on her breasts. She was the milk we drank, the air we breathed. She was the arms we ran to when we fell and the last voice we heard before falling asleep.

My eyes and my heart screamed that my mother was there – but my mind couldn't quite believe it, and the dissonance made me feel cut off from space and time, existing in a dimension where space didn't matter and time didn't flow.

*Mum!*

The first word I'd ever learned to say, the sweetest word, was stuck in my throat, my lips unable to form it.

Fireworks exploded in my brain with contrasting messages: *run after her, stay, she's dead, she's right there, run to her!* The crowd moved like one body, melted, came apart again. The red-haired woman was nowhere to be seen.

I was about to take a step, to look for her, when someone held me back.

'Lucresiah?' Claude pronounced my name with the accent on the last syllable, the French way, and he now called me in a low voice, with that irritable edge I knew so well. What he meant was *we're on stage: perform.*

I brought a hand to my cheek, and I was surprised to feel it wet. I'd melted into tears without noticing.

I hadn't cried for a long, long time.

'We're about to go live, *Lucresiah.*' I could see a red halo around Claude – he was angry, even if his tone was calm and measured. Being able to see auras, like I could, was a gift and a curse. A gift, because it helped me to read people – a curse, because sometimes I learned things I didn't want to know.

'The light made my eyes water.' I summoned an excuse. Claude's face morphed from irked to TV-ready, and he beamed at the world as he returned to the table. The cameras were on – one minute – thirty seconds – count back from ten – and we were live.

My gaze wasn't on Claude's performance, but beyond, to the crowd, as I half hoped, half dreaded to see the red-haired woman again. I was rooted to the spot, my face composed, but my chest heaving – *thud, thud, thud*, went my heart, and with each beat more unshed tears swelled behind my eyes. The handbag at my side felt hot and heavy, pulsating with a life of its own: inside was a letter from Bianca, from Casalta, the first after a long time.

I didn't even know why I kept it in my handbag and carried it around with me, when I'd cut all contact with my family years before.

Claude's demonstration came to an end; voices rose to signal that the event was over. I brought a hand to my mouth; I was trembling so much that an assistant laid a hand on my arm, murmuring something about sitting down and getting me a glass of water.

It took all my willpower not to run into the crowd and scream her name, to look for her among all those strangers' faces.

This was the second time I thought I'd caught a glimpse of my mother.

The first was twelve years ago, not long after she died.

# CHAPTER 2

## CASALTA, TUSCANY, 12 APRIL 1973 – TWELVE YEARS EARLIER

LUCREZIA

Matilde, our housekeeper, was at the stove stirring a sauce, her apron tied in a bow at the small of her back, her wavy dark hair in a low ponytail. Beside her was my twin sister, Bianca, dutiful and sweet as ever, holding a bowl of parmesan she'd just grated. The air was full of the aroma of tomato and basil, and the golden rays of sunset came through the door that opened on the courtyard.

I sat at the table, barefoot and dirty from spending the afternoon in the hills around our home, my hair a tangled nest. My father had sent one of his men, Diego, to find me and take me inside; now I was waiting to be summoned to my father's study, most likely about my behaviour since Mum died. I skipped school, I refused to wear shoes, brush my hair, go to church with the family or step inside the house at all until night fell. Also, I was almost sure someone had grassed about me spending time with the son of my father's enemy, Vanni Orafi.

I didn't care about my father's stupid feud. The Orafi family

had been our allies for two generations, until my father fell out
with Gherardo Orafi over something that was never spoken
aloud. Us daughters didn't know the details, of course – we
were told only that they were after our lands, they wanted to
destroy our family and business, and we were forbidden to have
anything to do with them.

Bianca kept throwing glances at me, her bottom lip quiv-
ering in that way she had, irritating me and breaking my heart at
the same time. She hated it when I was in trouble and doubled
her efforts to be docile and dutiful, as if she could cover me in
her good behaviour to make up for my rebellion. Since our
mother's accident I'd grown uncontrollable, and she'd grown
even sweeter, more pliant.

We'd always been different, but the last few months had
carved a chasm between us: we both tried our best to cope with
what had befallen us, but we'd chosen opposite ways to do this.
Bianca tried to appease circumstances in any way she could, as
if life was a wild beast you could *endear* not to devour you. I
baited the beast, waiting for the consequences to rain on me and
shake this cage we all lived in, shake my father's pockets so the
keys to the cage would fall out. I reasoned that the worst thing
in the world had happened already, after all. I was wrong, of
course.

The irony was that our father didn't like Bianca more, for all
her meekness and acquiescence. She was almost invisible, to
him. Looking back, maybe that was exactly what she wanted, so
she wouldn't get hurt. And she wanted me to follow the same
strategy, so that I wouldn't be hurt either.

'Can you not just *behave*?' she'd asked me in every possible
tone, from exasperated to pleading, from indignant to
despairing.

I couldn't. My mother had always called me *fierce*, Matilde
called me *wilful*, my father didn't call me anything at all, but
swelled with resentment a little more every day.

I'd been lost in grief for three months now, since my lovely, beautiful mum had died of a fall on rugged ground, not far from the house. I was a tightly wound ball of loss and loneliness, and nobody could reach me in this barbed, droughty place I'd found myself in. I couldn't have done what Bianca asked of me – my own will had been replaced by bereavement and fury, and they growled and paced inside my mind, giving me no rest.

There was a cloud of wrath over the villa that day; and the origin point was a slight, skinny girl of twelve who perched on a chair with her arms around her knees and her eyebrows knitted together. Me, the bad twin, the one who defied her father's authority and stalked around like a wolf child.

It seemed that Fosco Falconeri, my father and the head of our family, whose authority had always been undisputed, had finally grown weary of the rebel child. Since my mother's death, he'd called me to his study twice already. Twice I'd stood on the rug in front of the heavy wooden desk, head bowed to hide my contempt, listening to his calm, poised words of warning. I could feel the fury behind that calm, that poise, like the low growl of a beast that any second would erupt in a roar.

It was the third time I'd been summoned: I knew in my bones that this time would be different. *Worse.*

'Signor Fosco is ready for you.' Laura, our maid, came into the kitchen and offered me her hand as if I were a little girl. I refused to take it and walked out by myself, the stone stairs cool under my feet, step after step down the corridor lined by wide wooden beams. The faint image of me and Laura reflected in the glass of the floor-to-ceiling windows walked alongside us, and beyond it, the rose bushes that my mother had planted.

My father didn't usually give out punishments. Nor praise, really. Just orders. We hardly ever saw him, except for Bianca, who occasionally received a word or a pat on the head, like a well-behaved dog. All matters of discipline regarding us girls were delegated to my mother and to Matilde: there was hardly ever any need for Father to intervene, because we all knew that his word was law, and nobody dared contradict him.

Except me.

We were almost at my father's door when out of the corner of my eye, through the glass, I saw a figure behind a rose bush. For a moment I thought it was my reflection, or Laura's – then I realised it was neither.

Roses encompassed her with a crown of petals and thorns, the golden light of sunset at her back and her eyes on me. Her chest was rising and falling, like she was panting, like she was afraid. It was my mother. I was too shocked to throw open the French doors at the end of the corridor – I screamed and launched myself at the windows, hitting the glass with my fists. I wasn't strong, but one of the glass panels was loose and freed itself from its metal encasing. My hands and arms went right through it, and I fell face first onto the gravel, in a shower of shards of glass and blood. There was a cacophony of screams and shouts and the sound of running feet, with my father's powerful voice above all others, barking to Laura to call the doctor.

I found myself lying on my back in my father's arms, looking up at his face. There was a black aura around him, and it frightened me more than I could say.

'I saw Mum...' I whispered.

His eyes widened, and without a word he let go of me. In a seamless gesture, Matilde took my head on her lap and Bianca's hand was on my forehead.

My father disappeared into his study and stayed there throughout whatever happened next – I don't have any memories of the aftermath, of the ambulance coming and being taken to the hospital.

I never saw him again.

~

When I came to, I was in a strange bed, pleasantly fresh under my body. A woman dressed in green was bending over me, and the white light of the sun seeped through half-closed blinds.

The first thing I whispered was: 'My mum is alive.'

A small gasp came from the other side of my bed, and I turned to see that Bianca and Matilde were there. Bianca looked stricken and Matilde was clasping a hand to her mouth.

'*Piccola*, she's not,' Matilde said. 'I'm so sorry, but she died on the hills above Casalta, and you need to accept it, we all need to accept it.' She lightly touched my bandaged arm.

'I saw her. She's alive,' I insisted. 'Bianca, I swear, I saw her!'

The nurse made her discreet way out.

Bianca sat there, clean and tidy in her short-sleeved shirt with the little bows on the shoulders, her hair, strawberry blonde, cut in a neat bob to her chin. 'Don't say that. Please, Lulu, *don't say that*. Father will be so cross.' There were tears in her eyes.

'All you can do is cry!' I shouted. 'You pretend to be good, but you really are just a wimp!'

'Lucrezia!' Matilde reproached me. 'Your sister doesn't deserve—'

'I'm not a wimp,' Bianca said in a way that made me suck my breath in. She sounded so much older than her years. 'I'm trying to keep you home with us.'

*What? Where else would I be?*

'What do you mean?' My voice came out small, and I was mad at myself for showing weakness.

'Just stop saying you saw Mum. And start behaving,' Bianca pleaded. '*Please!*'

I turned my back to them, my face against the wall. 'I saw her.'

'You didn't!' Bianca jumped up and began shaking me by the shoulder. I yelped with the pain from the cuts in my arms.

Matilde held Bianca back – she looked shocked. My sister never behaved this way.

'Let's go, Bianca. Lulu needs to rest. Sleep now, *piccola*...' I heard Matilde say, but the medicine coursing through my system was taking over anyway, and I felt sleepier and sleepier. The door had barely closed when Bianca ran back in and kneeled beside me.

'Maybe it was... you know, the way we are. The way I hear voices and I see people, maybe you saw Mum because it's part of your gift,' she whispered urgently, and turned towards the door.

'No,' I managed to say, slurring my words and feeling my eyes close.

'Maybe that's what it was! And maybe I'll see her too...' Matilde didn't let Bianca finish, because she took her by the arm.

'Bianca! We need to let her rest!'

'No... She was there...' was the last thing I said before sleep took me.

Next time I awoke was when the nurse came to check on me; I was alone. I thought it must be not long later, because there was still light coming through the window – but I must have slept all night, because she was holding a breakfast tray and bid me good morning. I was starving, and devoured the bread and jam with the mug of warm chocolate milk.

'Am I going home today?'

'We'll see what the doctor says,' the nurse replied with a reassuring smile. 'You seem to be doing well. You have an appetite, that's for sure!'

I nodded, my mouth full of bread and jam. I was sore from all the cuts, but I didn't want her to know, in case they kept me there longer.

I'd just finished my breakfast when the doctor came to see me. He wasn't as reassuring as the nurse – his smile was tight.

They refreshed my bandages while I bit my lip not to cry. The cuts were healing nicely, he said. Then why did he look at me in that strange way? As if he felt desperately sorry for me.

'May I sit?' he said and patted my sheets. I nodded, and he took his place beside me. 'Well, signorina. You gave us all a big fright.'

'I'm sorry.'

'You don't need to apologise. You and your family have been through a lot, recently. When something so awful happens we all react in different ways. We wish for everything to be all right again, don't we?'

I nodded.

'Sometimes we wish so hard we might even see things that aren't there... Do you understand what I mean?'

I nodded again, even if no, I didn't really understand what he meant, because I didn't see something that wasn't there. My mother *was* there. It hadn't been a dream, it hadn't been part of my gift.

'Your father is concerned. He wants you to recognise that your eyes played a trick on you, and that's how you got so hurt. There was nobody there. You threw yourself against the glass... through the glass... for nothing.'

'But my mum *was* there.'

The doctor's face fell. 'Oh, Lucrezia.'

I knew that I'd disappointed him, that I'd said the wrong thing. But it was the truth.

'Well. Not to worry. Your dad will sort this whole thing out, yes?' He lifted his fingers to my chin and looked at me. 'You're a brave little soul.'

'I'm not little. I'm twelve. Is my father coming today to take me home?'

The doctor gave me another tight smile. 'Not to worry,' he repeated.

I took it as a *yes*.

It was clear to me that I had to stop acting up, stop skipping school and not coming in for meals. I would try so hard to be better. I had to unravel the thoughts in my mind like Matilde did with yarn before knitting, sort it all in a tidy ball and be a good girl. If I showed Father that I was willing to behave, then I could tell him that I was sure, *completely sure* about seeing Mum behind the red rose bush. He'd believe me and look for her. If I endeavoured to be as perfect as I could be, he would listen to me, they all would. There had been a terrible mistake, and I had to right it. Our mum wasn't dead, and it was my responsibility to make sure everyone knew.

I wanted to be dressed nicely for when my father came to get me. I asked the nurse to please brush my hair, because I couldn't lift my arms properly yet, and to help me get dressed. The clothes I'd worn when I came in were ruined, but the nurse gave me a little bag that Matilde had sent. Inside I found a pink top, denim shorts and white sandals, together with a headband. It was a little girl's outfit, and I rolled my eyes. Matilde didn't understand that I wasn't a child any more.

I stood on the hospital steps with the doctor and the nurse who'd been taking care of me. When I saw Father's car approaching, my heart jolted. I was half apprehensive, half elated to be going home.

I smoothed my hair down with a bandaged hand.

Martino, our driver, appeared out of the car. I expected him to open the other doors and let Father and Bianca out, and maybe Matilde too, but he didn't. He avoided my eyes as he greeted me and took my little bag. I followed him down the steps, a bit unsteady on my feet – and when he opened the boot to put my bag in I saw that there were two big suitcases there, and a wicker basket all tied up with string. My winter coat was there too, folded in two and encased in a plastic covering. A red and white blanket was rolled on the side, and on top of it rested Bernardo, the stuffed dog I'd slept with since I was a baby.

At that moment I realised that wherever I was going, it wasn't home.

# CHAPTER 3

## PARIS, 12 APRIL 1985 – TWELVE YEARS LATER

LUCREZIA

I stood on the balcony of my apartment, leaning on the wrought-iron banister and watching the sky over Paris turn lilac and pink, slowly swallowed by twilight. A grid of graceful buildings unfolded in front of me like the backdrop of a theatre. Usually I was a restless soul, always busy; it wasn't like me, to stand in contemplation. I had work to do, but my agenda sat untouched. My thoughts were held captive by the woman I'd seen today.

The woman who was *not* my mother.

A whole world of yearning had opened before me again: yearning for home. And it had all happened in an instant, barely enough time for the whip of a layered skirt, the glimpse of a face turning away, the glimmer of a red plait...

The first time this happened, in the rose garden at Casalta, my life had fallen apart. This time, I wouldn't let a figment of my imagination, a daydream or whatever it was, destroy me again. I'd accepted long ago that the trauma and pain of her death had conjured up the image of my mum that night in the rose garden. Even if it seemed so real, it was simply a product of my longing. Finally, I'd come to acknowledge that it had been so.

But now it had happened again, and doubt was worming its way into my mind once more. I *knew* that the red-haired woman in the crowd was not her, that my mother was dead and gone forever. *But...*

But oh, the shape of her body, the hue of her plait, now interspersed with silver – and those eyes, as big as Mia's but blue, Scottish blue. All her family, she'd told us – the family she'd been estranged from and who lived like a legend in her stories – had blue eyes.

*And yet, it happened before!* I told myself angrily. *For a while every red-haired woman you saw had to be your mother. You made a fool of yourself more than once. Nothing happened today, not really. For a split second the memory of your mother's face was superimposed on a stranger's, that's all. You're not losing your mind again. Don't let any misgivings ambush you, tear you apart. Not again.*

Memories of my mother and my sisters were held back by the wall I'd built around my heart. It had to be this way, otherwise heartache would sweep me away. But thoughts of them were always there, in the back of my mind, like the cosmic sounds that reach our Earth, but we can't hear – inaudible, and yet pervading everything.

I was alone, but I was still a fourth of something and always would be. While I watched the first stars appear in the evening sky, I saw us four as a little constellation, impossible to break apart.

*Bianca, Nora, Mia.*

I whispered their names under my breath, and they rolled off my tongue, bittersweet, something much loved and lost.

'Did you say something?' I flinched at the sound of Claude's voice – I'd been far away. The smell of his cigarette reached me, a habit I couldn't stand, but he couldn't lose.

'No, nothing.'

'Are you not feeling well?'

'I'm good.'

'Are you sure? Today at the event, you were all over the place. You were... *crying.*'

'I told you, the sun made my eyes water. And the heat made me woozy.'

'It wasn't that hot. Or that sunny.'

I sighed. He wouldn't let this go. I knew he cared, in his own way, but I truly didn't know what to say.

*I thought I saw my dead mother, Claude.*

'We all have our moments...' he said.

'I know, I'm sorry.'

'But we have an image to maintain. *I* have an image. And you're part of it. You can't...' he made a gesture with his hand to signify tears falling.

It was a sucker punch. Of course, Claude was always Claude. He simply *had* to remind me that I shouldn't have had a meltdown thirty seconds before his event, whatever the reason.

I looked at him, and suddenly this person I'd shared my life and my bed with for the last two years, the man I lived and worked with, felt like a total stranger to me.

Likewise, the yellow buildings like dominoes on the boulevard, the rows of urban trees and lampposts – this graceful, enchanting city – was an alien place.

A red-haired woman in the crowd, a glimpse of the past, a flood of memories: and suddenly, in the space of a day, I felt like a stranger in my own life.

Or maybe this wasn't so sudden. I read somewhere that before an earthquake, strange lights might be seen in the sky – and the letter I received from Bianca, with the invitation to our father's wedding, had been just that, an earthquake light. Today the tremor had come.

'It hasn't happened before, has it? It was just a moment. Now, can we move on?'

'You're angry,' Claude said and pressed what was left of the cigarette in the ashtray he kept by the window. He put his hands up. 'I'll let you be.'

He disappeared into the kitchen, where he invariably took refuge when things weren't going his way. With him, I always had to keep my composure. He had no patience for frustration or negativity. He wouldn't entertain any distraction from his pursuit of both success and life's pleasures, and to be fair, I'd always liked it that way. Maybe it was the very reason I was with him.

My childhood had enough drama for a lifetime, and I craved his ability to be impervious to distracting emotions. The relationship between us was safe, because we kept our distance. I didn't want to share my innermost feelings and emotions, and he didn't really want to know either.

But there was a price to pay. It was safe, but it wasn't intimate. We were together, and yet we weren't close.

With a sigh of frustration I took myself to the bedroom, closed the door and fished out from my handbag the letter Bianca had sent me a month ago. I sat on the bed, the letter in my hand. Since I'd received it, I'd carried it with me everywhere I went, like a talisman; but I had never replied.

Bianca had written to me for the first few months of my exile, but she stopped abruptly, and never replied to my missives again. Her silence devastated me. None of them, none of my three sisters, ever wrote after that.

Bianca knew nothing about my life: I had no idea how she'd found my address in Paris.

*My dear Lulu,*

*I know we haven't spoken in a long time, but I must tell you that our father has decided to remarry. The bride's name is Gabriella Manto.*

*There will be an intimate ceremony here at Casalta, in the rose garden, on Sunday, 3 March. All the details are in the invite.*

*I hope, more than words can say, to see you there. But if you choose not to come for the wedding, maybe you could come and see us anyway?*

*There's no need to tell you how much I miss you, and how much I've missed you all these years, because you know that.*

*Your sister,*

*Bianca*

*PS Here's an updated picture of us.*

There's no need to tell me how much she missed me? How was I supposed to know that she missed me, that they missed me, when shortly after I went away they stopped answering my letters, they never got in touch with me again, as if I was dead to them?

I scrunched up the little blue envelope that contained the invitation – I wasn't interested in my father's wedding. But the photograph played all the chords of my heart.

It had been taken in the courtyard of Casalta, against the fountain that rose in the middle of it. How many times I'd sunk my hands into that cool sparkling water, glittering in the sunlight – I could almost see my childish hand under the water, on the slippery stone...

My sisters stood in a line, with Nora a little apart from the others. It was a surreal experience to look at Bianca and see *my* face, framed by strawberry-blonde curls down to the middle of her back – my hair was more the colour of mahogany, and came to my chin. Bianca and I took after our Scottish mum, with our fair skin and freckles, while Nora and Mia looked like our father's side, with their brown hair and dark complexions.

Nora had become the beauty of the family, I observed, tall and slender, with delicate features exalted by a boyish cut; Mia was as small as a pixie, her black hair down to her waist. She was born with eyes of different colours, one blue and one brown, and this made her look a little otherworldly.

I counted in my mind. Nora was now twenty-one and Mia was twenty, and I hadn't seen them since they were little girls…

I never could bring myself to go back to Casalta, the place I loved to hate, only to be thrown out again by my father. I couldn't bring myself to even see his face at all.

But there was more, more than my father's presence, that kept me away.

My sisters had been allowed to stay there, to be brought up in their own home, while I'd been rejected and left alone. I was jealous of them; I resented them for having been the chosen ones while I was the black sheep. I knew that when I left Nora and Mia were only little, and Bianca not much older. And deep down, I also knew that it wasn't their fault. It made my resentment ugly and unfair, but it didn't make it go away. The silence on their part had been the nail in the coffin.

And still, Casalta was… my *home*.

I longed for it, and yet the darkest part of me also longed to see it disappear, destroyed with all the awful memories it carried.

'*Lucresiah?*' Claude's face peeped round the door. I hadn't had time to put the letter away, and I sat there with the piece of paper in my hand, almost guiltily, as if it'd been from a lover.

'I've been insensitive. You can talk to me, you know,' he said and shrugged his shoulders in that very French way of his. His gaze fell on the paper in my hands. Could I talk to him? Could I talk to *anyone* about my family? Because apart from what I'd confided in countless therapy sessions, the rest was all tangled up and unspoken.

But Claude was there, waiting for me to confide in him; he was making a gesture of reconciliation after our little spat and rejecting him again felt unfair. I tried to find the words that would tell him what was going on, but that would allow me to remain in not-too-deep waters.

'It's a letter from my sister. My father remarried.'

Claude came to sit on the bed beside me. 'And that's... good? Bad?' He paused. 'Of no importance?'

*Option A, B or C?* How could I fit the whole story and the complexity of my feelings in a little box? I imitated him, and shrugged my shoulders, too.

'You know, you never speak about your family.' Claude wasn't that close to his parents and his only brother, but we still saw them once in a while. We never saw my family, so I'd had to explain to him that they weren't in the picture, but I'd kept it vague. 'You don't have to, if you prefer not to...' He took my hands in his – his palms and fingers, and the backs of his hands, bore little scars from cuts and burns. A chef's hands. 'But it's quite clear that you're not at peace. Is there anything I can do?'

Efficient as ever. Pragmatic.

'I appreciate it, Claude. I really do. But no, thank you.'

'Are you going to go to the wedding? I'll come with you, if I'm free, of course. Why don't you check my diary...?'

'It was a month ago.'

'Oh...'

All of a sudden, I felt my hair standing on end, as if cold fingers had just tapped on my neck and run down my spine. The air seemed static – I thought that had I been a cat, my tail would have been twice its normal size. I was sure I'd see lightning through the window at any moment...

Something was coming, but I didn't know what.

The phone rang and I jumped, startling Claude.

He turned around and grabbed the receiver on my bedside table. '*Allo?*'

A suspended moment, and then – 'It's for you.'

I was still feeling my skin tingle when I brought the receiver to my ear.

'This is Lucrezia Falconeri,' I said while Claude hurried to smooth the creases on the covers where we'd sat. He needed everything to be just so, unlike my messy self.

'*Lulu?*'

When I heard the voice at the other end of the line, and a name no one here called me by, a wave of emotion engulfed me, before I could raise all my walls up and harden my heart. My eyes filled with sudden tears, pouring out without warning. Claude gasped at seeing me unravel so suddenly, so incongruously. For the second time that day.

'It's... Bianca,' the voice said.

A pause, while I tried to get my breath back.

'I know. How did you get this number?'

My harsh words hid the storm raging inside me, a mixture of yearning and joy and anger and regret, regret, *regret*. My twin, the girl who was knitted with me in our mother's womb, who slept beside me in the same cot, whose scent I'd breathed since I was born. Her breath mixed with mine on the same pillow; we spoke a secret language before we had even learned to talk.

While I was exiled and alone, she was allowed to stay home. She was able to sleep in her bed and play in our garden, to see our sisters growing. When she was sick, she was given Matilde's soup and felt Matilde's hand on her forehead. When she cried, our sisters or Matilde comforted her. She went to the local school with our friends and neighbours, she played in the village square, she walked the streets of home.

When Bianca missed our mum, she could go to her rose

garden. Or open her wardrobe and smell our mother's scent from her dresses, read her books, sit at her desk. She could go into her studio and gaze at her paintings, breathe in the scent of paint and turpentine that was so much a part of our childhood. She slept in the room our mother painted for her.

Bianca had the chance to see Vanni, my best friend – a friendship that had been on the cusp of turning into something else... And, as she wrote in the letters I received in the first few months of exile, she *did* see him.

'Madame Aubert,' she said in the sweet, soft voice I remembered so well. The head of the boarding school I'd been sent to, after I recuperated. 'I know you didn't want to be in touch again...'

*Me?* She'd stopped writing. She never replied to my letters. They forgot about me! I steadied my voice. She couldn't know how upset I was. 'But our father remarried. I know, Bianca, I read the letter. You didn't think I would come, did you?'

'No. But I'm not calling about the wedding, Lulu. I'm calling to say that our father is dead.'

# CHAPTER 4

## PARIS, 13 APRIL 1985

LUCREZIA

In the space of half a day, I held a train ticket in my hand.

Now that my father was gone at last, the time to go back to Casalta had finally come, and I couldn't wait. I wanted to *devour* the distance between me and home. Oh, the butterflies in my stomach were more a hurricane than a flutter. I could go home!

There was no Fosco Falconeri there any more. My father was dead, and I was free.

Claude watched me as I prepared my bag. Even though he had offered to go with me, I sensed he was annoyed about this disruption to his routine. Nothing had ever interfered with my work before. Nothing until now. I could see a hint of scarlet around him now. He was irked by this whole thing: he could mask his true feelings, but his aura, a thin but bright halo of red, spoke the truth.

'You'll have to hand over everything to Sophie,' he grumbled.

'I will, don't worry. It'll all go smoothly,' I reassured him. I was going away, but all he could think about was how this would affect our work.

I examined a row of dresses before choosing three, a deep red one down to my ankles, a blue one to the knee, and a short turquoise one, each with matching high heels. I laid them on the suitcase, where Bernardo, my little faithful stuffed dog, waited already. Then I remembered about the funeral: I picked a black dress with a tulip skirt, black shoes and tights. My father's funeral. The thought was surreal.

'I'm sorry I can't come with you, I can't cancel things like this, at the last minute...'

'I know, it's fine. Don't worry,' I repeated. It was better than fine – Claude didn't do well in a supporting role. He wouldn't accept being a background character in the play that was about to unfold.

'Well. Sophie will do the work that you should be doing.'

I thought we'd established that already. Never mind. 'Well, yes. Thank you.'

'Let me cook you something nice and light, yes? And then off to sleep for you. It'll be a long journey.'

'I'd love that. Thank you.'

We looked at each other – for a moment, I felt we were on the verge of a real conversation between a boyfriend and a girl-friend, one that would go beyond formalities and discussing who was going to handle the agenda while I was away... an authentic connection between us.

But the moment passed.

And it wasn't the right time to elaborate anyway. There was already so much happening, it wasn't wise to talk relationships now, when everything was intense as it was, and confused, and I was about to take such a huge step.

No. Our relationship would have to wait until I came back.

∼

I took out Bianca's letters from a drawer in my dresser. There were precious few, and I'd read each of them so many times, I knew them by heart.

I didn't even know why I kept them. I suppose that even if they caused me so much heartache, they were my last and only link to home. The first letter was decorated with flowers and butterflies and stickers. It was so Bianca.

*To Lucrezia Falconeri*
*Istituto Lugano*

*15 May 1973*

*Dear Lulu,*

*I hope this letter gets to you!*

*I miss you so much. I'm sleeping in your bed because I need to feel you close, but it doesn't really work. Father said you're in a very good school and you're lucky to be there...*

A school? A *very good school*. Indeed.

*Matilde says you shouldn't be there. It's one of those things she says that must never be repeated to Father. I don't think you should be there either. I think you should be here with us. I just want you home.*

*I saw Vanni in the village. I hope I'll catch him alone sometime so I can explain what happened to you, even if I know I can't really tell him the whole story...*

The mention of Vanni made my heart skip a beat, just like it did back then. Knowing that he was looking for me, that I'd left him without an explanation, without saying goodbye, killed me then and did again now. How many times I'd wondered if he remembered me.

In my reply, I'd decided back then, I would reassure her that the Istituto Lugano was *a very good school.*

I didn't want them to know the truth.

*3 June 1973*

*Dear Lulu,*

*I miss you so much. The house is empty without you. I try to help Matilde as much as I can, and look after Nora and Mia. Father said that with Mum gone and you away I'm the lady of the house. I don't like that much, but I don't think I have a choice. I hope you'll come home soon. I asked Father when you're coming back, but he said not to be inquisitive. He never tells us anything. I suppose it's for our own good. I try to believe it, but I don't think that you being away from home is good at all, for anyone.*

*Matilde is angry with Father. The other day she was talking to her sister on the phone and she said she would have looked for another job if it wasn't for us needing her. I got a real fright: imagine if she left us, too!*

*I met Vanni in the bread shop, and had a chat with him. I was scared that someone would see us, but it was a few days ago and Father hasn't punished me yet, so I hope nobody told him I spoke with an Orafi. You know the way his men are everywhere, especially Diego. It's like he has eyes all over the village.*

*5 July 1973*

*... I miss everything about you, but especially when we used to sit on the stairs at night and look at the stars. Nora and Mia fall asleep early, and it's not safe to sit there with two little ones. So I sit on my own. I used to hear the long-ago voices there, but since you've gone, I don't any more. They're just whispers and I can't make out the words. I miss my gift. But not as much as I miss you...*

Learning that Bianca had lost her gift made my heart ache for her. I knew how important it was for her, for her identity. I wrote back to her saying that she shouldn't worry, that it would come back soon, when we were reunited. That I'd come home as soon as I was allowed, to please ask Father to let me come back.

I went through the next few letters. Every time Bianca mentioned Vanni, it was like a stab in the heart. I couldn't write to him, of course – I'd get him into huge trouble. And when she told me about having a good time with our sisters, I was taken by a bout of envy so sharp, so cruel, I didn't know what to do with it.

*... Time flows so fast. We are good, but missing you as always. I spend many afternoons at the hazelnut tree...*

*... we're all at the seaside, as you can see from the postcard! We're all getting very brown and my hair is turning blonde with all the sunshine! Every evening I need to drag Nora away from the beach because she never wants to go inside! Mia sits in the shade with her sketchbook all day long...*

*... I'm sending this Christmas card early because I really want it to get to you in time! Merry Christmas! I wasn't sure they sold chocolate duckies there in Switzerland so I bought you a packet and you can put the shiny wrappings on the tree!*

She sounded so cheerful in this one. There was a card each from Nora and Mia. Nora's was a stick tree with a big, bold 'Merry Christmas' written in red above it, while Mia's was an exquisite gouache snowy scene. It was incredible for an eight-year-old; she'd inherited our mum's talent.

> *Happy birthday to us! Even if you're not here, I can feel you close... I think of you every day. I wish you were here, so much, you can't imagine. But I still go to the hazelnut tree, and it makes me feel better. It feels good not to be alone. I know I have our sisters, but...*

This affectionate reference to Vanni slayed me. Even if I knew it was unwise, I couldn't resist: I wrote a note to him, a simple hello, and a little sketch of our tree. I asked Bianca to give it to him. But either she never did, or he didn't bother to reply, because there was no answer.

And then, there was the last letter she ever sent me. It'd been written hurriedly, Bianca's usual pretty handwriting turned into a scrawl.

> *My dear Lulu, I know these words will hurt you, but it's for your own good, I promise. It's better for you and for us that you stay away. This will be my last letter.*
>
> *Oh, Lulu, please know now and always that I love you.*
>
> *Bianca*

*It's better if you stay away.*
But I couldn't! Even after all that happened, I couldn't stay away from Casalta, from my sisters! I had to speak to them. I wrote and wrote, but they never answered. Bianca wanted me away; they wanted me away.

It was then that I began to build my inner wall. I piled all my emotions behind it, and hid them from view. From everyone, and from myself too.

Lying in my bed at night, sitting in the common room doing those inane jigsaws, walking alongside the lake I'd grown to hate, I played my daydream over and over again in my mind, like an obsessive film. Walking up the path to Casalta, seeing my sisters, dipping my fingers in the fountain, climbing up the stairs where I used to sit with Mum...

Soon after, I was allowed to leave the Istituto Lugano – the *very good school* – for a boarding school where I'd stay until the age of eighteen, the École Aubert. There, in the Swiss Alps, I found some peace.

My sisters had moved on, Vanni had moved on. Even Casalta had moved on.

Without me.

∾

I was sure I wouldn't be able to sleep; I lay in my bed for hours, until finally I drifted off – and then opened my eyes at the darkest hour of the night, after a dream so sweet, I felt my heart had liquified.

I was at the hazelnut tree with Vanni, sitting side by side with our legs dangling. We were children again, on the cusp of adolescence, innocent and yet on the threshold of feelings that went beyond friendship. He came closer to me, and I looked into his hazel eyes, green on summer days, like the leaves around us. I laid my head on his shoulder, and he wrapped his arm around my waist. I closed my eyes and we stayed like that, in silence and peace.

He kissed the top of my head. It was then, with that kiss, that my dream ended, and I opened my eyes in the dark.

I lay waiting for dawn, and the time to go home.

# CHAPTER 5

## ON THE WAY TO TUSCANY, 14 APRIL 1985

LUCREZIA

The landscape ran away from me through the train window, until night fell and all I could see was my reflection in the glass. I travelled in the dark across the Alps, and it was as if crossing the mountains meant crossing an enormous gate, on the other side of which was Italy.

The sky lightened slowly, and I saw the first dawn in my own country after all these years. The last time I'd been a girl of twelve, driven into Switzerland and away from home – and now I was a woman of twenty-four, returning to Italy.

A woman exhausted, with purple shadows under her eyes, I had to admit as I tried to apply some make-up on the layers of tiredness; I'd been too excited to sleep for more than two, maybe three hours. I bought a coffee from the trolley and sipped it, drinking in the landscape that became more and more familiar, sweeter and sweeter to my eyes and to my heart.

Finally the hills of Tuscany, crested with cypress trees and dotted with stone farms and hamlets, appeared. The beauty and gentleness of the landscape filled me whole and took all weariness away – weariness of the body and of the heart both. It felt like I'd never left... everything was so familiar, everything spoke of home. My flesh was moulded from this soil and my bones carved out of these stones: the hills called my name.

I opened a window and closed my eyes to the wind – the scent of laurel and oregano and juniper, of sunbaked grass and perfumed thickets, filled every receptor of my mind.

I was going home at last. There was no Fosco Falconeri there any more, nobody to bully me and punish me. I was free.

Santa Maria Novella, Florence's train station, was covered with glass panels that let the sun stream through. Could it be that the sun of home shone more golden than that in Paris?

I stepped outside, my head spinning a little from the lack of sleep and being seated for so long. Just like I'd planned, nobody was there, waiting for me. Bianca knew that I was coming home, but I didn't tell her when: I needed to be alone to have the time to compose myself. I found a taxi, and my voice was a little shaky when I said to the driver with a hint of a French accent: 'I'm going to Casalta, please.'

Casalta was both the name of my home and of the tiny village at the foot of the hill. Once upon a time, the owners of Casalta were the local squires. My family were squires no more, of course – but something in the ancient system, when the powerful families ruled the land, had certainly remained. My father and his friends and associates had woven a web of power over the territory.

'You going to the funeral of the Falconeri boss?' the taxi driver asked. At the mention of my father's name, my heart began to gallop. The old reflexes of fear and dread.

*Boss.* I wasn't sure I liked that word. But it probably described my father accurately.

'I don't know what you're talking about, sorry,' I said, and thankfully the driver let it go.

It occurred to me that my hair wouldn't go unnoticed in tiny

Casalta, that I'd be recognised or mistaken for Bianca. And I wasn't ready to speak to anyone until I saw my sisters again. So I slipped on my sunglasses and tied my hair back with a silk scarf – it was the best I could do.

There was a little over an hour's driving between Florence and Casalta – I knew every inch of that road, every street sign, every house we drove past. I asked the driver to leave me at the foot of the hill, right in front of the village; I paid quickly and watched the car disappear, until I was alone. The early morning had turned into the fullness of noon, and the warm spring air enveloped me. I would have liked to make my way through the narrow, winding roads to the square, and see the village I'd left long ago and pictured so many times in my mind.

Was it crazy? I hoped against hope that Vanni would materialise from somewhere... But I had no idea where he was now, what he was doing – he might have moved away, he might have got married. He certainly wouldn't be here now, by some bizarre, serendipitous coincidence...

My gaze followed the alley in between two rows of houses, to the church steps – where we'd spoken for the first time...

'Excuse me?'

I jumped out of my skin – I turned around and saw a tall man, his face darkened for a moment, against the glare.

'You forgot this,' the taxi driver said, and handed me the leather ticket holder I'd used on the journey.

I almost couldn't articulate a *thank you* – really, for a moment I'd thought it was him...

Enough – the lack of sleep and excitement were playing tricks on me – he wasn't there, he couldn't be there, he'd likely forgotten all about me, and I had a lot more to worry about.

I reached the orchards and vegetable gardens at the back of the village, where the path that climbed up the hill opened in between chestnut and hazelnut trees.

I'd taken that same path I'd walked so many times in my

dreams, up and up the way towards... *home*. I could almost see the dream-me at every bend, sitting among the wildflowers, lying in the grass to watch the clouds and guess their shapes, stinging my hands on chestnut shells, gathering them to bring to Matilde.

Every step took me closer to home now – I took off my scarf, letting my hair flow free – and my sunglasses, so I could see all the colours. My suitcase felt light, almost weightless – the bends became sharper, until Casalta came into view – I almost ran, my heartbeat and breath fusing with the spring music, birdsong and buzzing of bees – until finally, I was there.

I set my suitcase down.

At last.

'I'm back,' I whispered to the dryads on their pillars.

I couldn't believe I really was here. I really was home, the place I'd dreamed about when I was all alone. The place I'd grown to hate when I realised that nobody was coming to get me and bring me back. I loved it, I loathed it, I longed for it, a combination that pulled and tugged at my heart so violently, it left my head spinning. I couldn't wait to see my sisters, and yet I wanted to take it all in by myself until I felt a little more composed, a little more myself.

For the first time, I saw Casalta with the eyes of an adult. Now more than ever, I realised what a thing of beauty it was.

The front was all straight lines and harmonic symmetry, in typical Renaissance style with its stone arches over the main entrance and evenly spaced windows. Everything was perfectly geometrical and elegantly arranged in an orderly, constant visual rhythm.

But the house was just like our family had been when I was growing up: perfect on the outside, chaotic behind the scenes. I lifted my bag again and made my way along the perimeter, on the carefully cut grass bordered with shrubbery tended just as carefully, until I reached the gardens.

The villa rested on a natural terrace, but at the back of it the ground crumpled, rising and falling in small hills and ridges, like velvet cloth thrown on a table. Here the remains of a castle built, destroyed and rebuilt in the Middle Ages were still visible: ghost walls had left traces everywhere, in small mounds of stone and marks on the land that seemed natural, but were man-built. A set of stairs with high, uneven stone steps leaned against the back of the house, all the way from the ground to the roof, with a small window opening on the second floor into my room.

It was here that Mum, Bianca and I sat to look at the stars. And just like the stairs rose up along the house, a web of cellars upon cellars opened underneath Casalta; we weren't allowed there as children, except the main cellars where food and wine were kept, but it was said that a web of tunnels linked the castles in the area and extended to the city of Florence and all the way to the sea.

The gardens followed the uneven shape of the grounds. I stood on top of the flat, rocky steps that led to my mother's rose garden, which was nestled in a small, round plateau paved with stones. The stone had that unique hue that went from brown to pink in different light and seasons – now it gave out an opaque, restrained glow as if absorbing the sunrays and giving them back alchemically transformed into something dense, almost solid. I sat on a stone bench among the roses. I knew it was just a matter of time until someone spotted me, so I closed my eyes for a second and breathed in this moment alone with my memories before facing whatever was ahead.

I could have opened the French doors to the hall that ran along the length of the house and made my way inside the house from its heart, springing my presence on my sisters like I belonged there, as if I had never left. But I chose a less dramatic entrance. I made my way around to the front again and entered the courtyard slowly, savouring every step, the same way I'd walked a thousand times as a child, running in after playing outside or back from school. I had this little ritual I followed every time I came home – I dipped my fingers in the fountain, its water cool in the winter and warm with sunshine in the spring and summer... And I did it this time too, twelve years after the last time, my fingers now long and with red painted nails, not a child's chubby hand any more.

The kitchen door was open as always.

Just like I'd imagined, not much had changed. The same old photograph of Padre Pio and the blessed olive branch hung over the door; there was a pot simmering on the stove and carefully cut vegetables wrapped in kitchen towels on the marble slab.

Matilde was there. Her hair was shorter, and she was a little thicker around the middle, an apron tied around her waist as always. It was like a glitch in time, and I was transported back to when a younger me sat at the kitchen table, with Matilde standing at the stove, both waiting for the master of the house to summon me...

Matilde's voice brought me back to the present, as a young man in boots appeared at the door, carrying a fruit box full of yellow pears.

'You can leave it there, thank you, Paolo!' Matilde called, still stirring the pot.

It was then that she saw me. She hesitated for a moment, her eyes wide, wondering, maybe, if I was Bianca, or a product of her imagination. 'Oh, *Signore mio*... is it really you? Is it really you... *Lulu?*'

Her cool hands, smelling faintly of cut vegetables and hand cream, were on my cheeks. Her eyes filled with tears, and she held me to her, her head coming barely to my chest. 'Oh, Lucrezia! We've all dreamed of this moment! You've *returned!*'

A hairline crack appeared in the wall I'd built around my heart – it was almost a physical sensation – and all the pain wound up in a knot inside me began to unravel.

'Father is dead,' I said simply, because after all, it was that that summed it all up.

'Yes. The funeral is tomorrow. You'll be able to say goodbye, to be there with your sisters. Oh, Lulu! It's been so long, *bambina mia*! But it doesn't matter, it's all in the past. You're here now! Bianca will be so happy, she missed you so, everyone missed you so...'

*If everyone missed me so, then why did nobody try to keep me home? Why did nobody try to defend me and stand up to Father, when he sent me away?*

Yes, it did matter, and no, it *wasn't* all in the past. Everything that had happened was very much present, in my very soul, in every aspect of my life.

'You're *bellissima*, Lulu! Look at your dress, it's like you're an actress out of the TV! But then you were a beautiful child! And your *mamma* was like a Botticelli, with that hair of hers,' Matilde said. The mention of my mum threatened to break my barriers, here in this kitchen, in this house, where memories of her were everywhere.

'Thank you,' I said in a low voice.

Matilde slipped her hand into mine. 'I thought of you every day, *bambina*. But now here you are, this house is free, and you're back.'

'It will never be free of the memories...'

'Ah, but there were so many good ones, Lulu. Before...'

Her voice trailed away.

*Before.*

'Are my sisters home?'

'They are. Come,' she said, Matilde's hands going to her wet cheeks, to her hair, to compose herself. She took the apron off, as if I were a visitor to be welcomed formally.

I followed her down the corridor that led to the living room, passing a wall of family portraits, and finally the antique mirror across from the living room door; in the glass I saw a twelve-year-old girl in a pink top and denim shorts, waiting for her dad to take her home...

*Breathe. Lucrezia, breathe.*

A voice rose, sweet, delicate. I would have recognised it among a million voices. My sister Bianca was there, and suddenly I found my body frozen, incapable of deciding whether to run in and hold her to my heart, or run away. The flood of emotion was drowning me.

Matilde was behind me, and I turned around to see that she was looking at me expectantly, waiting for me to step inside the room.

And I did.

The room was empty, but for a young woman in a blue dress sitting by the window. She had my features, my build, my same hair colour, albeit lighter – it was like being in two places at the same time.

I was blind to everything except her, as if the sun was in my eyes and only she moved against the light.

My twin, my other half.

*Bianca, Bianca, Bianca.*

My heart howled in longing and abandonment and grief of all those years apart – I just wanted to hold her and feel her close – but the wave of love was too strong, it was drowning me – my frozen heart couldn't take it without shattering into a million pieces and so I closed it, and swallowed back my tears.

A moment when she raised her face and saw me – a blink, and she was running towards me, her arms open – I stood cold and rigid as she held me – I tried to remain so, distant – I never wanted to be hurt again – but in an instant I was clutching her back, breathing in her scent of roses, her scent of Bianca and of me. Of home.

# CHAPTER 6

## CASALTA, 14 APRIL 1985

LUCREZIA

'You're back, you're back!' Bianca whispered in my neck; I pulled away from her and we took each other in. A beautiful aura, light blue dotted with silver like a twilight sky, emanated from her.

'You have no idea how much I've dreamed of this moment. Oh, *Lulu!*' She held me tightly again, and I couldn't breathe but didn't care.

How could I put in words all that was in my heart? How could I tell her all that had happened in those years?

What do you tell your sister, your twin and the other half of you, when twelve years of absence stretch between you? *Why did you stop writing? Why didn't you answer my letters?* All I could do was hold her to me again, and we rocked from side to side, smiling like nothing bad had ever happened, like we'd just been parted for a little while...

Our moment was diffused by a soft, silvery voice behind me.

'You're here. At last!' A small girl, all dressed in black and with long, dark, wavy hair, threw herself in my arms. Little Mia, the youngest of my sisters.

'*Mia!*'

'I *knew* you'd come!'

She was a whirlwind, as small as a fairy, with those huge eyes, one brown, one blue. 'I need to show you something,' she said before I could find my bearings.

Mia radiated pure joy in seeing me, and this surge of affection and tenderness warmed every corner of my heart. I didn't quite have time to say anything before she slipped her small, tanned hand in mine and almost *dragged* me outside. I walked after her, her hair bouncing on her back, through the garden, towards the back of the house.

'Mia, Lulu has just arrived, we're not even giving her the chance...' Bianca began, but her words trailed away as we arrived at the small thicket of maritime pines behind the house, and stepped through a fairy-sized arched door. This was where my mother's studio used to be, though she mostly painted outside.

The pungent smell of paint, so familiar to me, filled the air – it was a little eerie, as if my mother's spirit lingered there... Now the place was empty of furniture, apart from a few pieces covered in white sheets. Its walls were covered in frescoes that hadn't been there when I was a child. Mia must have painted them. But I didn't get the chance to see them properly, because Mia pulled me on: they passed on both sides of me, like the view from a train window.

We climbed the winding stairs to the turret – butterflies of different species and colours had been painted on the wall – it was as if a cloud of butterflies flew alongside us as we climbed. We came to the top, round and stone-floored, with a window opening on the grassy hill it leaned against. Here there were canvases everywhere, some finished, some works in progress, bright splashes of colour against the grey stone. A ladder leaned against one of the walls, painting materials were meticulously organised on a table and the floor was covered in white, paint-stained sheets.

Mia stopped in front of a rectangular canvas that sat just underneath the window. I couldn't normally see the aura of objects, but this painting gave off such strong vibrations I could see a small rainbow around it.

And the subject of the canvas was me.

The Lucrezia in the portrait was vibrant, alive, her eyes looking straight at the viewer, and not withdrawn like I'd become.

Perhaps this was the woman I *could* have been.

'Do you like it?' Mia asked. She was beaming. This girl I didn't know, so full of talent and joy, was my sister, my baby sister...

'It's amazing. But I'm not that beautiful, in real life!' I smiled.

'You *are.*'

'I never sent photos of myself. But the resemblance with me is uncanny,' I said. Yes, Bianca and I were identical twins and Mia could simply reproduce her face, but the portrait was unmistakably me, down to the hairstyle, long and wavy, and the exact shade of red. Even stranger, I recognised the top I wore, a red and white short-sleeved shirt with a high neck that I'd bought not long ago in Paris.

Her gift. Of course.

'I knew you were coming back,' Mia said cheerfully. 'I saw you.' I couldn't help noticing that she didn't seem touched by grief. It didn't seem to me like my father's death had broken her heart, or even really affected her.

Finally, as our heads were close together while we admired the portrait, I had the chance to look at little Mia properly. She was little no more, but a vibrant young woman. I could see the family resemblance, and yet she didn't quite look like our mother nor our father, but seemed to have been born from a shell, like Venus in the painting by Botticelli. She was tiny while Bianca and I were tall, and fine-boned like a little bird. She seemed childlike and ancient at the same time, somehow.

'You saw me?' I asked, all the while contemplating this wondrous sister of mine, this stranger who was so surprising, and yet shared my blood.

Bianca and I exchanged a glance. Once again, I recognised my mother's family's gift, and the way it manifested itself in different ways in each of us.

'She inherited *this* talent from Mum too,' Bianca said with a smile.

I turned around, taking in the canvases of all shapes and sizes, the landscapes and portraits, the scenes of ordinary life – gathering of the olives, cutting of the grapes, the cellars full of bottles – Bianca sitting outside with a stripy cat by her side, Matilde on a small ladder dusting in my father's study, Nora looking to the viewer from a field, caught by surprise like a wild animal on camera.

'These are... what can I say? It's like I can see all this happening right now, in front of me,' I said.

'Her art is *magical*,' Bianca said simply. 'Just like her.'

Mia smiled towards me with total trust, as if there had never been any separation at all and she knew me like the back of her hand.

'Sorry, we're talking about you as if you weren't here. Big sisters, I suppose!' Bianca laid a hand on Mia's back. The bond between them was palpable. There was a little stab in my heart... The wall inside me was beginning to crumble. And what was behind that wall was endless love... and endless resentment and regret.

'I... I think I need a little fresh air...'

Mia fussed over me. 'I'm sorry! You do look a little pale... Must be the paint fumes. Sometimes they get to me, too...'

'The paint fumes. That would explain the way our family is,' I murmured, and Mia laughed heartily.

'Well, you've seen two sisters out of three! Nora is at the stables as always,' Bianca said. 'Let's go.'

We walked back through the frescoed room on our way out. Two walls of the four were divided into squares, each representing a little scene. While the paintings were colourful and spontaneous, all wide brushstrokes, the frescoes were precise, meticulous, almost geometrical. They reminded me of medieval paintings, each figure detailed to perfection.

'What will you do when you run out of space?' I asked Mia.

'Paint the rest of the house,' she said without missing a beat. 'I'm working on this, now.' She crouched and showed me a little tableau that bloomed near our feet, although the word 'tableau' is a little too gentle for the scene. There was a richly dressed woman, a gold circlet around her head, holding a sword – and lying beside her, a man in agony with a wound on his neck, his head thrown back.

It was a brutal representation, in contrast with the peacefulness of the other scenes that were all calm, domestic.

'Can you guess what it is?' Mia asked.

'Maybe... is it Judith and Holofernes?' I guessed. 'From the Bible? He was a cruel king, wasn't he, and Judith killed him?'

'Yes. She chopped his head off,' Mia replied calmly. 'And he didn't bother them again.'

# CHAPTER 7

## CASALTA, 14 APRIL 1985

LUCREZIA

Bianca and I made our way into the hills, under a gentle spring sun. We took our high-heeled shoes off and advanced barefoot, like we'd done so many times as children.

Since I'd stepped back in this house and seen my sisters, time had turned into an accordion, expanding and narrowing and expanding again, flowing and halting and restarting, so that past and present were woven together and I kept going back and forth between reality and memories. I threw my head back and took in the blue sky, and the smell of grass and herbs, and the distant song of some brave cicadas that were opening the season so early.

*Home, home, home.*

'When I called Madame Aubert to find your number, she said you were a secretary. A chef's secretary,' Bianca said.

'Well, yes. An assistant, more like. A secretary sounds like an office job, but we travel around a lot. He's very successful, he's on TV, he works non-stop.'

'It sounds glamorous!'

'It sounds more glamorous than it is. Mainly I keep his diary and I tell people off on his behalf if the parsley is not fresh, or if a pan isn't the right size.' I laughed.

'Why did you choose it?'

'It fell in my lap. When I finished boarding school...' A pause.

*When I finished boarding school, I wanted to come home and see you, see my sisters. But I was angry, and afraid.*

'Madame Aubert knew someone who knew Sophie, Claude's manager. They were looking for an assistant, and I got the job. I didn't really have time to think; I needed to find something to support myself quickly. What about you?'

Bianca shrugged. 'I wanted to study art. But I'm not clever enough, of course...'

'Of course you are! What are you talking about? Who said that...? Oh.'

'Yes, well, Father always said you got the brains, and he was right. I was never good in school; I was always preoccupied with what was going on at home... Also, I didn't want to go to university and leave Nora and Mia, just in case. You know...'

I didn't know. But I could guess.

'So, I stayed home to run the house and, with a bit of time on my hands, I started helping people in the village, you know, elderly people, or people who were sick or disabled. I did simple things, getting their groceries, taking them to hospital, cooking and cleaning for them, whatever their needs were. Even just lending a listening ear. I ended up founding a co-op with a friend, Renata, remember her? She was at school with us.'

'Oh, yes. That sounds wonderful, Bianca.'

'Ah, it's small stuff. But it's so good when you see people getting out of ruts, with a little hand. There's a few of us now, two are nurses, so we can do a little more.'

'Sounds very you. And it suits you. *You look happy!*'

'*You look lovely!*'

We'd spoken at the same time. It was hearing the same person speak twice, simultaneously. Something shifted between us. I saw her aura shimmer silver.

We came to the top of the hill, and from there we could see the expanse of vineyards on one side and the olive groves on the other. The stables were there, a cluster of stone buildings where the Falconeri horses were kept, and from where the soft sound of neighing could be heard. And beyond them, beyond our grounds, in a small, secluded valley between Casalta and the Orafi estate, was the hazelnut tree where Vanni and I used to meet...

All of a sudden, it all came crashing down on me: this bittersweet return, this volatile mixture that was bound to explode, sooner rather than later. A flood of emotion left me shaking.

I grabbed Bianca's hand to make her stop, and she did.

My twin and I stood in front of each other.

'Why did you not fight for me, Bianca?'

'*Fight* for you? I was *twelve*. I was a *child*. What did you expect me to do?'

'You *wanted* me to stay away. I know it. I could feel it. At the beginning you wanted me to return, but then...'

'Oh, Lulu. There's so much you don't know...'

'This, again? There might be a lot I don't know, but there's also a lot I *do* know! And you kept sending me those letters about everything you did, and how everyone was doing, and you wanted me to answer as if we were pen pals! You have no idea what I went through.'

My outburst was followed by another bout of neighing coming from somewhere behind us, this time louder.

'Because you never told me! You never answered my letters! It was guesswork, for me, for us...'

'I did! I answered *all* your letters, you ignored everything I said...'

Bianca froze. 'You wrote to me?'

It began to dawn on me. On us.

'You never received my letters, did you?' I said.

Bianca shook her head slowly, disbelieving.

I should have known. We should have known! '*He* intercepted them. And either hid them, or destroyed them!'

'Sit down!' Bianca whispered suddenly, the kind of whisper that sounds more powerful and intimidating than a shout. I was taken aback.

'What?'

'I said, sit down.'

'Oh. You're ordering me about, now? Not like you.'

'Very funny. How do you know what's like me and what's not like me? We haven't seen each other for twelve years. And now, sit down. Please, I'll tell you everything.'

I obeyed, and let myself fall on the grass, suddenly drained. I bent my legs beneath me, and dried tears that refused to stop. My chest was rising and falling fast.

The grass was warm, and in front of us were the sweet, sweet view of vines covering the hills, and the bluest of skies. In the distance, far away, were crests of cypresses and the silhouette of more hills melting into each other under the sun – and, beyond those hills, the Florence skyline. The light of this Tuscan afternoon was so golden, so warm, that I raised my face and closed my eyes to soak it all in. Everything was still complicated, and emotional, and the mixture of joy and guilt and regret I carried around my sisters made my thoughts tangle in twisted threads – but deep down, almost at a cellular level, my body and soul knew that I was *home*. This was the light of home, the food of home, the first sky I ever had above my head and the first air I ever breathed. I felt a little like Ulysses returning to the island of Ithaca, except there were no greedy pretenders to spoil my return: the agent of chaos and upset was gone.

Tears kept flowing out of my eyes of their own accord. I'd

kept them in check for too long to rein them in. Beside me, Bianca was crying too. I wondered what Claude and the people in our circle would say, seeing me in the middle of all this drama, barefoot and puffy-eyed. Me, his ice queen.

'What happened to you? You *never* used to order anyone about. It's like hearing a hamster roaring,' I muttered.

'Try living with Fosco Falconeri, with a little sister who needs looking after like an eternal child, another sister who believes we all wronged our father and should make amends, and a twin who's disappeared. Believe me, you'll develop some character as well.'

More neighing in the distance. One of the horses had been spooked, probably.

'But you got to stay home! All this time, I was alone...' I exclaimed, but stopped abruptly. The neighing was joined by the din of someone, something, panting, snorting, displacing the grass around us.

'Get up!' Bianca bellowed.

'Sit down, stand up! Stop telling me what to—' My sentence ended in a scream. An enormous horse was careering towards us, charging us. It was such a surreal scene that I was frozen. My whole body was rigid, and I was wide-eyed, staring at the galloping beast.

'*Get. Up!*' Bianca yelled again, dragging me to my feet. The horse was now so close, I could almost feel its hooves on my body. I threw myself on Bianca and we rolled together down the slope. When we finally stopped I opened my eyes, thinking I'd see the animal stand upon us, poised to squash us under its weight; but it wasn't there.

Instead of the horse, standing above us was a young woman, straw in her hair and mud on her boots, her expression somewhere between concerned and amused. 'You overreacted,' she stated, and didn't bother hiding a smile.

'*Nora!*' Bianca took the hand that Nora was extending to her. 'That beast was *charging* us!'

'He wouldn't have trampled you. He would have avoided you instinctively. He was just a little spooked.' She shrugged. 'He just moved here; he's acclimatising. Bianca, when will you stop coming out on the hills in a dress? You look like you're going to church...'

Then she saw me, and stiffened. Her eyes moved from me to Bianca and back.

'*Lucrezia?*' she half-declared, half-asked. Her beauty struck me once again, even more than it had when I saw her picture: she could have walked out of a film or a magazine, with her amber skin and freckles, moss-green eyes and slender, colt-like figure. She wore riding trousers and a long shirt, and her hair was short, with a mop of dark curls on top. A single earring, shaped like a feather, played hide and seek in her hair.

I was still too shaken to be able to speak, so I just nodded. She was quiet, but the way she studied my face, the way she stared at me, betrayed the intensity of her surprise, beyond the silence. And then the stare turned into something else – a glare, a look of plain hostility that passed on her face like clouds on a hill, and disappeared. But the cold vapour of her aura, a dark, acid green, betrayed her. I felt Bianca almost squirming beside me. She was uneasy.

I searched for words to defuse the moment, but none came. Bianca and Mia had made it easy for me, but not Nora. I couldn't blame her, but I wasn't ready to make it easy either.

'He *was* charging us,' I ended up muttering.

To my irritation, Nora laughed, a fearless, forthright laugh, as direct and devoid of embarrassment as her gaze was.

'No, he wasn't,' she said matter-of-factly. 'You were in his path, that's all. Ettore is incapable of deliberate aggression. He's as sweet as they come; you just don't know him.'

'Where is he?' Bianca whipped her head around.

'I have him!' a dark-haired man called from behind us: I turned around, and his eyes widened slightly when he recognised me – it wasn't difficult, I supposed, given that I was identical to Bianca. 'Signorina Falconeri.'

I tried to say hello, but bits of dry grass in my throat made me cough instead.

'I'm Matteo, the stable manager. It's nice to meet you.'

No point in trying to be dignified, sweaty and dishevelled as I was. 'It's nice to meet you too,' I croaked.

Matteo had slung reins on the horse and was holding them, all the while stroking its muzzle. He was awfully close to its teeth, I thought, but both he and my sister seemed unfazed. Had I not been so scared I would have appreciated the beauty of the animal, its shiny brown coat and the white diamond on its forehead, and those liquid, liquid eyes. But I wasn't familiar with horses, and my knees were still having to work to keep me standing. I plucked out some more grass from my hair.

'How come your horse-whispering didn't work this time, Nora?' Bianca said good-naturedly. 'That's her gift,' she explained to me. I supposed that simply mentioning a gift was vague enough not to make Matteo wonder.

'I don't have any gifts,' Nora stated simply, and her eyes were dark for a moment. 'Ettore is a Maremmano horse. They're an independent breed and want to be *almost* completely free. I say almost because they still like having their fresh water and somewhere warm and dry to come home to at night. We have to work together, so they understand the boundaries. They're wild at heart, but we still need to co-exist.'

'You're the same breed then, *cara*,' Bianca said with a smile, and the look of admiration she was giving Nora nullified her attempt at sarcasm. It was clear to see that Bianca doted on Nora, just as much as she doted on Mia.

'And you're Marie the little white cat in *The Aristocats*,' Nora retorted without malice, and she turned to me. 'It's almost like meeting you for the first time,' she said, her moss-green eyes studying me.

While both Bianca and Mia had come close at once, Nora kept her distance. The awkwardness I felt was such that my ice-maiden persona returned to me. Nora seemed unfazed.

'I'm glad you're back,' she said simply and walked away with Matteo, Ettore the horse in between them, snorting. Ettore had a swagger about him, like a little boy who'd misbehaved and was quite satisfied with himself.

'Nora is wild,' Bianca commented. 'She doesn't like having four walls around her and almost lives at the stables.'

'Where were we?' I said, still fishing grass out of my hair. My dress was ruined. Suddenly, unexpectedly, Bianca started laughing.

'What?'

'Your expression. You look so... *outraged.*'

'You can say that again! That horse owes me one.'

And just as unexpectedly, I started laughing too, and we laughed and laughed until the laughter mixed with tears and we fell into each other's arms.

# CHAPTER 8

## CASALTA, 14 APRIL 1985

LUCREZIA

Later that night, Matilde gave me one last hug before going home. 'I made dinner for you, though I had no warning, it was the best I could do! It's in the oven,' she'd said, and left us four sisters alone.

Nora was coaxing the fire, welcome warmth on the chilly spring night. Mia was sitting close to me, her legs bent underneath her, and Bianca was pouring us some nocino, a liqueur made with walnuts. The bottle carried our label: *Falconeri Estate.* She gave us each a tiny glass, then sat back.

'You never wrote to us,' Nora said. She may have wanted to sound nonchalant, but the dark green aura gave her away.

'She did, but the letters never arrived!' Bianca exclaimed. 'I should have known. *We* should have known.'

A sudden thought hit me. If they didn't get the letters... Then Vanni never received my note. He didn't choose not to write...

'That's what Lucrezia says,' Nora rebutted.

'Why would I lie?' I said coldly.

Nora shrugged. 'Bianca has been in charge all this time. She would have seen the letters.'

'Do you think Matilde...?' I began.

Bianca shook her head at once. 'No, I'm sure. But who else? Father never concerned himself with the post. It was either Matilde or me sorting it out for him.'

'Dad wouldn't have done that,' Nora said. She didn't seem to know what our father was capable of. I had never told her. Maybe Bianca did, but Nora didn't believe her... she seemed to need the illusion of a wise, loving father.

She was the only one who called him Dad. For Bianca, Mia and me, he was Father.

'Why did *you* stop writing to me, Bianca? And why were you two never in touch?' I looked from Mia to Nora.

Mia seemed stricken – guilt squeezed my heart, but I had to know.

'I told them not to,' Bianca murmured. 'I wanted to protect you, Lulu. *We* wanted to protect you. I was afraid for you.' She nodded and looked down. I needed more than that, and Bianca must have guessed it, because she said in a low voice: 'I promise I'll explain. Later.'

Nora intercepted her whisper. 'You all kept secrets from Dad! You never understood him,' she cried out and got up. Her aura was flashing red, but there was a deep blue in its heart. The deep blue of sadness. 'He wanted to help you. After Mum died, you were all over the place. He sent you to a nice school in Switzerland where you were happy, and they looked after you. But instead of being thankful, you cut all contact!'

My mouth fell open.

'Nora, that's *not* what happened!' I managed to cry.

'Spare me your lies,' she said and strode out, leaving me with my mouth agape. We all jumped when we heard the door banging.

'Give her time,' Bianca pleaded. 'Please. It's been hard for her, since Father died.'

*It's been hard* for her? I wanted to shout. But I bit my lip.

'She doesn't know anything.' I looked down. 'And you don't either.'

I downed my nocino in a few sips, and a pleasant warmth, an artificial calm, filled me. The question that had been brewing inside me finally came to the surface.

'How...how did he die?'

'His heart gave way in the middle of the night,' Bianca explained. 'Gabriella left the room for a little while, and when she came back, he was gone. His pillbox was open and there were pills everywhere.' She paused. 'The doctor said that had he managed to reach them, he would have survived. Gabriella blamed herself, of course... if only she'd come back a few minutes before, if only she hadn't left the room... It was a blow for her.'

'And a relief for us,' Mia added.

*You can say that again.* 'Why is the house so empty, anyway? I thought it would be full of sycophants coming to pay their respects.'

'We thought it'd be best to have time to... you know. Digest the whole thing. The funeral will be private. Gabriella and I agreed.'

'When is it?'

'Tomorrow. You arrived just in time.'

I was looking forward to it. I know, who looks forward to a funeral? But I was. It would open old wounds, but also lay a whole world to rest, the old world where my father had dominion over all of us. He'd be lowered into the ground, and all that hurt me, all that separated my sisters and me, would be in the past.

With a marble slate on top.

'Father wouldn't have liked this. He would have wanted hundreds of people, a grand affair,' I remarked.

'Gabriella said it's best to think of the living, not the dead. And none of us wanted to go through a *grand affair*, like you said. Also...'

'Also?' I encouraged her after a pause.

'It's difficult to explain, but it feels like the sentiment towards our family has changed. Remember when we were little, it was like everyone was our friend? Everyone wanted to be near us. But now... it's different. Maybe it's because Father had to scale down the business, and so he had to let a few people go. But they were then hired by the Orafi family, Matilde told me...'

I took a deep breath. It was so hard, so hard to feel the emotions I'd pushed down for years, pressing against my inner walls and threatening to bring all my defences down, anger and tears mixing and releasing me at once.

'I tried to ask him,' she continued. 'But having his daughter being involved in his work? Would have been a sacrilege.'

I nodded. 'Father lived in the eighties like us, but truly he was in the *eighteen*-eighties.' I made a little joke, and it ended in a sigh.

Bianca squeezed my hand. Her aura was becoming more and more luminous, the more time she spent with me. Her light, gentle blue was now tinged with silver all around. She stroked my face. 'You haven't slept, have you?'

'Just three hours on the train.'

'Food and sleep for you. And then I'll tell you everything,' Bianca said. 'Like I should have done years ago.'

Matilde had gone all out with dinner: cannelloni with a ragù sauce that tasted of heaven followed by a fragrant polenta and orange cake. Claude and his posse of celebrity chefs weren't a patch on her home cooking. Once again, it seemed to me like time had reversed and we were back to being children, eating in the kitchen on a night that Father wasn't there, and we were spared the formality of the cold, grand dining room.

'Well. *Buon appetito!*' Mia called cheerfully.

I wanted to pretend I didn't care, but it stung that Nora wasn't there. 'So... Nora won't be joining us?'

'Please, don't take it personally. Besides, tonight she volunteers at an animal shelter,' Mia said.

'What is Gabriella like? Father's new wife?'

'She's sweet,' Bianca said. 'She's with her son now – she has a grown family.'

'A grown family? So, is she Father's age? I thought she'd be younger. You know, young and blinded by the Falconeri wealth,' I said, trying, and failing, to keep the sarcasm out of my voice.

Mia shook her head and swallowed a bite of cannelloni. '*M- mm.* She's older and kind and I like her a lot. I think she was disappointed, you know? She loved Father and then she found out what he was *really* like.'

I could feel Bianca cringing. 'Mia tells it like it is.'

'That's a good thing, no?' I said. 'She's transparent.' I smiled in Mia's direction.

'Not the best thing when you're in company.' Bianca laughed.

'I'm *never* in company,' Mia said cheerfully. 'I prefer being on my own and painting, or with my sisters. But really, I wish Father had died long ago...'

'*Maria Falconeri!*' Bianca exclaimed, but Mia was undeterred.

'So you'd come back, Lulu,' she continued. 'I used to set the table for you, you know? When I was little. I used to put a plate and a glass and cutlery for you, but...'

'Then I took everything away quickly, so that Father wouldn't see it,' Bianca reminisced.

'So we came to a compromise and we set a place for you in the kitchen, where Father never went,' Mia said. 'Every night, you had your little place here, at this table.'

I was speechless. They'd set the table for me every night, for all these years.

'And for Mum?' I asked, a lump in my throat.

'No,' Mia said. 'Because I was sure that you'd come back. I'm not sure she will.'

'You're not... sure?'

I looked at Bianca, who shrugged imperceptibly. 'Well, let's get this cleaned up and I can prepare your room, *va bene, cara?*' she said quickly.

'Do you mind if I make a call? My boyfriend, in Paris...'

'Of course. And then we need to know everything about this *boyfriend*,' Bianca quipped while gathering our plates.

'It's more of a...' A *work partnership*, really. But I didn't say it aloud. It sounded sad and unsatisfying. 'Well, I won't be long anyway.'

I wanted to ask Bianca if she had someone, but I was afraid of the answer, somehow. Because I hadn't forgotten what she mentioned in her letters: her meetings with Vanni at the hazelnut tree, while I was away. Childish, maybe, but childhood wounds cut deep.

'Take your time. I have a phone in my room.'

'Thank you.'

I made my way upstairs for the first time since I'd returned, and stood for a moment at the top of the stairs. The master bedroom and bathroom were at the end of a corridor on the right; ahead were our bedrooms and bathrooms, lined along a corridor; beyond there, the oldest part of the house with Mia's turret studio.

I made my way inside Bianca's room and inhaled my twin's

scent, the same that exuded from her clothes: lavender and rose. The window was a square of black dotted with stars over the profile of our hills. I switched the light on and the frescoes on the walls came to life: wildflowers and aromatic plants, bees and butterflies, and over the window and along the ceiling, pink roses trailed and bloomed. It was bright and yet soft, like stepping into a meadow just before twilight turns the sky lilac, in the last rays of sunshine.

The phone sat on Bianca's bedside table – I lifted the receiver and prepared to turn the dials...

But I didn't.

I didn't want to hear Claude's voice. I didn't want to break the spell of being here, and be told how much work had been accumulating while I was away, how much my absence was inconvenient for him. Maybe I was being unfair: but I was almost sure that was how our conversation would end up going.

Claude would have to wait, and anyway, I was sure he wouldn't be worried. Most likely, he was taking advantage of this time to work even harder...

*This is not the way I should feel towards my boyfriend.*

Being with Claude was perfect for the frozen, frightened Lucrezia who'd anaesthetised herself against emotions – our relationship was safely formal, scheduled just like the work we did together. If we were to break up, there would be no devastation, no heart-wrenching sense of abandonment. Perfect, for the child who'd been abandoned once and never wanted to feel like that, ever again.

You can't feel a frozen limb – the pain begins when it thaws. And now that I was thawing, ever so slowly, I was beginning to wonder if, beyond the pain and fear, there would be more.

More than a life that revolved around making sure I would never get hurt again, a life besieged.

And Claude, did he not deserve a woman who missed him terribly when they were apart?

I leaned on the windowsill, and the night, so deep and peaceful, relaxed my thoughts and made me sleepy. What a day.

I must have lost track of time, because Mia's small figure appeared in the doorframe, holding the portrait she'd made for me under one arm and my suitcase in the other. She'd come to me silently, in her cat-like way.

'Lulu?'

'Yes, come in.'

'I wanted to help you make your bed and be sure you had everything you needed. I'll wait in your room, if you haven't finished.'

'I haven't even started. I didn't phone after all.' I shrugged, and took my suitcase from her. 'Thank you for carrying this.'

Mia tilted her head. I guessed she was wondering why I'd decided not to call my boyfriend, but she didn't ask any questions – and for that, I was grateful. 'Are you ready to see your old room?' she said instead.

'As ready as I can ever be.'

I preceded her, and she stood silent as I lowered the door handle...

And here it was, the room of the red roses, the place I left one morning twelve years ago without knowing I would not return until now. I switched the light on, and the trails of roses seemed to quiver and ripple around and above me.

Nothing had changed.

My old desk was untouched, with its pencil holder; the ripped page from a notebook with a list of stationery I wanted to buy; a mint lip gloss that, I remembered clearly, came free with a magazine; a small folder with matching paper and envelopes; a flower press for a school project, still with flowers inside; my schoolbag on the desk chair, with the doodles I'd drawn on it in biro. The clothes I'd left on the back of the dresser, neatly folded – I certainly didn't leave them that way – someone must have folded them.

Everything was spotless.

'Look! It's perfect, here!' Mia said, and sat the painting on top of the desk.

The canvas was still shining with its radiant, rainbow aura. I didn't usually see auras emanating from objects, but this painting seemed to be the exception, because the rainbow-like iridescence wasn't fading. The more I looked at the woman in the painting, with those bright eyes, and that vibrancy, the more I thought she was the person I could have been, had it not been for the chain of events that destroyed our family. Almost as if she was the road not taken.

'I can see it shining,' I whispered, and dried a rogue tear which I hoped Mia wouldn't see – but I was sure she did. 'What I mean is, I can see its aura. It's like nothing I've ever seen, all colourful and bright. That's my gift. Did you know?'

'No... There's so much I don't know about you, Lulu. And don't cry. You're home now, and we love you so.' She dried my tears with her finger, and I blinked. Suddenly I didn't feel like crying any more. Mia's eyes were enormous, almost swallowing her face, and the difference in colour was startling. Her high forehead and long dark hair reminded me of a Renaissance girl, someone belonging to another time.

'There's so much I don't know about you, too.'

'Well, my gift is some kind of clairvoyance, I think that's what they call it. The best way to describe it is that I know things I'm not supposed to know. Also, sometimes I see Mum's paintings or my paintings change. But it's not always clear to me what they're trying to tell me.'

'Sounds fascinating. And a little confusing at the same time.'

'It can be, yes. It's why I don't usually leave the house. When I'm outside, so much information comes to me. About what people are thinking and feeling, what they went through or what's ahead of them. It gets overwhelming. But I'm happy, here at Casalta. I don't really want to be anywhere else.'

'You look like you belong here, in fact. Like you grew in the garden.'

'That's a perfect way to put it!'

'What about Nora? Bianca mentioned some kind of horse-whispering?'

'She has a connection with living things. Animals and plants. I think that one day she's going to sprout deer antlers, or develop leaves for hair.'

'Like the dryads,' I said with a smile, thinking of the statues at our gate.

'I never thought of that! Yes. She insists that she doesn't have any gifts. You see, she wants to be a Falconeri only, and to have nothing of the McCrimmon. She pretends she didn't inherit anything from Mum. She's the one who looks the least like her. So... I don't know. She's very independent; she doesn't spend much time with us. She doesn't let Bianca look after her and Bianca gets so annoyed. You know, Bianca...'

I looked away. Now that Mia was in front of me, with those truthful eyes that seemed to look through me, I was almost ashamed of the contrasting feelings I had towards my twin sister. It'd been almost easy, blaming her for not fighting for me harder, for saying I shouldn't write any more, for meeting Vanni when I couldn't see him. But now that I'd seen her again, in front of this girl whom Bianca had brought up like a mother, my resentment seemed petty.

And still. It was so hard to get over the awful feeling of betrayal when I read that sentence in her letter: *I met Vanni at the hazelnut tree...* Right at that moment when I felt so alone, so abandoned.

'What about her?'

Mia smiled a little smile, with a touch of mischief. 'She

thinks she's the one looking after everyone, especially me. I let her believe it...' I had to laugh. Mia spoke those words in a half-serious, half-playful way – the tenderness she felt for Bianca was unequivocal. 'But she needs to be looked after too. Can you see what I'm trying to say?'

'Yes. I'll try. Now that I'm back, I'll try.'

'Thank you. Sweet dreams, *sorella mia*,' she said, and hugged me goodnight. I hadn't been called *sister* for so many years, and I felt my heart constrict at the thought.

When I heard the door close behind her, I thought I could have fallen asleep there and then, on my feet. I took my clothes off and threw myself on the bed, in my silken slip.

It'd been one of the longest days of my life. Early that morning I was still in Paris, and now... I was in my childhood bed. I'd forgotten how deep the darkness was here, how complete, without the city lights.

I curled up on my side.

Sleep claimed me fast, and I had a dream within a dream: that I was still in Paris, and dreaming of Casalta.

And then – I don't know how much time had passed, because it felt like an instant – I was awakened by someone shaking me softly and whispering in my ear.

# CHAPTER 9

## CASALTA, 15 APRIL 1985

LUCREZIA

'Lulu...'

I opened my eyes and in the half-light – *is it dawn already?* – I made out Bianca's silhouette, bending over me and shaking me gently. She sat on the edge of my bed.

I sat up. 'What happened? What's the time?'

'Early. I just wanted to speak to you in peace. Everyone is asleep. Come outside with me?'

I slipped on my short satin dressing gown and we tiptoed to her room. I followed her outside by sitting on the windowsill and turning around until my feet touched the stone. The world spun a little when, as I settled on a step, I looked down to the ground below. I didn't remember the stairs being so steep, and with such a low banister, carved in the stone – Mum was a brave woman to come out here with toddler twins.

The sky was limpid and full of stars, and the air was drenched in the scents of the night. But over in the east a thin pink-orange line was rising on the hills – dawn was not quite breaking yet, but preparing its arrival. We sat side by side, shoulder to shoulder and cotton against silk, our bare feet lined up, mine with painted red nails and hers mother of pearl.

Only then I did I realise that Bianca had perilously carried a cup of coffee and, by some miracle, she'd managed not to spill it. 'For you.'

'Heavenly,' I said, and took a long sip. Caffeine coursed through my veins, and everything became a little sharper.

'I think there has been too much silence and too many secrets already, so I'm not going to wait any longer,' Bianca began in her soft voice. Her words, though, were bold in a way I never thought she'd muster. I still wasn't used to the grown-up version of my timid, mild twin, timid and mild no more.

I held my breath.

'You're right. I *did* want you away from here. Not at the beginning, I tried desperately to stop Father from sending you away and then get him to let you come back. But then I started doing the opposite, doing everything I could for you not to return to Casalta.'

My stomach knotted up. Suddenly I was cold, and the coffee tasted bitter. There was a pause where I felt utterly lost, in free fall, as if those stairs might give way and crumble under me. *Because you wanted Vanni for yourself?*

'Father did terrible things. Worse than any of us could ever imagine. We knew he was a tyrant, of course. We all could see it. Maybe Nora refused to, but, deep down, she knew.'

'Yes.'

'But there's more than that. When I wrote you that last letter, when I told you not to come home, and I stopped writing to you... I was trying to *protect* you. I was afraid for your safety. I've been so afraid all these years, until the night he died. I was afraid he'd do to you what... what he did to Mum.'

My hands tingled in panic and the sound of my heavy breathing filled my ears. I was cold. So cold. 'What did he do to Mum?'

But I knew the answer. Had I always known, in a way? Had I deluded myself, like Nora, that Father couldn't have done it?

'Mum's accident *wasn't an accident*.' She was whispering, even though we were alone, even though the whole house was asleep. She spoke as if the hills themselves were listening. 'Do you understand?'

'I don't know.' The icy feeling spread from my heart to all my limbs, numbing my head.

Our noses were almost touching, and our eyes were searching the other's gaze, with me trying to swallow what she'd just said, and her trying to gauge if I'd grasped it: I could only stare at her. Her skin had a slight blue tinge, in the eerie light of dawn.

'That day on the hills, Mum didn't fall. She was *murdered*, Lulu. By our father.'

# CHAPTER 10

## CASALTA, 15 APRIL 1985

LUCREZIA

Bianca's whispers felt like screams to me. The word – *murdered* – seemed to dance in front of my eyes in shiny, cruel letters.

It couldn't be.

And yet...

Before I could stop them, my fingers uncurled and couldn't hold onto the cup. It fell silently, cleanly, in a perfect drop, and shattered on the ground below.

'Remember how he used to call Mum a *witch?*' Bianca continued, her voice so thin, it almost faltered. 'Because sometimes she had dreams and what she dreamed came true, and how the men at the vineyards wanted her to be there at the opening of the season because the vines would grow well...'

'I remember those things she did, but I don't remember Father calling her a witch.'

'He did, and he thought *you* were one too. He thought that when you saw Mum that night, it was because of that, because you're our mother's daughter. And that you knew... what *really* happened.'

Oh, God. How could I not have thought of that? I could see Father would be capable of it; why then why did it not occur to me? Had I shut that possibility away because it was too awful to contemplate?

'How do you know? How did you find out?'

'He told me. He seemed proud of it, Lulu! He said Mum had betrayed him, and he punished her. He said he pushed her down the hill. He *told* me, Lulu.'

How scared our mother must have been! To see her husband's face as he sent her to her death...

Did she fight? Did she beg for her life? The idea of her accident had been terrible, but it seemed almost painless now compared to the agony of having your life taken away by a loved one.

'And that if I was to tell anyone, if any of us said anything, we'd end up the same way. I was terrified that if you came back, he'd take you for a walk on the hills, and...'

'And that he'd do the same to me.' I finished her sentence for her. 'Because he knew you wouldn't dare speak out, but *I* would.'

'I'm no coward, Lulu. I've never been. I'm the eldest daughter, even if just by a few minutes, and I couldn't put any of you in harm's way.' There was a steely edge to her tone.

'I know. I know. I don't blame you for not saying anything. Who knows what would have been the right thing to do, what we could have done to cause the least pain to each of us? You did what you could.'

I felt Bianca exhale beside me, like the burden of the blame I'd laid on her shoulders for so long had been lifted. We took each other's hands, at the same time. The dawn, clear and pure, lined the hills with pink, and its beauty filled the silence between us.

This sheltered space where Casalta rose seemed so peaceful

and safe, and yet, it had been neither peaceful nor safe for Mum. Nor for Bianca, or any of us, really.

Five women annihilated by one man, and all this because we used our strength and courage to *endure*, instead of use that courage and strength to rise up. I wondered how many daughters and wives, how many women in this ancient house and its thousand years of history, must have gone through the same. I wondered if any of them ever sat on the stairs and held hands, drawing support from each other, or alone in sorrow or hope, watching cold, distant stars.

'It's strange, you know. It should be this big revelation that changes everything. And it is a big revelation, and it *does* change everything. But it doesn't feel absurd, impossible. It feels like he *would* have been capable of it.'

Bianca nodded. 'Our family business hasn't always been... straightforward. It took me years to twig. Father's men coming and going, and people treating him like a little emperor. Like the lord of the land. When we were children, I used to think that Father's men were simply our friends. That we sat in the first pew in church and that everyone treated us with deference because they *liked* us. But it took me years to understand that... the powerful families they speak of on the news, the men who are above the law, the clans that control pretty much everything in their territory. We're one of them. Or we were.'

Every word Bianca spoke was another piece of the jigsaw – how obvious the whole picture is, once you've put it together. I'd grown up away from Casalta, working and reworking fragmented childhood memories, trying to finish the jigsaw when there were so many missing pieces.

'Do our sisters know the truth?'

'I didn't tell anyone what Father said to me. Mia goes from having no filter whatsoever to being unreadable, so I have no idea whether she knows or not. Nora rejects Mum completely;

she refuses to be anything different from a Falconeri born and bred. She always looked for Father's approval.'

'Yesterday Mia said she wasn't sure if Mum was coming back.'

'I think sometimes she lives in another world. I can't always make sense of what she says.'

I looked down at the pieces of the broken cup. Pieces of my memories, my assumptions, my mistakes, coming together to tell the story. My mind was still wrapping itself around those pieces. 'I saw her again in Paris. *Mum*. The day you called me.'

'You *did*?'

'She was in the crowd at an event I was doing. Dressed in one of her long skirts... All those years ago they tried to convince me that I was hallucinating. But weirdly enough, Father was right. I hadn't really seen her. It was my gift. It must have been.'

Silence filled the space between us while I processed what Bianca had said. Father had confessed to Mum's murder...

'But if he sent me away in case I'd found out the truth and told anyone... why did he confess to you?'

'Because he was afraid of you. He wasn't afraid of me. And he didn't confess, he *boasted*.'

'I know that letter by heart, you know? The one where you told me to stay away.'

Even in the half-light, I could see Bianca's eyes glimmering.

'I'm so sorry. I didn't see another way.'

'He was wrong about you, you know? He thought I'd be strong, but you wouldn't. He was wrong.'

Bianca smiled a half-smile, sweet and wistful. 'I wish I could see her, Lulu. Or hear her talking to me. My gift disappeared when you left, you know? With you and Mum gone... I don't know. I lost it. Remember the little girl I used to hear, Viola? I pretended she was an imaginary friend for so many years.'

'Yes, of course I remember.'

'I haven't heard her since you left. Sometimes I still catch whispers on the wind, or when I go to see someone we look after, I sense snippets of conversation in their homes. But apart from that, I have no gift. Nora refuses her gift, but I loved mine. I miss it.'

'Oh, Bianca! Did you not consider that I could help you... That together we could do something? Fight for a better life?'

'Something like what? Dismantle Father's domain? At twelve, fourteen, sixteen? We were children, and then teenagers. This wasn't a book or a film where everything ends in glory, Lulu.'

'I could have helped you shoulder the burden. We could have carried the situation *together*!' Our whispers and our breath mixed, our faces close.

'I wanted you to be somewhere free of danger, Lulu! And I was going to stay here and look after Nora and Mia. This was the plan. Except you hated me for it. What I wanted, what I needed... having my twin with me... didn't matter anyway. Practically speaking, I mean. Father would have left you at that school no matter what I said or did.'

'Bianca... I'm sorry,' I said, and for once, it wasn't the hurt, lost child who spoke for me, but the woman I'd become.

'I'm sorry too! I should have come and looked for you. And spoken to you. But we thought you never wrote, and I thought that meant something... I thought you'd come back, after boarding school, and then we'd be old enough to know what to do. Except you didn't come back. By then, it was all broken, and I didn't know how...' She threw her hands up. 'You didn't even tell us you went to Paris...'

'I wanted to disappear. At least for a while. It sounds cruel, it was cruel, I can see it now. But I felt like nobody wanted me here.'

'Oh, I wanted you here. I felt like half of a person.'

'In your letters, you always seemed so happy. It was like you were rubbing my face in it. That you were home, and I'd been exiled. I know you didn't mean it, but it was hard to read about Casalta. I was terrified, Bianca...'

'I was nowhere near happy, Lulu. I didn't want to worry you, and I didn't want to say anything against Father in case he'd harm you. I should have come to you, told you everything...'

'We both did our best. And we're here now,' I whispered. 'What I'd like to know is... did he know you'd sent me an invitation to the wedding?'

'I don't know. I didn't dare bring it up. But I was still afraid, you know? I wasn't sure if you'd be safe here. It was Gabriella who insisted, and convinced me.'

'I see.'

'Lulu, towards the end... he'd changed. When he met Gabriella, or maybe just before. I let Gabriella convince me because I hoped he'd be harmless, now. And then, well, he died.'

'Not many will miss him,' I said coldly, but there was a pang in my heart anyway, because we could have been father and daughter, we could have had each other, and now we never would.

I was desperate to ask about Vanni. How was he, where was he? Were they friends, or even something more? She'd mentioned him in almost all the letters. But then, it was many years ago...

'Bianca...'

'Oh, look! That's Gabriella back,' she said, and I followed her gaze to a woman in a blue jacket, carrying a small suitcase and making her way through the French doors. 'You'll like her, I'm sure. I'm going to make more coffee; it's going to be a long day,' she said quickly, and gave me a peck on the cheek.

I shivered in the fresh morning air, and slipped inside to get dressed. I'd have to go retrieve the pieces of the broken cup – the metaphor wasn't lost on me.

I hadn't called Claude yet but now Gabriella was here, and I wanted to meet her – we were to get ready for the funeral – there was so much to do... Easily, seamlessly, Claude slipped from my mind again.

I looked at myself in the mirror, in my black dress and black Alice band, and slipped on a pair of earrings. Talking with Bianca had been the sweetest reconciliation, but at the same time I was chilled to the bone: Father boasted about pushing our mum to her death? Could it really be? Could he have done that to her?

I recalled the day my mother died, and my instinctive answer was yes.

He could have.

# CHAPTER 11

## CASALTA, 15 MAY 1973 – TWELVE YEARS EARLIER

LUCREZIA

I crossed the gardens, returning from seeing Vanni after school – in secret, of course. I often spent a little time outdoors before coming home anyway, to shake off the school day, so I had a ready-made excuse for being out longer.

It was then that I saw my mum coming out of the house with her bag on her shoulders, on her way to the hills. I ducked and hid, even though I knew she wouldn't have stopped me from seeing Vanni, as *she* had nothing against the Orafi. But if I were to be discovered, I didn't want her to be involved and get into trouble on my behalf.

There was a precedent. Once, Mum exchanged a few words with Signor Orafi in the tailor shop: this came to my father's ears, and I still remember the shouting that followed.

Mum often wandered in the hills carrying her painting materials with her, an easel under her arm, wearing her wide-brimmed hat, so I thought nothing of it. But just as I was considering whether it was safe to come out of my hiding place and go home, I saw my father go after her. He was taking his time, like he wasn't in a hurry to reach her. In hindsight, I would say he was stalking her like a hunter with a deer, in the way he walked slowly and silently after her – but at the time, I didn't think there was anything untoward happening, because Father enjoyed walking around the Casalta estate, too, on the hills and in the vineyards and olive groves. He said he wanted to see in person what everyone was doing.

When they were both out of my sight, I slipped out of my hiding place and made my way to the kitchen, where I knew Matilde would give me milk and a slice of bread and jam, and settled down to do my homework. Bianca was already there, her school materials on the table, carefully arranged the way her things always were.

'If Father finds out you're talking to Vanni Orafi he'll be angry,' she whispered. Looking back, this had always been her worry: that Father would be angry.

'Well, he *won't* find out!'

Matilde turned to look at us, but she said nothing. Years later, I was to describe her stance towards my father's authority to my therapist as half feisty, half pragmatic. Feisty, because I could see she loathed him, and she showed her rebellion in half sentences and pursed lips; pragmatic because not only did he pay her wages, but her family was employed by the Falconeri in various ways. Laura, our maid, was her niece; her son, Diego, was one of my father's men, even if he was young still; an assortment of nephews and cousins worked in our estate.

We resumed our homework. It was a peaceful afternoon. So peaceful, it seemed like nothing could ever disturb the harmony of the five of us together: Bianca and me studying the Roman emperors, Nora and Mia playing in the courtyard under Laura's watchful eye, the familiar scent of Matilde's cooking in the air.

And then, suddenly, the sound of Mia's crying seeped in

from the courtyard. Matilde and Bianca rushed to see what was wrong, while I lingered on the doorstep – Mia never cried; she was usually very quiet and not prone to outbursts. The sound of her desperate sobs was so upsetting, so *wrong*, I almost covered my ears.

Nora was standing there, eyes wide. 'I don't know what happened!' she said over Mia's sobbing. 'I didn't touch her!'

'Did she fall?' Matilde asked, inspecting Mia's knees. Mia wrapped her arms around Matilde's neck and wouldn't let go. We were all aghast. This had come out of nowhere. She was crying so hard, she was almost howling.

'No. We were just playing,' Nora replied, and her eyes were full of tears too. 'I haven't done anything to upset her!'

'I know, *tesoro*, don't worry,' Matilde said, and Bianca took Nora's hand.

Matilde felt Mia's forehead for a temperature, asked her if her tummy was sore, but my sister wouldn't answer, just cried and cried.

Mia's despair was contagious, and for a little while all of us sisters were in tears. The peace was broken, and we became tetchy, anxious. It took a long time for Mia to calm, and when she did, she lay listless and pale in Matilde's arms, sucking her thumb, even if Mum and Matilde were trying to help her grow out of it. Nora was back outside, skipping – she always hated being indoors, confined. We could hear the *snap snap snap* of the rope as she jumped.

The sun was setting and making the copper pots and pans hanging on the walls shine golden red. 'You need to get off me, *tesoro*, it's dinnertime,' Matilde said gently; Mia rested her head on Bianca's lap instead. 'The Signora should be home any time now; there's not enough light for painting,' she said. Mum was never out in the dark.

When the evening shadows began drawing in, Matilde

stepped outside, waiting... I put mine and Bianca's books away in our bags. Nora joined us inside.

No sign of Mum.

And no sign of Father, either.

He was usually strict about his routine and liked his meals at the same time every night, in the dining room, with a table-cloth and the good crockery. Dinners were always a formal affair, even when us girls were little; we were expected to have the table manners of mini adults. Often Father's friends or associates joined us at the table, and he sat like a king over-looking his kingdom, and held court.

We were so much happier when he was out and we were allowed to eat in the kitchen with Mum, warm, cosy and free to be children; but it hardly ever happened. We needed to be given explicit permission to do that, and now there was no instruction.

Us girls were chomping on breadsticks and Matilde was fretting, going in circles between the courtyard, the inner door and the stove where dinner was spoiling, grumbling under her breath about whether she should go and speak to Father or not.

'He likes his meals on time,' Bianca whispered, apprehensive as she always was. She was the one most affected by his moods and his explosions; she couldn't stand anyone even raising their voice, so Father's wrath was the equivalent of the end of the world for her sensitive soul.

Matilde threw her hands up in the air. 'I *know*. But he doesn't like me going to his study and disturbing him, either. You know he hates being interrupted when he's working.'

'He's not working. He's out on the hills with Mum,' I piped up. 'Unless he's back and went straight to the study and we didn't hear him.'

I remember both Matilde and Bianca stiffening, and Bianca's aura appearing before my eyes, scarlet with alarm.

'What are you all babbling about?'

Father's tall, imposing frame appeared on the kitchen doorstep. We all fell silent, and Mia sat up. He was smiling in a way that disquieted us even more; I remember his expression to this day.

'Dinner's ready, Signor Falconeri, the table is set – we were just waiting for the Signora. Would you like it to be served now? I didn't want to...'

'Don't fret. Please feed the girls. I'll send Diego up to see if Emmeline lost her sense of time while painting, as she often does.' That wasn't true. She was always home before dark. 'I'll go down to the village to look for her, in case she's visiting a friend. Is the little one all right?' he added, seeing Mia's face, which still bore the signs of her tears. His benevolent expression was confusing. Usually it was reserved for friends and clients and associates, not for us.

Bianca stood in front of Mia at once. 'She's fine, Father.'

'Good, good. Well, *buon appetito*, girls. Thank you, Matilde.'

Again, in hindsight: he never felt the need to tell us what he'd been doing – Mum never lost her sense of time because she knew the consequences – she would never have gone to see a friend at dinnertime, for that exact reason.

Time stretched; that evening seemed to last days. The house was empty without Mum, and Father had disappeared, too. Matilde said she'd stay over and put us all to bed, but as soon as she'd tucked the little ones in we all piled up in Bianca's little bed and waited. We were so young, we couldn't resist sleep: it took us, despite the worry and weirdness of it all.

The next morning, when we were still in Bianca's bed, half asleep and bundled up like puppies, Matilde ran in, still tying her dressing gown. She was followed by Father, who told us that Diego had found our mother's broken body, up on the hills.

After the funeral, Father's friends gathered in the living room to drink and smoke, while us girls were supposed to be in bed. I don't know why, but I slipped downstairs and stepped into that room full of men, a little girl in a polka dot nightdress, traumatised and in pain.

When they realised I was there, everyone quieted. I also don't know why I said what I said.

'You weren't in your study, working. You went to the hills with Mum. I *saw* you.'

Mia's sudden upset came back to me: I was sure, then, that she'd felt the exact time it happened.

'I'm so sorry, Signor Falconeri!' Matilde ran in to take me back upstairs, and the little kingdom of men reprised their business.

I still have no idea why I did that, why I dared interrupt a gathering of adults – my father's friends, in particular – in my nightie, barefoot and half-dazed.

Like a small avenging angel.

It was just for an instant, but my father looked almost afraid.

Everything was coming back to me now, all the memories that I'd struggled to recall even during my therapy sessions in Paris. It made sense. What Bianca had told me made sense.

Father *murdered* her. I knew he wasn't home, that afternoon. That was why he sent me away. And yet, why be afraid of what a little bereaved girl would say, when the Falconeri family was so powerful as to have everyone who mattered in their pockets? So much so that nobody challenged my father's account. My mother died on those hills, and nobody asked any questions.

But he'd been afraid of a little girl. And I found the thought grimly rewarding.

My father had been afraid of *me*.

# CHAPTER 12

## CASALTA, 15 APRIL 1985

LUCREZIA

Everyone was in the living room, dressed in black, stiff and waiting for this day to be over. Coffee and pastries were laid out on the low table. I scanned the room until I found Gabriella, the unknown quantity.

'Oh, you must be Lucrezia!' Gabriella exclaimed and came to embrace me.

Gabriella wasn't like I'd expected – Bianca had told me that she was Father's age, and not young as I'd imagined her – but she simply didn't look like my father's type.

'You look just like Bianca!'

*Er, yes, we're twins.* But I refrained from a smart answer.

'This is my son, Giulio.' She opened her arm to indicate a quiet-looking middle-aged man.

My mum had been stunning, and Father had always liked everything showy, shining, from his clothes to his cars. Gabriella was dressed in a suit jacket and sensible shoes, she wore her hair in a grey bob and her face was clean, free of make-up. Her eyes were deep blue and calm, kind – she was looking straight at me, almost through me. I noticed that Mia, sitting on the windowsill a little removed from everyone, was watching us.

I held Gabriella's gaze.

'Nice to meet you,' I told her, and nodded towards Giulio. My tone was non-committal.

So this was the woman who, according to Bianca, had changed my father for the better? First impressions weren't always reliable, and people could be deceitful, but my impression of her was the same as my sisters': that she was mild-mannered, calm, reassuring. She seemed grieved by her new husband's death, but not devastated, not broken.

To think how I'd pictured her when I received Bianca's letter in Paris: *fake blonde opportunist marries old man for money*. A sudden thought made its way into my consciousness: I'd been wearing grey-coloured glasses for a long time, but maybe, just like *pink*-coloured glasses, they lied. Not everything was potentially painful, not everyone potentially out to hurt me.

'So, is it just us?' I asked Bianca.

'Just us, and a few distant relatives meeting us there,' she said.

'We let everyone know we preferred a private ceremony and no home visits. To give us privacy, a chance to grieve,' Gabriella intervened while Bianca was nodding her approval.

I was sure that tongues would wag. I could hear them already: *Falconeri should have a sea of flowers, authorities in attendance, a full church with latecomers left outside, what are they thinking?*

'Dad deserved better than this. I need to go and see to the horses,' Nora said in a clipped tone. I could hear tears in her voice.

'What? Now?' Bianca protested. 'You'll smell of horse! In the church!'

'Nobody will be there to smell it, Bianca! It's not even a

proper funeral, and it's not even in a proper church! I still can't believe you did this!'

'I suppose animals don't go by our commitments and sched-ules, do they? Whatever happens, they need to be seen to...' Gabriella said mildly, but Nora looked at her with narrowed eyes and strode out. Her peacekeeping attempt had failed. Mia ran after Nora, and I could see Bianca trembling with anxiety.

'Bianca, why don't you sit in peace with a cup of coffee? I'll clean all this up,' I said.

'I'll help you,' Gabriella offered, and Giulio busied himself with a cup for Bianca.

A moment later, Gabriella and I were standing at the kitchen sink together, washing cups. *Who is Gabriella really trying to relieve from the ordeal of a crowd of mourners and a big family reception, us or herself?* I asked myself as I looked across at her from under my lashes.

'You know, Lulu. It's what he would have wanted. A small ceremony, away from the village's eyes. I can assure you.'

'It doesn't sound like my father, but I suppose you knew him better than me at the end. I was away for years.'

'He'd changed.'

'So Bianca told me. She said *you* changed him.'

'Oh, no, it wasn't me. It was guilt. And that's the real reason for his death. He missed your mother; he missed you. Believe me. You know what he said to me, the night he died?'

'What?' I wasn't quite ready to feel sorry for him.

Because of what he'd done to Mum.

Because he'd sent me away.

Because of the year I'd spent at the Istituto Lugano, the *very good school.*

'That he got everything wrong. That he'd ruined his life.'

I was about to say that he was right, that he had, indeed, ruined his life, and mine, and ended my mother's – when thank-

fully, Bianca interrupted us. She did a double-take, as she saw
me flushed and flustered.

'Lulu, there's someone on the phone for you. Someone who
can't speak Italian.' Of course, it had to be Claude. I instantly
felt guilty for not having called him yet.

'Want to take it in my room again?' Bianca offered. 'It's the
only private place aside from Father's study.'

Father's study held so much trauma for me, I never wanted
to see the inside of it again.

'It's fine, I'll take it in the living room. The cars are nearly
here.'

I held the phone to my ear.

'*Lucresiah?*'

Already it was strange to hear my name pronounced the
French way again.

'Hello,' I said. 'I'm sorry I didn't call, I...'

I... *what?* I was trying to work through the idea that my
father murdered my mother, to unravel years of misunderstand-
ings, to get to know three young women who were my sisters
and yet were strangers. How could I explain all that? The wall
between Claude and me was higher than ever, and I had no
way, no words, to confide in him. I didn't even think he'd want
to know, or be faced with all these complications.

'I have been so busy,' I finished the sentence.

'I can imagine. It was busy here too. How are you?'

'Good. It's all a little complicated, but good,' I said. Sophie's
forty-cigarettes-a day voice said something in the background,
and Claude laughed.

'Sophie here says to please come back, that she can't deal
with the workload all on her own. I think she means she can't
deal with *me* all on her own.'

'Tell her I'm coming back soon.' My eyes met Bianca's,
sitting on the sofa. She pretended not to hear what I'd just said.

*Am I?*

I supposed so. Once my father's affairs were sorted, I'd go back to my life while staying in touch with my sisters. I'd return to the Paris apartment I shared with Claude, and there would be no daydreaming of Casalta any more, because I'd been there in person and broken the spell.

'Anyway, I miss you. You'll tell me all when you come back, *bien?*'

'*Bien,*' I replied. It didn't escape me that he'd called me with Sophie there, therefore it couldn't be a private conversation – that there had been no *I love you*, nothing tender in our words or tone except a quick *I miss you*, more because of my absence in the workplace than because I was his girlfriend. This was the way things were between us.

'I need to go. I'm about to go to my father's funeral.'

'You... what? Oh. I'm sorry. It really was a bad time to call.'

'I'll call you later. I probably won't catch you at home, but I'll try.'

But thoughts of Claude, Paris and my life there were quick to fall out of my mind as we climbed into the black cars on our father's final journey.

Now I understood what Nora meant: the funeral firm's cars stopped at one of the small chapels at the edge of the village, a cramped little building that was opened only once a year, in August. The rest of the year, leaves and dust accumulated on its steps, and even now that it'd been cleaned it still looked a little neglected. How different from the patron saint's church, laden with frescoes, statues and decorations.

It was a small crowd that attended, and the whole thing was pervaded with a strange feeling, almost furtive. There were the four of us daughters, Gabriella and her son, Matilde with Diego, a few long-lost relatives – two elderly cousins and a young woman who looked eerily like Nora. Some of Father's men were there too, but none of his old friends and associates, the people I used to see at the parties in our house.

The coffin, by contrast, was covered in flowers, and a purple and golden garland that said 'Amatissimo Fosco' – 'Beloved Fosco'.

That had been Gabriella's choice, for sure.

I sat between Bianca and Mia, both stony-faced, and beside them were Nora and Gabriella. Nora was the only one in tears, though Gabriella's face was full of wistfulness... as if she was missing something that never was.

It all finished quickly. The mass was short, the walk to the cemetery a stone's throw, and after a few words, Fosco Falconeri was gone, sealed away in our family's marble tomb. Nora bent down and laid a little bouquet of wildflowers against the plaque with his name engraved. She looked so desolate, and I wanted to go to her and hold her, and tell her how sorry I was that she was suffering. But I knew I wouldn't be welcome, so I just hovered there awkwardly. It was Mia who went to her, and then Bianca, one at each side of her.

I was so surprised when Nora turned her beautiful face to me, and freed one of her arms. She extended her hand to me, and I took it, and my sisters welcomed me into their embrace.

'Emmeline McCrimmon Falconeri', said the plaque just beside my father's. I'd never been at my mother's graveside until today... I'd never wanted to. She wasn't there, anyway, for sure – not in that silent, cold place, when she'd been so vibrant and full of life.

My eyes were full of tears, and the breeze was lifting up dust and soil – I couldn't see properly. It was definitely an illusion, the head of bright red hair that appeared behind the cypresses and disappeared just as fast. My heart galloped for a little while, but I didn't move; I didn't say anything.

*Hello, Mum. Look at us, we're together*, I told her in my mind.

*You're gone, and I'm here, in Casalta*, I said to my father. *It turned out that your daughters were, ultimately, stronger than you.*

It was time to go back and offer refreshments to the few relatives in attendance – that would be Bianca's and Matilde's territory. I wondered how the small talk with long-lost relatives would go: *Yes, he sent me away for a few years, I don't know exactly what he told you, maybe that I was unruly? Uncontrollable? Mean to my sisters and disrespectful to him? I'm back now, though. Because he's dead.*

Oh, God. I really hoped I could find a way to avoid all of this.

'I'd like to walk home,' I said to Bianca, and she nodded in agreement. I couldn't face sitting in that black car again, ready to swallow us like an enormous crow, hot and claustrophobic, but mainly I was hoping to get home after everyone had already left.

'Don't worry. I'm holding the fort. Take your time,' she said, and I was so grateful. Coming back to Casalta like this, with a cloud over my head, not knowing what my father had said about my absence. Soon I'd go to the village and see the people I used to know, walk in the places I used to walk... but not today, not yet.

Before taking the road home, I looked around one last time... I *knew* that Vanni, and any representative of the Orafi family, would not be there.

And still, I looked around me as discreetly as I could all the way to the church and then to the cemetery, hoping against hope to see him.

But it was someone else who came up to me before I could get away, someone I didn't want to see or speak to.

'Diego,' I greeted him with forced cordiality, because he was Matilde's son, and she didn't deserve any less.

*He* did, though. This wiry, pinched man with cigarette-stained hands had been my father's factotum. He wasn't one of his friends, the men who had access to our home when Father held court – he was relegated to the kitchen, or slipped in and out of my father's study on errands. I was always wary of him, even as a child. I remembered seeing him outside my father's study, playing with the pocket-knife he always carried, waiting for orders. He made my skin crawl, and my sisters had always been wary of him too.

'Lucrezia.'

Oh. He always addressed me as 'Signorina' when my father was alive.

'We lost a great man,' he said, his tone grandiose.

What should I say to that? 'Thank you,' I whispered, while asking myself if there was any polite or even just acceptable way to tell him to go away, without hurting Matilde's feelings.

It seemed impossible that a kind, honest woman like Matilde had given birth to him. Matilde's husband, also one of my father's men, had disappeared many years before, leaving her alone and penniless to raise their son. No wonder Diego was so loyal to the Falconeri; Fosco had given his mother a job and taken him under his wing.

'I hope you know you're not alone. I'm here for whatever you need. I know the business inside out,' Diego said. He didn't *know* the business, not really; all he knew were the tasks my father gave him.

'*We'll* take charge.' What was I saying? I was going back to Paris as soon as I could. Wasn't I?

The snort of laughter he made when I spoke about taking

charge made me want to slap him. Except I would have had to touch that greasy skin.

'Of course, we'll make sure to look after you until you find another place to work,' I said, summoning all my good manners. I didn't know exactly what he'd done for my father all these years, but it certainly wasn't about wine and oil making. As dramatic as it might sound, he was the henchman to the villain, and with my father gone, he had to go, too. No more shady business in Casalta.

Diego went pale and took a step back. 'I've worked for your father since I was a boy.'

'Please, Diego, this is not the moment... Like I said, we'll make sure you're looked after. And your mum is staying with us, of course.'

'Casalta needs me.' He now looked and sounded almost menacing.

'My father needed you. We don't,' I snapped. I didn't want to be cruel, but I also couldn't stand the subtly threatening way he was talking to me. I didn't want him anywhere near my sisters.

It was Gabriella who saved me the embarrassment, taking me by the arm and leading me away with a mild but firm excuse.

'He seems bad news,' she whispered.

He stood by the side of the church, cigarette in hand. His eyes were still on us. We would have to speak to my father's men. We would have to take charge. Someone would. Could I really go back to Paris and let Bianca have everything on her shoulders... again?

'Do you mind if I walk with you?'

'No, not at all. Where's your son?'

'I asked him to go home. He has a family, a job; I don't want him to be away for long. He told me to say goodbye to all of you.'

*What are you going to do?* I wanted to ask her, but it seemed an intrusive question, right now. And a loaded one. Now that my father was dead, who'd own Casalta? Gabriella, us sisters, all of us?

We walked together along the village borders, and up the hill. A gentle spring wind was blowing, light and fresh and new. White fluffy clouds flew in the sky, and a hint of grey over the hills told me that rain was preparing to fall.

'Lucrezia, I have to tell you... I'm so happy you came back. For your sisters, but especially for you,' Gabriella said.

She was being so kind to me. I was surprised – she was my father's widow, after all; did he not convince her that I was the devil, the black sheep of the family who brought only trouble to his door? But then, he'd told her that he regretted what he'd done. That he missed my mother and me.

Should my heart soften towards him, now? Because it didn't.

'Thank you.'

'I know you suffered much, Lucrezia...'

*I don't think you do. Nobody does.* Unless... Had he told her? Had he told her *where he sent me?*

I closed my eyes in the sunlight for a moment, and then my gaze followed a Vanessa Atalanta fluttering among the wild fennel. I didn't want to think about that place now – it was all over, my father was in the ground and there were blooms and blossoms all around us. A new era was beginning.

'There are easier times ahead for you, now. I'm sure,' Gabriella continued.

'Yes. For all of us.'

'But if that shouldn't be the case, you can count on me. I promise.'

It was a sweet thing to say – but I couldn't help thinking that it sounded a little ominous. Maybe it was just my paranoia, but for a moment it seemed to me that Gabriella knew something I didn't.

Bianca was in the kitchen, uncorking another bottle of our wine.

'They're still here. *Hide!*' Mia murmured with a half-smile. She'd guessed I didn't know what to tell my father's family. Or that I was worried I'd end up saying too much.

I slipped upstairs to Bianca's room: I had a promise to keep. I was almost sure he wouldn't answer – when he did, I stuttered for a moment.

'Claude? Why are you home?'

'Because you promised you'd call after the funeral. Why did you call home if you thought I wouldn't be here?'

Good question.

His tone softened. 'How are you? Has it been crazy, with the family and everything?'

'Yes. It's all finished.'

'Are you coming home?'

*Home?* For a moment, I was confused. I *was* home.

I rubbed my forehead. 'I don't know. My sisters need me, I think. There's a lot to sort out...'

'I understand. But there's a lot of work to be done here too.' *Are we together, Claude? Or are we working partners who happen to live together?*

Neither of us had said anything about missing each other.

'I know. I'm sorry. But I really have to stay a little longer.'

A sigh. 'Fine, of course. Do you have an idea how long...?'

'No. Not yet.'

The question burned on my tongue, but I was too overwhelmed by everything that was happening – changes that were so fast, so deep. It was just like I'd thought the night before leaving: the Lucrezia who returned to Paris wouldn't be the same Lucrezia who left.

Silence fell: it wasn't often that Claude was at a loss for words.

We had nothing to say.

'Say hi to Sophie for me,' I scrambled, and then, just as he was putting the phone down, I called his name – but it was too late. He'd gone.

I realised that what churned my stomach now wasn't only the sense of loneliness that the conversation had given me – but guilt.

Because since I'd arrived in Casalta, I'd dreamed of seeing Vanni, as absurd as it was. A man who might have had ties to my sister, whom I hadn't seen in twelve years, who could be married – who was still a sworn enemy of my family, and even if that meant nothing to me, it might mean something to him...

Vanni's face had been behind my eyes every moment, since I'd arrived. I could picture him so clearly, his mellow smile, his constantly tangled brown hair, his sun-kissed skin – but I pictured a boy, the boy I knew – not the man he was now...

Right in that instant, something caught my eye.

Over Bianca's desk, pinned to a corkboard, were postcards, tickets, photographs. One in particular made me do a double-take. I stood and stared at it. *Vanni?* She had a photograph of Vanni hanging on the wall?

I blinked. His hair was tamed, he looked more confident, his eyes smaller and sharper. But he hadn't changed much. His face was still, unmistakably, an Orafi face. An Orafi face, yes; but not Vanni's.

I unpinned the picture and looked at it more closely – that was Lorenzo! Vanni's older brother. They looked very much alike, but I could see the difference, now. I breathed out a sigh of relief – it would have been so hard, to see him and Bianca together. But this was a true mystery – why did Bianca have

Lorenzo's picture pinned up? Was there something between them?

Now that would be a strange turn of events, if it was the good sister, the well-behaved one, falling under the Orafi boys' spell.

A sudden noise made me jump, and I pinned the picture back. As soon as I found a good moment, I'd ask Bianca for an explanation. But I was happy that the picture wasn't Vanni's. That was something.

Unexpectedly I slept like a baby that night, in spite of everything. And if at some point a tear came down my cheek for the death of my father and the love I never received, the love I gave him and wasted – if I mourned him in my own way... nobody would ever know.

# CHAPTER 13

## CASALTA, 16 APRIL 1985

### LUCREZIA

It was as if a weight had been lifted from us all, a weight we didn't know we were carrying, because in the morning everyone looked lighter. Even Nora, who was composed, serene, like someone after a good, liberating cry.

It was a moment of calm before the storm, as we sat together on the patio, looking out to the rose garden. Matilde laid out croissants and pastries she'd brought from the bakery, and a wonderful smell filled the air. Bianca followed with a tray of espressos and Mia with a fragrant teapot and a jug of milk.

Today we were all to attend the reading of Father's will. I hoped this would be the last dreg of the past, and then we could all put my father's affairs behind us and get on with our lives. Whatever that might mean for me.

'Lulu?' Bianca asked.

I realised that I'd been staring at her. Today was also the day I'd ask about the Orafi. I wanted to know. I *needed* to know.

'Sorry,' I mouthed, and waved my hand to signal nothing was up.

I looked around the table and considered how different us sisters were. But there was a red thread that ran through us, a subtle likeness. A stranger would have been able to tell that we were siblings.

I wore my red dress and drank black, bitter coffee. Bianca wore a flowery dress, her hair half up, half down, strawberry blonde curls escaping like wispy clouds around her face. She was drinking a cup of tea and eating a small pastry.

Nora stood leaning against one of the stone pillars, munching on her second croissant and downing cold milk. Her T-shirt and rolled-up cargo trousers told me she intended to spend the day at the stables, even if she had to drag herself away to come to the reading of the will with us.

Mia sat beside Bianca, looking half-gothic princess, half childish in a long dress, dangling earrings and bare feet – her skin was sun-kissed too, her unique eyes, one blue, one brown, resembling those of a cat, much like her demeanour.

Nobody wanted to move, hypnotised as we were by the golden sun and the perfume of the roses, but we had to. We helped Matilde clean up; Nora went to see to the horses – 'Can Matteo not do it? You're always hairy and smelly every time we have to do something formal,' Bianca protested, to no avail.

'Why were you staring at me?' Bianca whispered as we washed dishes.

'I—'

At that moment, Mia and Gabriella stepped in with stray cups, and we were interrupted.

'I'll just put some make-up on, and I'm ready to go,' I said, and made my way upstairs.

Sitting in front of the mirror, I considered the practicalities of our situation, maybe for the first time. The question that'd made an arc across my mind while sitting in the church – who will get Casalta – now sat a little heavier on my heart. Was there a chance that my sisters couldn't live in Casalta any longer? The thought was terrifying for their sakes, and yet...

Could there be a world where we'd be free of this place, heavy with memories, the place that had seen our mother's demise?

All of the answers would come this morning.

My foot was on the first step, when I froze – there were male voices coming from downstairs and something in that sound made my heart beat double time. Emotion overwhelmed me and I found myself sitting on the step.

I knew who that voice belonged to...

The Orafi brothers were here, at Casalta.

I laid a hand on my chest, trying to calm my heart – I was about to see Vanni again – the Orafi were here, they were not allowed, they'd get in trouble, my father would be angry – but no, my father was gone – what were they doing here, anyway? *I'm about to see Vanni again!* My head spun, and I almost hid behind the banister. *Lucrezia, nobody will get in trouble, you're not a child any more, and this is a courtesy visit.*

It'd been instilled into us that the Orafi were our sworn enemies, even if we didn't know why, and now they were here.

Of all the swirling thoughts in my mind, the loudest was: *I'm about to see Vanni!*

*Who* was he, now? So much time had passed, so many things had happened. I wasn't that wild little girl any more, climbing trees and hanging upside down from their branches, and he wasn't the sweet, quiet boy who listened to me and sat beside me with that steady energy, capable of calming me down. Our paths had split, and we didn't really know each other any more.

There was no reason to be nervous now, when I was simply about to meet a stranger, was there? No reason at all. I was a woman now, not a child. I'd learned to be in control of my emotions.

I took a deep breath and retreated into myself, behind my safe, unconquerable walls – only then, when I felt detached enough, did I get up and make my way downstairs.

Bianca was greeting the two brothers at the front door, but the morning sun shone in such a way that the glare almost blinded me – I could see only their silhouettes, black against the light. One stood tall, the other half his height – was he seated?

A tall and broad-shouldered man stepped in and kissed Bianca on both cheeks.

'We came to pay our respects.' His voice was gentle, but somehow imperious, even if it seems contradictory that it could be both. It was the voice of a man used to having authority.

Bianca took his hand. 'Thank you. I didn't expect you to come, but... thank you.'

I was confused, and I had to blink once, twice against the glare, until the two men came into view, and I realised what I was seeing.

Lorenzo Orafi, the older brother, was the one who'd just spoken and kissed Bianca. Vanni was sitting in a wheelchair. I grasped the banister with both hands. In a second, the wall I'd retreated behind crumbled and lay in ruins. My heart was exposed, raw and fragile, and I wanted only to run to him.

Just before I was sent away, I'd seen the tanned, scrawny boy morphing into a quiet teenager who spoke with his eyes more than with words; but I hadn't been there to see the teenager turn into a man.

Now his lithe, long frame was folded in the chair, his legs covered by a blanket. He still had a head of unruly chestnut curls, and a dimple on his right cheek... He'd changed, and yet, he was the same. I could see the wheelchair, yet it wasn't there – it didn't matter, it didn't exist.

After the first shock, all I could see was him: Vanni.

*My* Vanni.

He greeted Bianca, and she leaned over to kiss him on both

cheeks; when she straightened, there were no more obstacles in our line of view.

He saw me.

We looked at each other for what seemed like an eternity – it seemed like neither of us could look away. I knew immediately that he had not forgotten me.

On a summer evening long ago, I'd slipped out of the house to go see Vanni at our treehouse. We'd never met in the evenings before – he and his brothers were allowed to play outside until late, being boys, but us girls had to stay home. I was excited, and scared, and then excited again to be out when I wasn't supposed to, and when darkness was falling! By the time I arrived at the hazelnut tree, the sky was deep blue, stars dotted here and there. We sat together in silence, holding hands, too young and innocent for even just a kiss – and before we knew it, there was perfect darkness. The sky was ink black and covered in stars, stars like silver dust. We lay back on the blankets we kept there to make the treehouse more comfortable, and it was like falling upwards, falling in the Milky Way. I could hear him breathing beside me, feel the warmth of his body and my hand in his, and the sky above us was like a blanket, a blessing.

Looking back, I think that was the purest moment of my life.

Now, it seemed to me that the starry sky was above me again, that the silence of night enveloped us as if there were only the two of us in the world.

He was staring at me with those hazel eyes I knew so well, his chin a little raised. For a moment, those eyes belonged to the child I used to know – but then I blinked, and I saw they had hardened a little, as if the child inside had pulled back, and left his place to an adult who knew diffidence, who knew disappointment. The Milky Way dissolved, and silence gave way to words that broke the spell.

Step after step, I went down the stairs and stood in front of Vanni, Lorenzo on one side of me and Bianca on the other.

'Hello, Lucrezia,' Vanni said. His voice was deeper than I remembered. The voice of a grown man, of course – but still Vanni's voice, the voice I knew so well. He opened his hands ever so slightly, almost imperceptibly – but I noticed. It seemed to me like he was gesturing to his chair, as if to say: *this is me, now.* His aura appeared slowly as if he'd been struggling to contain it – the scarlet of anger, the light blue of sweetness and a touch of silver. The strange mixture of colours betrayed the contrast of his emotions, and flustered me even more.

*Oh, Vanni, what happened to you?*

A million questions crowded in my mind, too many to ask them all now, with Lorenzo and Bianca standing there. I was trying, and failing, to look away from Vanni, to raise my defences again.

'I'm glad to see the family reunited,' Lorenzo said towards me, and then kissed me on both cheeks, the customary way. He was dressed impeccably in a dark suit, and his demeanour was smooth, calm. He seemed in control, while Bianca and I were flustered, Vanni unreadable, a dance of colours around his head like northern lights. His aura hit me intensely, more intensely than any other's. I thought that if I'd extended my hand, I would touch solid colour.

Everyone had greeted each other formally, the Italian way, except Vanni and me. I bent down so that my cheek would touch his, and then the other side, and his aura enveloped me, the red weakening and the blue intensifying, ripples of silver wrapping themselves around me.

When what I really wanted was to hold him against me, and say how sorry I was, how desperately sorry, that I had disappeared without saying goodbye, that I had left him there alone at the treehouse, waiting for me...

'Thank you.' Bianca mercifully spoke for me. 'Please,
come in.'

We were almost in the living room when Mia's voice piped
up, calm, even. She'd been there all along, but she could be so
still and silent, she almost merged with the house. Whenever
we played hide and seek, even when she was so little, she always
won. We looked for her for hours and then she materialised
from somewhere, having forgotten we were playing at all.

'They want our house,' she said now.

Just like that.

Everyone froze. The embarrassment that filled the room
after Mia's candid words could be cut with a knife. Mia seemed
to have this effect on people – she stripped away the artificial
layers, the social conventions and polite lies, added a touch of
that unearthly clairvoyance she had, and unsettled everyone.

I *loved* it.

'Mia! Please, come in, sit down,' Bianca said after the
longest pause. Her cheeks were suffused with pink, and, I
guessed, so were mine.

I felt as if I was hovering above the sofa, instead of sitting on
it. I had to make an effort to stop myself from staring at Vanni,
striving to absorb the changes of twelve years of life in a few
minutes, to reconcile the memory of the running, jumping boy
with the man in the wheelchair. The northern lights of his aura
had diffused a little, now.

'Let me get some refreshments,' Bianca offered.

'We don't want to put you out...' Lorenzo began, merely as a
formality, because he knew that it'd be impossible to come as a
guest to an Italian home and not be offered food or drink.

'Please, it's really no bother,' Bianca insisted. 'Coffee?
Wine? I'll get both. Mia, *come with me*,' she added in a clipped
tone, and Mia followed, meekly. I was left alone with the
brothers.

'Thank you for welcoming us so kindly. Considering the history between our families,' Lorenzo began. 'Your father was a man with many friends... We thought you'd be overwhelmed with visits, and that it would best to wait until after the funeral before coming to pay our respects.' He spoke slowly, enunciating every word. He reminded me a little of a feline, the way they move slowly and lie about, perfectly relaxed, only to pounce fast and suddenly.

'We chose to keep it all private. For everyone's sake, really,' I said. My voice was a little shaky, and I hoped they wouldn't notice. I could feel Vanni's presence with every fibre of my body, and I almost didn't know what I was saying. It was like hearing someone else talking, but that someone was me.

'I understand,' he said, but his expression told me the opposite. He didn't understand, and he was surprised – or should I say, intrigued – by the deserted house and the small funeral. Because of course he knew about that – in Casalta, not many secrets could be kept.

'You said my father was a man with many friends. He was also a man with many enemies... but none of them are ours. We make our own choices.'

'That is good to know.' A brief smile.

I thought of what Mia had blurted out, that they wanted our house. Why would we give Casalta away? The thought of what would happen after had brushed me, but the idea of Casalta not being in the family any more was so remote as to be almost impossible. It took my breath away with both desire and dread: the release would be immense, for me. All those memories gone. But my sisters would never want to do that. And even I... even I would feel the ground rumble under my feet. Being in Casalta, dreaming of Casalta, hating Casalta – the house was a part of me.

I saw no reason to even think about such a thing. Mia's

words were mysterious indeed. But why were the Orafi here at all? When I'd been growing up, having them or any of their men here would have been like having a dragon rampaging in our corridors. Instead, here we were, sitting civilly like our parents hadn't hated each other with a vengeance for years.

Bianca and Matilde came carrying a tray each with coffee, sweet wine and biscotti. Lorenzo accepted a glass of sweet wine and a biscuit, while Vanni lifted a cup of black espresso. Vanni's hand was shaking – I had to hold mine in my lap, to stop them from trembling as well.

'They tell me that your little business is doing well,' Lorenzo said. 'How nice.' He seemed sincere, like he wasn't *actively* trying to be demeaning, but he managed anyway.

Bianca was unfazed. 'It's not a business, it's a co-op. We don't make a profit; we try to help people in need.' Lorenzo looked at her as if she came from another planet. Bianca's generosity wasn't something he'd be familiar with; maybe he believed such people couldn't even exist. There had to be something behind any act of kindness.

'Very noble.'

I took a sharp intake of breath. There was something about him, something in his tone... it was hate.

He hated our family, after all this time.

And there it was, the black aura appearing around him like smoke.

Bianca looked at me for a moment – she must have sensed my distress. 'And how are the Signora and Signor Orafi?' she asked quickly.

Small talk: Bianca's work, their parents' health, exchanging pleasantries.

But Lorenzo was oozing *hate*.

And Vanni was in a wheelchair, and there was no polite way to ask directly what had happened. Had Bianca known all along, but never told me? There was turmoil beneath the surface; beneath every word spoken there were another thousand that wouldn't be.

'Our parents are divorced, as you most likely know already...'

'I didn't,' Bianca said. 'I'm sorry to hear that.'

'Mum lives at our seaside home, now. And Father is not keeping well, unfortunately.'

'I'm very sorry to hear that,' Bianca repeated.

Gherardo Orafi, the head of the Orafi clan: I remembered him as a man my father's age, therefore, to my eyes, an old man. But when I left, he must have been just middle-aged. These Titans that had ruled our lives were now being shrunk to human size...

Once, Gherardo Orafi met my eyes on the church steps, and I'd trembled in terror. The Orafi patriarch was our archenemy, and I'd expected lightning and hellfire to shoot from his eyes. Instead, he'd smiled a kind smile, and this had taken me so much by surprise that I hadn't been able to look away. His aura began to appear around his body, and as a child I rarely saw auras: only when the strength of someone's feelings met my readiness to perceive them. When us daughters stepped out of the church door with our mother, Gherardo's aura had shone *gold*. I'd never seen such an aura before, and never have again.

Lorenzo laid the cup back on its plate. 'After the accident, he was never the same.'

*The accident.*

'What happened?' I asked in a small voice.

Lorenzo looked at me, and he seemed to truly see me for the first time. Surprise filled his face for a moment, and then amusement, bitter amusement. 'You don't know?'

'She's been away for years,' Vanni said, and there was reproach in his tone. As if it'd been my choice.

I felt everyone's eyes on me as I searched for something to say. *I was sent to boarding school* would be a neutral, shallow, polite reply. But it got stuck in my throat. How much did he know? How much had Bianca told him? I knew they'd met up while I was away, but how frequently, and how important these meetings were for them, I had no idea... and I was afraid to ask. Because it was Lorenzo's picture hanging on her desk. Not Vanni's.

And what happened to them? *What accident?*

I was desperate to tell Vanni everything that had happened, maybe all of it, maybe even what I hadn't told my sisters, apologise for my silence, tell him he'd been in my thoughts always, always.

I was desperate to ask him what had happened to him, about this accident that seemed to be part of everyone's knowledge except mine.

I opened my mouth to speak but couldn't find the words. I took a sip of sweet wine, my cheeks hot. If Claude and the people I worked with had seen me now, they wouldn't have recognised me. The composed ice maiden who never smiled and never cried was left behind, and this woman whose hands were shaking around her glass was left in her place... Bianca came to my rescue.

'Lulu, I believe Vanni has never seen our gardens. And it's such a beautiful day,' she said gently. Had I been a little less flustered, I would have thought it funny: Bianca and Lorenzo, the older ones, were sending the children out to play and letting the adults discuss things.

My eyes met Vanni's again, and I searched for an answer. It was clear how angry he was with me; there was no need to see the scarlet film of his aura to know that. But he laid his hands on the sides of his chair, ready to move. He followed me to the French doors, the same ones I'd gone through, literally, that day twelve years ago, and the rose garden seemed to welcome us.

Maybe the sweet scent of the roses, maybe the sunshine, unknotted us a little. The suffocating atmosphere of the living room and all its formalities was behind us, together with Lorenzo's disquieting gaze.

'The red roses,' Vanni said as we moved along the path, his strong arms pushing the wheelchair forward. 'You told me years ago.' He turned around and stopped in front of me, and I sat on the bench across from him, among the rose bushes and all their thorns.

'I remember.' I was tormenting the hem of my blouse with my fingers, and Vanni's hands were flexing on his knee.

There was more silence than words in our conversation, and so much unspoken. We were like two people on different sides of a rushing, deep, bridgeless river, trying to find somewhere to cross and meet. I tried to summon the other me, the icy woman I was in Paris, the person I'd become, but seeing Vanni had turned me back into the girl I was before, open and vulnerable.

'You never said goodbye,' he blurted out suddenly, and it felt like he'd wanted to speak those words for a long, long time.

'I couldn't. It was all so sudden—' I began, but Vanni exploded.

'Where were you, Lucrezia? One day you were here, and the next... you were *gone*. I couldn't speak to your sisters; I wasn't allowed. It was months before I caught Bianca alone in the *panetteria* when I was buying bread, and she said you'd been sent to boarding school, but never told me why. Was that true, were you in boarding school? Or is this another one of the Falconeri's secrets?'

Not my sisters, not even Bianca, had suspected that there had been something more than a boarding school. Something worse, that I had never been able to put into words. But Vanni had come close to the truth.

'Had it not been for Bianca, I wouldn't have had any idea of—'

'Well, I'm glad Bianca kept you informed!'

A pause. 'For real?' he said slowly.

I looked down. Whenever I mentioned Vanni, Bianca had changed the subject; even after all these years apart, I could feel there was something she couldn't or didn't want to put into words. And yet now, under Vanni's open, honest gaze, it all seemed like petty jealousy on my part.

'Lucrezia. Please, tell me. I need to know. *Why did you leave?*'

I couldn't bring myself to tell him about seeing my mother in that very same garden, and all that had happened after.

'My father sent me away because I wasn't... *obedient.*'

It was a child's answer. It was all I could give now.

'I don't understand. Was it because of me, because you were seeing me...?'

'No, no. It's hard to explain.'

'Well, *try*! I waited for you at the treehouse, for hours, every day. You vanished, from one day to the next. I know you couldn't help your father's decision. But why not write to me? Especially when this happened...' He looked down at his legs, at the chair.

'I didn't know! I sent you a note, but it never got to you, my sisters didn't get my letters either, someone made them disappear... I'm sorry...'

All the anger seemed to flow out of me, leaving me deflated. Added to the mixture was guilt, and floating thoughts of Claude – because I knew very well that the storm of emotion between Vanni and me, right now, shouldn't be happening, wouldn't be happening if my heart fully belonged to Claude.

*Why, why had I rocked my tidy little life, why had I come back to Casalta?*

'Oh no, I made you cry. I... Lucrezia, I'm sorry...'

'I'm so sorry too...'

He touched my cheek and, with that, he dried my tears. I

held onto his hand and kept it against my face, my eyes closed. When I opened them again, the scarlet hue had gone from his aura, replaced by blue.

'Lucrezia...'

'Vanni... What happened?' I asked, dreading the answer.

'We were in a car accident, a few years ago. My mother, Lorenzo and our driver were unscathed, thank God. My dad was in recovery for a long time. And I ended up like this. Our car just swerved off the hill and all the way down the terraces. By itself.' He opened his hands, letting go of mine. I knew he had more to say. I knew there was more. 'Our driver, Maurizio... he's been with us for a long time. In fact, he still is. He swore on his family that he always made sure everything was in perfect order. But that morning, there was something wrong with the car.'

I took a breath, inhaling the fragrance of roses and the fragrance of him. Dots were connecting in my mind, and I didn't like the picture they made.

'We have no proof,' he said, tentatively. 'And I know you couldn't believe such a thing of your father, but...' He searched my face.

'I could.'

He waited.

'Believe me, I could,' I continued. 'The reason I was sent away... It was about my mother. Her death was an *accident* too, as you know.'

It was time to give a shape to all our ghosts. I hung my head, and felt his warm hand entwine with mine again. Our hands, his square, tanned one, and my smaller, freckled one, rested together on his wheelchair.

'Do you believe your father was involved?'

'He said so. To Bianca. Do you really believe my father tampered with your car?'

'I don't know for sure; it could be a coincidence. But

Lorenzo is adamant. He's convinced that Fosco Falconeri almost killed us, and put me in this wheelchair. We'll never know the truth, probably.'

'Only my father knew the truth, and he carried it to the grave with him. But not before confessing to Bianca what he did to my mum.'

'That is awful. And me, sulking because you went away without a word... when you were facing all that, living through all that. I'm so sorry.'

'No, no. Please, enough apologies. We all need to move on, I suppose. In one way or another.'

'Where do you live, Lucrezia? Do you work? Are you married?' Was it just my impression, or did his voice come out with a little crease when he asked me that question?

'I live in Paris. I'm a personal assistant to a chef. I'm not married. Me and Claude... the chef... are together, though. We've lived together for about a year, now. You?' I tried to keep a nonchalant tone, but mentioning Claude in our conversation seemed so wrong. For Claude, and for Vanni. Like two magnets meeting each other on the wrong side – not meant to come close.

His hands left mine.

'Well, I live in Biancamura as always. I saw someone for a while, but it didn't work out. I...' He shrugged. 'I try to help the family business, workwise, but Lorenzo is very... protective. Of both me and the business.'

It wasn't difficult, to read between the lines. To me, he seemed a little lost. I suppose some hide it better than others – my life was outwardly sorted, but inside... not so much. He looked away – and then threw a glance towards the glass doors.

'What your sister said, that we want Casalta...' he continued in a low voice. 'Well, I don't, but my brother does. He *says* our families' feud died with your father, but he doesn't really believe that. You need to watch yourself around him. Lorenzo does want Casalta, just like your sister said.'

'Would it be such a terrible thing? If we sold Casalta? It would be a fresh start for everyone,' I said. I was sounding it out to myself too, in a way. It seemed impossible, a world without Casalta. *And yet...*

The memories held by this ancient house wouldn't be ours any more; our shoulders would not be burdened by all that had happened; the thickness and heaviness of events that had almost destroyed us would be dissolved. My father's study, and the spirit of him with it. The rose garden where I'd seen my mother would be someone else's garden. The bedrooms where we'd cried after the accident, the kitchen where we'd waited in vain for her to come home, someone else's spaces.

All that would be gone.

But my mother's murals, different for each of us, each painted with her magic, and her love, and her wish for happiness; the stairs where we sat and watched the stars, snuggling in our nighties; Mia's studio and her incredible frescoes; the stables that Nora treated like a second home...

And what about our vineyards, our olive trees?

'I suspect you're the only one of your sisters who'd think of losing this house as a fresh start. I know little about your family – I mean, *really* know, beyond the façade – but I believe that Bianca and your youngest sisters would be heartbroken if they lost this place. I might be wrong.'

'You're right. It might not be our choice, though. Maybe my father left everything to Gabriella, his widow. In that case, she'd be the one who makes the decision.'

'You don't know yet?'

'The reading of the will is later today.'

The moment I'd told him about Claude, the conversation had turned more formal, more distant. It was inevitable.

'What a way to find each other again,' he said and smiled for the first time. I had a million memories of that smile. 'Conspiracies and testaments.'

'Yes.'

'Do you remember our picnics at the treehouse? I know it was a long time ago...'

I smiled too. 'If I *remember*? I remember our picnics as if they were yesterday!' We used to save the mid-morning snacks we were given at school to eat at the treehouse, our private little banquets. Sometimes we raided our respective kitchens and brought something more: bread and apples, cake, the exquisite jams that Matilde made. 'It was the best time of my life.'

'Really?'

'Yes, really.'

'Mine too... and it's finished. Now I can't even get there, let alone climb a tree.'

'We don't need a treehouse to eat together,' I said, then hesitated.

'Vanni? Are you ready to go?' Lorenzo appeared on the doorstep.

'You don't have to go so soon,' I heard Bianca saying behind him, but I knew she didn't mean it. We had to be at the notary's in a short while. All these reciprocal courtesies, painted over a boiling pot of resentment on Lorenzo's part and mistrust on ours...

As for me, I wanted to spend more time with Vanni. To kick my shoes off and be at the treehouse and be a child again, and savour the sweetest mixture of an innocent friendship and a first crush like I hadn't been allowed to do back then, because my life was interrupted and my world turned upside down.

But all that was gone, and it would never return. We were two different people now.

We were on our way to the door when Vanni whispered, 'By the way, you're right.'

'About what?'

'We don't need a treehouse to eat together,' he said, and the old spontaneous, natural connection passed between us once again, warming my very soul.

My heart lifted and soared up and up and up, over the hills of home.

# CHAPTER 14

## BIANCAMURA, 16 APRIL 1985

VANNI

Lucrezia is back.

Talk about a shock.

Twelve years is a long time, a long time growing up, growing apart. The girl I remembered is no longer there, of course; but I saw glimpses of her in the woman she is now.

I saw her astonishment when I appeared in this chair. What did she think, what did she *feel*? Pity, probably. Or maybe nothing but surprise, because, for her, I'm just a distant memory of little importance.

She has no idea that our friendship, and the loss of her, was the first turning point of my life. She has a full life, a glamorous life from the look of it, in Paris: she's left me behind like I could never do with her, even if many times I tried. I know it probably isn't healthy to have the ghost of a gone girl shaping your relationships – or lack thereof – but this is what happened to me.

The past can be a very difficult place, impossible to leave.

Lucrezia and I were born in Casalta in the same year; we were taken to the same places when we were babes in arms. But the first time I *truly* saw her was a Sunday of early summer, in church, when we were eight years old. She seemed a reserved child, wrapped up in herself – almost as solemn and quiet as her elder sister, Bianca, who looked and behaved like a china doll. I thought the Falconeri daughters were lofty, aloof, with their frilly clothes and noses up in the air.

The Falconeri were the unspoken leaders of our village, not just because of their wealth and the vast vineyards and olive groves they possessed, but also because their name could be traced back hundreds of years. Their blood was mixed with the Casalta turf. My family, the Orafi, were the newcomers, having emigrated from the south only two generations before. We challenged them with a small wine business that became bigger and bigger, more and more lucrative, until we could look at them, level in the eye, and from below.

Even as rivals, our grandparents, the heads of our families, always had an unspoken agreement: that they would help each other keep the position they'd spilled blood for, and make each other stronger instead of tearing each other down. They were pragmatic. Then something happened between my father and Lucrezia's, something my father never talked about; and the families fell out in a dramatic, awful way.

But back to that day in church, when the Falconeri daughters sat still and composedly, and I swayed and kicked my feet and turned back and forward as if being attacked by a swarm of ants. Lucrezia was in the first pew on the left, as always, and she turned around to look at me. I swear, something unspoken passed between us, a mutual understanding that I'd never experienced before and never did again. Something that even now, I can't translate into words.

Fate decided that at that moment my mother had had enough of me. In whispery and clipped words, she sent me to play outside while my big brother sat as well-behaved as always. He was a real little Orafi, the carbon copy of my father: they were side by side, my father in a perfectly pressed suit and my brother in an equally perfectly pressed shirt. I was never so well put together, always with my shirt hanging out of my trousers or a scuffed shoe, my mop of curls refusing to stay down even when my mother tried to tame it with hair gel.

I darted out and found myself in the sunshine, blazing and blinding after the gloom of the church. Having conquered freedom, I looked around. A few other children had been evicted from the service for restlessness and sent outside. There was plenty of entertainment for us there – the stairs were the perfect grounds for a competition of who could jump the most steps, for a start. The most daring of us, and the ones with a little pocket money, could run over to the Bar Piazza and buy themselves a clandestine *gelato*, to be finished quickly before mass was over – it'd be a huge offence to go for ice cream after having been sent out of church, but parents often chose to ignore the telltale chocolate stains on our Sunday clothes. Also, behind the church was a small thicket of maritime pines, a *pineta*, where we gathered resin off the trees' bark and then traded it between us children as if it was gold – a handful of resin could be exchanged for two hundred liras, which would pay for an ice lolly or strawberry bubble gum.

I considered my choices. A couple of boys sat on a step playing with football stickers, but it didn't interest me much. I'd turned around to reach a few of us small rebels in the piazza across the square, when I stopped cold: in front of me, immaculate in her dress, and unsmiling, stood Lucrezia Falconeri.

A Falconeri girl was joining the naughty squadron?

Out of the blue, one of the boys, Bruno I think, threw a pebble at her. It hit her shoulder, and she gave out a small yelp. Stuck-up or not, I didn't think throwing stones at her was fair at all.

'Leave her alone!' I shouted.

Lucrezia looked at me – but not with gratitude or even

recognition. More like surprise. Then, all prim and proper in her dress, she went up to Bruno and punched him. Straight in the face.

Everyone fell silent, including Bruno, who was too stunned to react. So much for the quiet child.

Lucrezia broke the silence: she called me with a simple 'Let's go,' like there was no need for any other words, and ran towards the thicket. I followed her, as if under a spell.

That was the beginning of our friendship. We met up the hills after school as often as we could; I built us what we called the treehouse, but was really just a few planks nailed over the middle of a hazelnut tree, which opened in a natural seat with its branches making a green, perfumed roof. We took things as they were, without asking ourselves why we fitted like two pieces of a jigsaw, why we seemed to never run out of make-believe and games to play, or even enjoyed sitting in silence while she read a book and I broke hazelnut shells in between rocks and filled her pockets with them.

A boy who couldn't sit still and a girl who couldn't stand wearing shoes, a boy who adored his parents and a girl who was afraid of her father; we were who we were, and didn't mull over the whys of the bond we had. I always had this feeling, weirdly enough, that my mum was more inflexible than my dad about me befriending a Falconeri girl. Until it wasn't a feeling any more, but a certainty, because one day my mother barged into my room and slapped me across the face. I was stunned.

'What have I done?' I shouted at her. I'd always been lively, maybe too lively, but I'd never got into serious trouble before. My mother and I were very close, and the guilt of having upset her was as painful as the slap.

'Now listen to me, Vanni. They want to destroy our family!' I knew at once who she was talking about. 'You'll never see that girl again, do you hear me?'

'She doesn't want to destroy our family! She just wants to be my *friend*!'

And then, something even stranger happened: my mum burst into tears and ran out of my room, leaving me confused and distressed. The next day, after school, I tried to stay home – but the thought of Lucrezia waiting for me there, trusting that I would arrive, gnawed at me. I jumped from my window to a branch of the tree below, and went. That day marked a change in my mother: she never brought up Lucrezia again, but it was as if I'd betrayed her. As if I'd made a choice between her and the Falconeri girl, which made no sense.

For Lucrezia it was the opposite: her father, the tyrannical Fosco Falconeri, was the intransigent one. She feared him and, to be honest, so did I: but not enough to obey his orders when it came to our friendship. We both defied our families, and neither of us understood why they hated each other so much.

Then, one afternoon, Lucrezia arrived at the treehouse pale and shaken, and burst into tears in front of me. She said that her mother had been found dead that morning. We sat in the tree and she leaned her head on my shoulder, in silence.

From then on, everything changed. Lucrezia began skipping school, and when I went to our tree I often found her already there, dazed and restless at the same time. She stopped bringing food, and when I tried to convince her to eat, she would refuse. She spent hours with her knees under her chin, looking out at the hills.

I was determined I would be there for her, no matter what.

I was thirteen, and my feelings for Lucrezia were beginning to colour into something deeper, something different. Not a child's feelings, and they confused me, scared me, and made me happier than ever at the same time. Through all that turmoil, I didn't have anyone to confide in, and maybe I didn't want anyone, either. My mum was spending more and more time at our seaside house, where she would later unofficially move, and

I could feel that all was not right between my parents – the tree-house, and Lucrezia, were a refuge for me.

One afternoon soon after, Lucrezia wasn't there. Sometimes it happened, if the coast wasn't clear and there was a danger of getting into trouble, or if she had something on, like family business or a doctor's appointment, or visiting relatives. But recently she'd been at the treehouse every day – escaping from home, and from her father. The day after I waited for her all afternoon; the day after that I stayed until dark. I saw the evening swallow the trees around me, and then night fall so dark and deep I couldn't see my own hands. No trace of her.

'I covered for you,' my brother hissed when I returned. 'But I won't do it again.'

And yet, I knew he would, and he did twice more. By now I knew that there was something wrong, but I wasn't allowed to go near the Falconeri. I recognised Matilde, their housekeeper, in the *panetteria*; but when I approached her she turned away and pretended not to see me. I knew that her whole family worked for the Falconeri, including her son, Diego, who was only a few years older than me but made me, somehow, uneasy.

'I just want to know what happened to her! Where is Lucrezia?' I murmured, trying not to catch anyone's attention.

Matilde turned and left without a word. I knew there was no point in persisting with her, so I kept spending time in the square, around the piazza and the handful of little shops, hoping to hear news. Until one day, in the *panetteria* again, I thought I saw Lucrezia – my heart was beating in double time, and I couldn't contain my happiness when I laid a hand on her shoulder and called her name...

Her face was identical to Lucrezia's, but her hair was lighter – it wasn't Lucrezia. Her twin, Bianca, was looking back at me.

She turned away at once, and I almost couldn't believe it when she whispered: 'At the treehouse.'

For a moment I thought it was my imagination. But no, she'd really uttered those words.

I ran to the treehouse and waited, but she didn't come. But the day after she appeared, pale and furtive. She didn't climb up: instead we stood at the foot of the tree. 'Lucrezia hurt herself... her arms. She had to go to the hospital...'

I froze, silent.

'She's fine now, but she needs a lot of peace and quiet, so our father sent her to a boarding school.'

'What? For how long?'

'I don't know.' She seemed desolate, more so than words could convey.

I was taught that boys don't cry, so I didn't. The tears I had remained stuck in my throat, refusing to either melt out or disappear. Weeks and months went by, until one day the car we were travelling in swerved and took us down a slope with it. It was a miracle we all survived.

And now, I'm in this chair. A half man, I believe deep down, though I don't say it: I don't want anyone to feel pity for me. A boy who couldn't sit still is now forever sitting. All my dreams involved being moving. Walking, running. My dreams have vanished, even if my father is adamant that they haven't gone anywhere, that it's me who disappeared the day of the accident. Retreated somewhere inside myself.

I didn't want Lucrezia to see me like this, but I had no choice: it was this, or not seeing her at all.

She was a child when I was a child, and in my mind, she's grown up with me. But the boy she knew could climb, jump, run. I'll never climb the hazelnut tree with her again, or jump any steps, or run anywhere.

The only thing I can run from now is myself.

# CHAPTER 15

## CASALTA, 16 APRIL 1985

LUCREZIA

When the Orafi brothers left, Bianca and I both had our cheeks on fire, while Mia looked at us with her arms crossed across her chest.

'Well,' Bianca said.

'Well,' Mia echoed, staring from me to her, and back again.

'I'm going to get ready,' Bianca muttered and ran upstairs, followed by Mia.

I found myself alone for a moment – I looked up to the wooden beams of the ceiling and ran my hands through my hair. Seeing Vanni today had been such an intense experience: my head was spinning with thoughts of past and present.

His eyes, his smile, that mop of dark, curly hair – it was him, it was my Vanni, wheelchair or not. Changed, yes, like I was, but still him. The car accident: had it really been my father's doing? Had he spread even more destruction than I thought? And it was never Vanni, for Bianca. My jealousy never had reason to exist.

But, Bianca and Lorenzo? *Seriously?* And... how? When had they ever had the time or the chance to know each other?

Oh, God. It was all too much. Maybe it's not so strange that the memory of Nora's Maremmano horse galloping towards me flashed through my mind now – my feelings a herd of wild animals I couldn't control.

The phone on the coffee table, grey and sturdy and with its round dial like a taunting face, stared at me. On the other end of that phone was Claude. And the way my heart had beaten when I saw Vanni, the promise to see each other again, couldn't exist in the same world where Claude and I were a couple.

It was just another sign of how our relationship felt like a plaster wall, and not stone.

~

We sat in a semicircle around Dino Cavalli's desk – our family's notary, like his father before him. Loyalties last a long time and have much power, in this part of the world.

The short trip there, in Bianca's little pod of a car, was a daze. So much was happening in such a short time, I could almost watch myself living, as if I were a spectator in a film.

Cavalli's mannerisms, from the way he plaited his fingers on the desk to the slow, careful way he spoke, would have been more suited to an older man, but he wasn't much older than me.

'Il Signor Fosco Falconeri was most certainly a remarkable man. I have long admired him, and so did my father, rest his soul. He's made a mark on our community, and, I'm sure you'll agree, on all our lives,' he said in a drone and swept the room with a grave look.

Not much of a *positive* mark, though. Cavalli probably expected us to nod and murmur words of agreement; he seemed surprised to be met with stony silence.

I looked around me, as discreetly as I could. There were

only women in attendance. Bianca sat composedly in her flowery dress down to her knees, and her eyes were shiny, but not with tears – she had that Bianca intensity, that restrained fervour that I knew from our childhood.

Nora was impassive, like this whole thing didn't concern her – she'd just come because she was expected to, having changed from her usual muddy cargos and boots to clean cargos and semi-clean shoes. But her eyebrows were knitted together, betraying her sorrow and, I assumed, her worry. Her beloved stables were at stake – and I knew that she didn't trust our father as much as she made out.

Mia was wide-eyed but calm, and she, too, in her usual black, seemed older than her years.

Matilde was there as well, looking rather ferocious – I thought I could see her feelings in fiery letters over her head: *at last*. Even if this left her miserable son without employment.

Gabriella looked like an old-fashioned librarian in a blazer and skirt, tortoiseshell clips in her grey bob, her head lowered. I could have been, in theory, cynical enough to believe that she'd married my father for his money: something told me that this wasn't true, but I could have been wrong.

The room was so full of emotion that instead of seeing individual auras, I could see a cloud of moving colours over our heads, dark and acid hues of alarm and apprehension. The exception was Bianca, who still gave out a light blue and silver aura, in spite of it all.

Cavalli moved on, accepting that nobody was going to agree with him on my father's all-round wonderfulness. 'Sometimes, even the most experienced and competent of businessmen are faced with the hard reality of a changing world. The eighties have seen big changes in the social and financial panorama, in Tuscany, in Italy and in the world.' He opened his hands, and I noticed a signet ring. An 'O' with a crown.

He was an Orafi man, now? So much for multi-generational alliances...

'Foreign firms, pale imitators of our wines and olive oil and gastronomy, challenge us on prices and scales of delivery. And please, forgive me if I dare utter these words – but your father, your husband, your employer, made some questionable decisions. He was badly advised, undoubtedly...'

Nervous shuffles all around.

*People have changed towards us. He wanted a small, almost secretive funeral. Workers were let go, but taken on by the Orafi...*

All the little clues were beginning to paint a picture.

'I know it might be a surprise to you, but I do hope I'll not upset you too much if I say—'

'I don't mean to be rude, but could you get to the point? These girls have been through enough,' Gabriella interrupted in her gentle tone. Gentle, but authoritative.

I was impressed.

'Of course. I'm sorry,' Cavalli said, and sounded outraged more than sorry. 'Well, to get to the point, like you said, I suppose it's enough to say that Fosco Falconeri left everything to one beneficiary...'

Gabriella, of course.

'His daughter, Lucrezia Cecilia Falconeri.'

I felt my lungs empty of all air, as if I'd been hit right on my collarbone. Five words that were like five punches. Everyone turned to look at me.

Gabriella lowered her head. 'Oh no,' she whispered.

Talk about misjudging someone. So she *was* after my father's money? I supposed I couldn't blame her. What else would there be for her in a marriage to my father?

But everything had been left to me. The black sheep.

I felt sick.

My eyes met Bianca's; she was smiling.

'He made up for what he did,' she whispered, so low that only us two could hear it. I gazed at Nora, who was unreadable, and then I turned towards Mia. I was aghast. She had a black halo all around her – her aura was almost the colour of the night.

'Mia?'

'I'm sorry, Lucrezia.'

'Well, I don't want any of this, but it's easily solved. I can give it all to you. To my sisters.'

'That wouldn't be exactly generous,' Cavalli said.

'What do you mean?'

'I wish I didn't have to be the bearer of bad news. But all that is left of your family's wealth is the house, Casalta, and a vast amount of debt. For which you're now legally responsible, Lucrezia.'

'*What?*'

'Sadly, this is the truth. And us lawyers' – dramatic pause – 'deal in truth.'

I heard someone growling something along the lines of 'sadistic old'... I think it was me. I felt Bianca take my hand, but it wasn't enough to help me out of the panic that was taking hold. The room was closing in, and the voices calling my name were distant and muffled.

'Excuse me,' I murmured, and bolted out.

Once outside, I leaned against a wall that was warm with sunshine, and tried to breathe deeply, slowly. I certainly would not cry. I wouldn't give my father this satisfaction. I was sure that even after death he was watching me with glee, as I crumbled.

So that was the reason for Gabriella's *Oh no*. Not because she coveted the estate, but because she knew what was ahead. She knew that my father was bankrupt, and in debt. And my father wasn't making amends; he was ensuring my life was ruined. I felt my knees give way – for a moment I pictured myself sliding down the wall, so I stood even straighter as my body and mind absorbed the shock.

And then I saw my sisters walk out of the building one by one, Matilde and Gabriella with them. All of them, even Nora, came to stand around me and, as they did, my racing heart slowed a little, my knees felt a little stronger, a little surer in holding me up.

'We'll face this together,' Bianca whispered as they all crowded around me, a tiny forest of women, helping each other stand strong.

# CHAPTER 16

## CASALTA, 16 APRIL 1985

LUCREZIA

Once the embrace was over and we were home, I felt alone.

I knew my sisters wanted to help, and Gabriella too, but this weight was on me. And I could only think of one way to shed it. I suppose the wise, reasonable thing would have been to sit and discuss a course of action, but I simply couldn't face it.

There was a cacophony of reassurances, fears, recriminations and sympathy – the only quiet one was Mia, and when my eyes met hers across the room, those young-ancient eyes, I remembered her painting of Judith and Holofernes. Why had she chosen that scene, that story?

I wanted a clear-cut decision. And considering that once again I was the scapegoat of the family, I would take it for myself.

'I need a walk to clear my thoughts,' I said.

'It'll be dark soon,' Bianca protested.

I didn't answer. I had to leave. I couldn't tell them that I had a plan, not yet. A desperate plan, but better than nothing, and certainly better than the situation I was in now.

Once again, years after I last did so, I was on my way to
meet Vanni – once again in secret, though for entirely different
reasons. The Orafi wanted Casalta – Lorenzo wanted Casalta.

They could have it.

The Orafi home was a little more than forty minutes away,
close to the village of Biancamura, but in the open countryside.
I took my high-heeled shoes off and climbed the hill behind
Casalta, past the stables, past our vineyards. Was it just my
impression, or did even the vines look a little neglected, not
perfectly manicured like they'd always been?

Now that my father's predicament had come to light, I saw
– or imagined – the signs everywhere. When I first walked out, I
was wrapped up in myself, my muscles tense and an iron grip
around my head – but with every step I took, my senses awoke
and my muscles began to relax. It was an unconscious process,
the way nature reached out to me with soft hands and caressed
my very soul.

The spring afternoon was drenched in sweet scents, and the
grass felt soft under my feet. It was impossible not to be touched
by this beauty, even in this mess I was in – the enchantment of
this place in the heart of Italy was impossible to resist. It
embraced me and comforted me, and everything seemed just a
little bit easier, or even just a little less important.

Everything will flow away, after all – all this will pass, our
stories and challenges and strife will all flow away, but these
hills will stay.

I saw it in the muted light, our hazelnut tree, in a thicket
that filled a low valley between my home and Vanni's. It was
still there, of course – nothing around here changed fast or easy,
not loyalties, not families, not landmark trees.

I ran to it, and rested my hand on the rough, gnarly bark – I
could almost see the children we used to be, sitting close to each
other... I looked up, the sky visible through the canopy that was
now wider and thicker – the planks Vanni had placed in a

hollow between the branches were now half-hidden, but still there.

The sky was darkening; I didn't linger further, and walked on. Aside from what I needed to discuss with the Orafi, the gentle pull towards Vanni, that simple, pure desire to be in his company, was still there.

Never before had I walked beyond the thicket where our tree was, but I was confident that I could easily figure out the way to the Orafi's. After twenty minutes of walking under the twilight sky, crossing the hills towards the belfry of Biancamura, I reached the Orafi estate. It was my first time there.

Although I'd passed by their villa in the car and spotted it from a distance, I'd never been inside. Now, standing on the hill behind it, I could see it from above. It was a far cry from Casalta and its ancient, atmospheric beauty. The Orafi's villa was modern and luxurious, with a wide terracotta terrace enclosed in high hedges, and a pool whose waters reflected the sky like a mirror. In the dusky light, the pool was silvery, like a lake from a myth or a fairy tale.

I slipped my shoes back on and made my way down the slope. My heart was beating hard against my chest; there was still a sense of furtiveness, almost transgression, at going to see our rival family. What would I find?

Even Vanni had admitted that they wanted to own Casalta. But on what conditions? I stopped and hesitated for a moment – and as I did a man dressed in a black suit and sunglasses appeared from nowhere and reached me in long, hasty strides. As if I were visiting a villain in a Bond film and security had spotted me. I rolled my eyes.

'Signorina Falconeri, *buonasera*. We prefer visitors to use the main door,' he said, and took my elbow. I shook him away.

'I was going to; I just came through the hills. I wasn't going to jump over the hedge! Please tell Signor Vanni that I'm here.'

He nodded, but didn't let go of my elbow, which got on my

nerves more than I could say. He led me all the way round to
the main door, at the end of a long, paved driveway. He took out
an enormous device he carried with him, a sort of walkie-talkie,
but more intimidating, and pressed a button. Wait – I recognised the guy...

'Bruno?'

'Yes, it's me, signorina.'

'I punched you once, remember?' I giggled, but there was no
laughter on his part.

'I'd rather forget. Lucrezia Falconeri, here to see Signor
Vanni. We're at the main door,' he said into the huge portable
phone.

'There's no sun, you know,' I said. I couldn't help myself.

I crossed my arms as I waited. This whole bodyguard thing
was absurd and slightly unnerving. A maid in a black and white
uniform came to the door, nodded at Bruno, and welcomed me
inside. If you could call this a welcome.

'Thank you, Susanna,' Bruno said with enormous self-
importance.

I glared at Bruno and his ridiculous walkie-talkie and
sunglasses at night, as he left me with Susanna, who walked in
front of me through a corridor lined with framed mirrors, and
into a sumptuous hall. The house was splendid, all marble and
dark wood.

I must admit that it was tasteful, not as obnoxious as it could
have been. Everything oozed luxury, solidity. Not my taste, but
beautiful, if you like that sort of thing.

It was only then that it struck me that everything looked
worn, back at Casalta. The curtains were a little frayed, the
doorsteps smoothed down, the furniture discoloured, the
banister chipped in places. The imperfections made Casalta
even more fascinating, but they did betray my father's financial
situation. Again, I thought that the family's decline was there to

see, if you knew where to look, if you observed. But none of us had – until now.

I followed Susanna through a reception room and across the terrace, along the side of the glimmering swimming pool, until we came to a one-storey outbuilding. She knocked and called: 'The Signorina Falconeri is here, Signor Orafi.'

The door opened and Vanni was there, a smile on his face, mixed with surprise – was he *blushing*? I probably was, because my cheeks felt warm. That easy smile was in such contrast with the circumstances of my visit, with the whole Bruno bodyguard charade and the maid's formality, that I had to mirror it. We stared at each other, smiling, for a few seconds – we must have looked quite daft.

'Thank you, Susanna. Come on in,' he invited me, and moved aside so I could enter. His place was different from the main house: it had a rustic feel with naked stone walls and wooden floors, and huge windows that opened to the hills, so big that it almost felt like being outside. The fire burned in an open fireplace, and the air was full of the fragrance of wood and pine.

'This place is beautiful,' I said. 'Very... *you.*'

'I'm lucky, yes. Everything is at my height and it's all on one floor,' he explained. 'It's my refuge. Did you come on foot?'

'Yes. Can you tell?' I laughed, looking down at my muddy shoes and the hem of my dress, damp with evening dew.

'I'm glad you're here,' Vanni said. 'So soon. I wasn't expecting...'

'Sorry, I...'

'No, don't apologise! It's great to see you, it really is. It's just that you went to Cavalli, this afternoon, and I hope you're good, you're all good.'

There. The uncomplicated joy of seeing each other lasted only a while – we both seemed to remember all that we carried with us, all at once. I looked down.

'You won't say no to a glass of Orafi-made wine, will you?'

'I have to walk back...'

'No way, Maurizio will give you a lift.' He made his way to a liquor cabinet and poured some wine from a bottle with their signature label, all golden – inspired by their name, *Goldsmith*. 'Come sit.'

With a fluid move, he lowered the wheelchair armrest and positioned himself on a leather armchair. I sat beside him and took hold of my glass. He was right. I needed a drink. Vanni's presence beside me, the burning fire, the warm liquor relaxing my muscles – everything seemed a little easier, a little more manageable... but not for long.

'May I come in?'

It was Lorenzo's voice, coming from behind the door. It immediately broke the spell between us, and I tensed again. As happy as I was to see Vanni, the purpose of this visit was to discuss business.

'Sure,' Vanni said, in a not-so-delighted tone.

I swallowed – I couldn't show how nervous I really was. I was used to being cool and in control in my job, and I hoped that I could slip into the role seamlessly again. I had to be on guard, because Lorenzo's smooth ways seemed to me like thin ice, deceitful and easy to break.

He poured himself a glass of wine and came to sit across from us, on the leather sofa.

'You're not worried our wine will poison you, Lucrezia?' he joked. *Hilarious*. He wasn't at all like he was that morning at my house, when he'd been courteous, calm.

'Is Orafi wine poisonous?'

'Only for Falconeri girls. Sorry, what a dreadful joke. Now let me guess,' he said, leaning back. 'You've been to Cavalli's.'

I bristled. 'Are you gloating?'

'Why gloating?' Vanni looked from one to the other. 'What are you talking about, you two?'

'You don't know?' I turned towards Vanni.

'*I* take care of work. Vanni and our father are not in good health. They shouldn't be exposed to stress,' Lorenzo said.

'Lorenzo. Can you please explain?' Vanni was holding onto the leather armrests, his fingers working at the fabric.

'I can explain,' I said. 'My father lost everything. We're neck-deep in debt, and it's all been left to me.' The weight of it, spoken out loud, overcame me – and the knot of tears I carried with me was threatening to flood again, not so much out of sadness, but out of anger. But Lorenzo was like a shark with blood – I couldn't let him smell mine. No tears.

'How is that even legally possible?' Vanni exclaimed.

I shrugged. 'I suppose, where there's a will... excuse the pun.'

'Lorenzo... You knew all along?'

Lorenzo nodded, a thin smile dancing on his lips.

'And you didn't tell them?' Vanni said, punctuating his words with his fist on his knee.

'Would they have believed me? And anyway, I don't owe anything to the Falconeri.' He turned to me. 'If anything, you owe *us*.'

'What?' I whispered so that I wouldn't shout, while Vanni was shaking his head.

'Lorenzo, don't go there...' Vanni growled.

'Who do you think did this, Signorina Falconeri?' He gestured to Vanni's legs. 'My father is almost bedridden, and my mother washed her hands of us. *Who do you think did this?*'

'Not me. Maybe my father did it. I can see now he was capable of anything. But not me, and not my sisters. And you were different, when you came to our house this morning. Now you're showing your true colours.'

Lorenzo's eyes widened for a moment. My remark had hit him where it hurt. But it was true: was it because of Bianca that he'd shown himself civil, even friendly, and assured us that the feud was over?

'I don't hold you and your sisters responsible,' he said slowly, looking at me straight in the eye.

'It looks like you do, if you throw what happened to your family in my face. You don't even know that it was my father who caused it.' He snorted. 'But even if it was, he's dead. It's finished. If only I could turn back time and stop it from happening, if I could heal Vanni...' My voice broke.

'Lucrezia...' Vanni murmured beside me.

'If I could change the past and bring back my mother and never leave Casalta... I would do all this. But I can't. I shouldn't have to make amends for what my father did.' Why was I arguing? I should have been being pragmatic. I should have been smoothing the way to offering him Casalta in exchange for settling our debts – my debts. But I couldn't help it. 'And anyway, I paid my dues already, believe me. My father almost destroyed me too.'

'By sending you to a boarding school in Switzerland? A genteel way of destroying someone.'

I took a breath. 'You know nothing. You really know *nothing*.'

'Lorenzo, you've gone too far,' Vanni said.

He got up and went to the fire, hands in his pockets. 'Well, I apologise.' We must have looked sceptical, because he added: 'I mean it. I agree with you, brother. I went too far. And for what it's worth, I'm glad to see you reunited.'

I had to end this conversation. I had to say whatever I had to say, and take whatever was coming next. 'All I know is that you've waited years to lay your hands on Casalta, and now it's your chance. If you want it, Casalta is yours.'

'You should hold your cards closer to your chest, Lucrezia. Make it a little harder for me, at least.' His tone was smooth, but dry as sand, as he added: 'There will be much to discuss. I'll be in touch with the details and the paperwork.'

The driver left me at the front door of Casalta. I tried to sneak through the courtyard to the kitchen, but Bianca was looking out for me and yanked the door open on the steps.

'Oh, thank goodness! It's dark; I was worried... You're so pale! You're not sick, are you?' She laid a warm hand on my forehead.

'Apart from finding out that I'm millions in debt at the ripe old age at twenty-four, I'm fine. Let me catch my breath; I'll tell you all.'

The Orafi's car started and left, the illuminated window framing Maurizio's face. 'You went to *them*?' Bianca uttered.

I took a breath, as deep as I could, and stepped out of my high-heeled shoes. I was exhausted. Between seeing Vanni again, finding him in a wheelchair, discovering we were bankrupt, and that my father might have tried to exterminate his rival family... I had nothing left to give. I just wanted to go back to Paris, where everything was regimented, contained, all my walls were safely up, and my heart was locked away.

'Please tell me you didn't offer them Casalta...'

Of course. Of course she'd know at once. I could see her aura forming around her head, dark blue with purple edges, drawing in like a storm.

I made my way inside. 'Can we discuss this tomorrow, Bianca? When we're all a little calmer...'

'Did you offer them Casalta?' she repeated. She was pale, but with a determined look on her face. She was saying: *If we have to, we'll face it.*

'We need to sell. There's no other way,' I said. 'If not to the

Orafi, someone else. If we don't do it, the banks will take everything to cover the debts. It's for the best.'

The devastation on Bianca's face killed me. Keeping my
heart locked away was harder and harder work, the more time I
spent with my sisters. The wall around my heart needed
constant maintenance, or it would crumble... already I could see
the cracks. And I was so tired, I thought I would fall asleep
there and then.

A cry, like that of a small animal, came from the other side
of the room. I looked up to see Mia briefly framed in the door
before she disappeared.

'You go rest; I'll see to her,' Bianca said.

I rested my forehead against the doorframe for a moment.
'It's for the best,' I repeated to myself – I was so tired I was
almost slurring my words – and made my way upstairs, to my
room.

The red roses on my walls seemed to sway and dance as I
came in. I didn't get changed; I didn't even pull the blankets up.
I lay on my bed fully dressed and fell into a fitful sleep, full of
agitated dreams that culminated in a nightmare.

My sisters and I were wandering around Casalta in a
strange half-light; cobwebs hung from the walls and dusty,
white-grey sheets covered the furniture. My sisters were children, all three of them wearing white summer dresses covered
with little flowers, and they walked barefoot on the debris
strewn on the floors.

I looked down at my hands, my feet – I, too, was a child in a
white dress and bare feet. Our mother appeared among us, and
we all ran to her – but as quickly as she'd materialised, she
disappeared. We began calling her name – she appeared on the
stairs, and we ran to her – but she was gone in an instant. Again
and again, we were lost children searching for our mother in the
cold and dark.

We were all calling, calling, until our calls became panicked

– there was no answer, and the light was fading – in a stream of unnatural light I saw her appear outside, in the rose garden. I banged on the glass, but my mother didn't seem to see me or hear me – I threw myself against the glass and went through it, a million shards exploding around me.

I awoke drenched in sweat, tears running down my cheeks, shaking with terror and cold, my screams resounding with my sisters' in my ears.

# CHAPTER 17

## BIANCAMURA, 1 OCTOBER 1985

VANNI

I remember the accident in all its details, and in vivid colours.

No merciful amnesia for me. I remember the car accelerating when it should have braked, the screams and the world turning upside down over and over and over again. When it stopped, there was silence.

I was awake; every breath was agony. My father was slumped in his seat, Maurizio with his face on the dashboard, both immobile. There was blood on them. I turned to my left to see my mother seemingly asleep: there was no blood on her.

I was completely alone in the world; there was nobody left on this planet but me: this was how it seemed at that moment, when everyone was unconscious or dead, I didn't know which.

Then I turned to my right, and I met my brother's open eyes. It was like a castaway seeing a boat. 'Vanni. I'm going to go get help, do you hear me? I won't let you down, I promise.'

I couldn't speak, but I nodded.

In all that terror and pain, my brother was there for me – this was imprinted in my brain that day, and the certainty never went away. It was he who scrambled out of the car, climbed onto the road and flagged down someone. It was he who held my hand when they lifted me onto a stretcher, and I realised that I couldn't feel my legs.

'I'll look after you. I'm here,' he told me. His face was the last thing I saw before closing my eyes and falling somewhere between sleep and death.

I was in that limbo for days, and I dreamed. Images of the accident kept coming back to me: I saw his face again and again, and heard his words.

*I'll look after you. I'm here. I won't let you down.*

*I'll look after you.*

His was also the first face I saw when I awoke – I was in a panic, believing I was still in the car, and I only calmed down with his voice, with him holding my hands.

'You're good. We're all good, Dad is injured but he'll be fine, Mum is fine, look, she's here... Maurizio only had a few bruises... We're all good, Vanni, I promise.'

He kept saying *I promise*, as if he had the duty and the power to keep everything under control, to make sure every member of the family would be looked after and safe. The moment they finished settling me, I saw the difference in my brother's face. His eyes had taken on a certain hardness that hadn't been there before – and beyond it, there was a permanent glint of anxiety.

I was the one who couldn't walk any more, but I soon realised that he was the one who'd been hurt the most.

During the months in the hospital, and then at home, being cared for day and night, Lorenzo was always with me. He made sure I took all my medicines, gave me blankets even when I wasn't cold, read me books even if I had no problems holding a book and reading, and watching endless action films with me. He announced to our parents – he didn't ask – that he'd study at home, so he could spend more time with me. He was close to Dad too, of course, who seemed to be affected by a mysterious ailment related to the accident, but that the doctors couldn't give a name to. Our parents' marriage was dissolving, but at that time, with me and my insensible legs and Dad's mysterious decline, it seemed the least of our worries.

Mum left for our second home, and this brought me and Lorenzo even closer. I began recovering some feeling in my lower half, I was fitted with a wheelchair, life still felt arduous and empty, but I was regaining hope, little by little. Lorenzo, though, didn't leave my side.

It took me a while to realise that he'd taken his role of protector so seriously, so desperately, that he wouldn't let me out of his sight. That he wouldn't let me get tired or hot or cold or hungry, not even for a second.

'You're ill, Vanni. Don't forget that.'

'You can't get too tired; you have physio tomorrow. You'll stay home.'

'Are you sure you want to sit your diploma? It'll wear you out. What do you need a piece of paper for?'

And then, after I did get my hard-earned piece of paper: 'Why would you want to work? I'll look after you. You focus on staying as healthy as you can. Don't worry about anything. Leave it with me.'

*Leave it with me* has been our refrain, growing up. First, it was my only lifeline, then it was easy, comforting; later, it turned suffocating. When the time came for me to work in the family firm, Lorenzo couldn't let go.

Month after month, year after year, he did all he could to keep me under his watchful eye, even if that meant I had no freedom. He was paranoid about me travelling in the car, even just to see my friends, even to go to physiotherapy for the many visits my condition required. My friends had to come to our house. Physiotherapists and doctors had to do home visits.

But I wasn't a child any more; I was a teenager who needed his space, and I was angry.

I suppose I surprised everyone because, having been a quiet, sweet-natured child, I became withdrawn and resentful. I rebelled with everything I had – against my father, who was still very ill, much worse than he is now; against my mother, who had detached herself from me and Lorenzo and treated us like friends – dear friends maybe, but not her sons – but most of all, against my brother and his control of me.

For months we argued constantly – and Lorenzo was forced to change. A little. Although I was young, he let me into our business's inner circle. I insisted I wanted to move out, even if it was going to be difficult to find somewhere adapted to the wheelchair. I began to go out more, even if Lorenzo waited for me, watch in hand, like an anxious mother.

And then I met Cristina.

It was a herculean effort for me, a swim against the tide, to open up to a relationship, letting a woman see the way I was now. But slowly, I came to trust her.

For a while, I thought that I'd managed to rip my life out of the hands of destiny: the accident had broken me in two, but I worked, I was engaged, neither the physical limitations nor the trauma had taken everything from me. I was just like some of the other paraplegic men and women I'd met during the years of doctors' appointments and therapies: they had jobs and families. They'd overcome. For years I hadn't thought I could do it, but I did.

Not long before the wedding, Cristina said we should talk. She burst into the worst, most heart-wrenching cry I'd ever heard – it was like her heart was breaking. She said she loved me, but *she'd come to the conclusion that she couldn't spend her life with someone in a wheelchair*.

Apparently, she'd only realised this *now*, when she was already wearing my engagement ring on her finger. She said she wanted a normal life. And children. And that it all seemed so real now, she just couldn't do it.

My answer to her was a straightforward, mild, *I understand*. I even comforted her. I reassured her that she had to do what was best for her, and that I didn't want someone to stay with me just because they felt sorry for me.

When I was finally alone in my room, I destroyed everything in sight with a rage I didn't even know I had in me.

My brother found me on the floor, in a corner, my useless legs dead in front of me – he cradled me in his arms, with a tenderness nobody would think Lorenzo Orafi could muster.

Since that moment, he has protected me more than ever. I slipped into the role of the vulnerable brother with a sense of inevitability. Looking back, it wasn't about what Cristina felt or told me – it wasn't about my feelings for her. That moment destroyed me because, down deep, I agreed with her. And so, it seemed, did my brother, who looked at me with the pity and sympathy reserved for a bird with a broken wing.

I had my apartment built on the property, all on one level, with the pool in front because only in the water do I feel truly free.

This is how I live today. My participation in the business is just formal, something my brother entertains to keep me busy, like giving colouring pages to a child. I've closed the door to relationships – never again will I put myself at the mercy of anyone.

I'm used to people looking at me with pity.

Only my father doesn't: only my father fights for me to rise from this endless swamp. A comfortable swamp, but a swamp nonetheless.

I know people think my brother is power-hungry. I know many, even in our inside circle, believe he's somehow triumphant, with our father so weak and me cut out from business.

But only we – Lorenzo, our father and I – know the truth.

It's us who hear him screaming in his sleep, when the accident returns in his nightmares.

We know that when he boasts, *Why settle down, there's many more fish in the sea* – he's really saying, *I can't have my own family; I'm responsible for this one, and I must live for them.*

My brother is still the little boy in the wrecked car, trying to save everyone in there, and forgetting about himself.

# CHAPTER 18

## CASALTA, 17 APRIL 1985

LUCREZIA

I woke up still reeling from my dream.

*Why, why, did my father choose to make me responsible for all this? There will be no forgiveness for him, ever. There wasn't before the reading of the will, and certainly there won't be now.*

And yet, when I went downstairs and into the gardens an eastern wind played with my hair, coming in from the sea and smelling of salt, pine and juniper, and my heart lifted. I took a deep, deep breath.

I belonged to Tuscany, and having been gone for so long made me look at the place with different eyes, like I was seeing it for the first time. The beauty of my surroundings made me feel like I was in the eye of a storm – a moment of peace and stillness after the crowded dreams and the complications of the day ahead.

Still in my nightie and barefoot, I strolled among the roses and finally sat on the bench, my eyes closed against the gentle sunlight.

'Good morning. I saw you coming down, so I made you

coffee.' I looked up, and saw Gabriella standing there with a coffee cup and saucer in her hand.

'Thank you.'

'Sugar, no milk, yes?'

'Yes. You noticed how I take my coffee?'

'I'm trying to escape the evil stepmum stereotype.'

I had to laugh. 'Keep me company?'

'Maybe you need some silence, some alone time?' she asked thoughtfully.

'You can't miss this sky,' I said, and patted the place on the bench beside me.

Gabriella settled in beside me with her calm, soothing energy. There was a suffused pink light coming from her. She was so different from my mum, I considered; Father had chosen two opposites for his two wives. My mum was a main character in every scene; she was colourful and wilful and a little eccentric. Gabriella was homespun, steady. She was tranquil.

She and Bianca were similar, I realised. I wore sharp couture to fit with my work, Nora was all rubber boots and outdoor gear, Mia was a variation on the theme 'gothic princess'. Bianca was all dresses and pink cheeks, and just like Gabriella she exuded nurturing.

Apparently, Gabriella was supposed to have changed my father – but it didn't appear so.

We were silent, contemplating the glorious morning sky, while caffeine did its job and woke me up properly. 'You really are failing, you know, in your role of evil stepmother,' I said.

She giggled. 'I'll try harder.'

I took a sip of coffee and felt it course through my veins, clearing my thoughts a little. 'Gabriella... I really must ask you.'

'Let me guess. Why I married your father? Why he married me?'

'I don't mean to be insensitive...'

'Not at all, my dear. We really were chalk and cheese,

weren't we? But I loved him. And I know for sure that he loved me. Plain and homely me.'

'You're not...'

She raised a hand. 'I know what I am, and I know my worth. I'm just saying that I'm different from the kind of woman a man like your father would go for. But I was what he needed. Was he what I needed? I don't know. No.' She smiled. 'But I fell for him at my ripe old age, after being convinced I would never, never marry again.' She swept a leaf from her skirt. 'You see, I've always been so sensible. In life, I always coloured by numbers. I got married young, had my son; I was devoted to my family. My first husband passed away, and I found myself alone. My son was now grown-up and independent, and I settled in a quiet life, alone. And then... then I met your father. And I fell in love for the first time.'

She turned to me, but I couldn't say anything. Her confidences were precious, delicate – after days of intense, almost violent sensations and feelings, she tiptoed onto the stage like a grey-haired ballerina.

'He was good to me. I couldn't quite believe he chose me. Isn't it unfair that women of a certain age are seen as past their best, while men seem to almost increase their prestige as they grow older? Your father was handsome, fascinating, always dressed as if he'd come off a film set...'

'Really?' In my memory, my father was the man who towered over me, and on his face were eternal discontent and disappointment with me.

'You probably saw him in a different light.'

*You can say that again.*

'He was fiery, as you know. With me, he calmed down. He used to talk to me for hours. About his youth, and the pressure to marry someone suitable for his family, not your poor mother, and how much he tried to mould her into the woman he wanted her to be. About his daughters and how disconnected he felt from them, about you...'

'He spoke about me?' I swallowed.

'He had a lot of respect for you. He said that even as a child, you were the only one who stood up to him.'

*Respect.* But not love...

'But things changed, between him and me.'

'What changed?'

'I saw how much Bianca and the girls missed you. I could only imagine what you went through. I learned things I didn't want to know.' I had the overwhelming feeling she wanted to say more, but she stopped. She looked away, biting her lip.

*Do you know, Gabriella? Do you know what happened to my mother?* The question was on the tip of my tongue, but I couldn't formulate it.

'I hope you don't mind me asking, but what will you do, now?'

'Not at all. I'd like to tell you, but I don't know. Everything happened so fast. Getting married again when I never thought I would, losing him so quickly. I own a house in the Riviera, up in Liguria. I suppose I'll go there. This is not my home.'

'Oh, Gabriella. I'm sorry. I'd love to say that this is still your home, that you can stay as long as you want, but... this place is not ours any more either.'

'Yes. About that. I have a little money set aside. It wouldn't make much of a dent, but...'

'Thank you, but we're going to need something radical. We need to sell *everything*... Maybe it's better this way.'

She turned towards me, mouth agape, but she controlled herself quickly. 'That's for you to decide, my dear.'

'The decision has been made already. There's no other option.'

'I... well, I still hope I can help a little. Give you some guidance, some clarity... because I'm a little removed, compared to your sisters,' she said.

She hesitated for a moment, then wrapped an arm around my shoulder and squeezed me gently. 'Thank you for being so welcoming to me. Even in these crazy circumstances. For not assuming...' I felt a little hot then, because at the beginning I *had* made assumptions. 'Well, yes. For being so welcoming to me. You know, your mum was very, very lucky to have the four of you. All of you are exceptional girls.'

'Well, thank you... we were very lucky to have her.'

'You were.' My gaze met hers, and for a moment it seemed like Gabriella was about to say something else. Instead she stood, an arm open to invite me inside with her. 'Lucrezia, your sisters are waiting for you. I think the moment has come to speak to them.'

My stomach churned. I nodded. 'Yes. It's time.'

All my sisters were in the living room, and all turned to look at me when I walked in. They reminded me of birds in a nest, looking up with their beaks open, waiting.

'I'll go get dressed,' I said more confidently than I felt. 'And then I'll explain everything.'

In front of the mirror in my room, I looked in my own eyes. I had to be strong. This burden had been placed on me; my father had chosen me to carry it, whatever the reason. I had to do the best by my sisters, and by myself too.

I had to sort this mess out in whatever way I could, so that my sisters would suffer as little as possible.

I reminded myself that there was *my* name on the terrifying document folder that Cavalli had given me – it meant my neck was on the line.

But it also meant that the last word would be mine.

~

Twenty minutes later, I went downstairs in my blue dress and heels, my hair done and make-up on. All this was my suit of armour; it made me feel more resolute and less vulnerable. I stopped on the stairs for an instant, gathering my strength. Bianca and Mia were sitting on an armchair each, while Nora stood leaning against the wall, as if ready to bolt at any moment, to go and find refuge with her horses. Which, I was sure, she was.

Everyone turned their faces to me. Bianca looked calmer now, Mia white and wan. Nora was clearly hostile, as if all of this was my fault.

'I'll get straight to the point. If we don't sell Casalta soon, the banks will take it. If we sell it at a good price, we can hope to settle the debts. Bianca, Nora, you both work, and Mia, maybe you can try and sell your paintings? I'll help as much as I can, of course. We'll make sure the house will raise enough funds to set us, *me*... completely free from all debts, and we'll start again. Hopefully there won't be creditors coming out of the woodwork. If so, well, we'll cross that bridge if we come to it.'

'You don't have a clue, Lucrezia,' Nora offered. *Well thank you, Nora.* 'What I earn from riding lessons is nowhere near enough to pay for new lodgings.'

'In that case, you need to sell some horses, or rehouse them somewhere safe, somewhere they can thrive,' I said slowly, steeling myself for her reply.

'We can't! They're part of the family! And they're my job, they're what I do!' I didn't need to see her aura to know how devastated she was. She was on the attack. Shame that she was attacking the wrong person.

'I'll have to leave my murals. Maybe they'll paint over them...' Mia whispered. A halo around her head and shoulders appeared, light grey, the colour of dismay.

I turned from one to the other. 'I don't see any other solution. We're *bankrupt*. And we owe a lot of money. Well, I do.'

Nora was staring at me – now I knew what the expression 'eyes flashing in anger' looked like. Her green eyes did seem to glimmer with her fury.

'Eleonora.' Bianca hadn't spoken until then. Her silvery voice had a touch of steel to it that I was starting to recognise. 'You're talking as if Lulu *wants* this. This disaster is to be laid at our father's feet, not hers.'

'She does *want* it! She *hates* Casalta. It's clear to see how much she wants to get rid of it. Don't you, Lucrezia?'

I saw no point in lying. If I started pretending now, everything else I said would be put in question.

I held her gaze. I'd been through years of exile; I'd been made responsible for my father's mess. I'd been forged in fire, and there was no way I would lower my eyes now.

'You'll be surprised to know that Casalta is in my heart,' I tell her. 'Yes, there *is* a part of me that will be relieved, but I hate seeing you so upset. And I wish I could find another way. I wish you could keep your horses and your murals, and Mia, your beautiful paintings! But there's nothing I can do. How else can we come up with that kind of money? If our father had chosen another one of us, what would you have done? Eleonora, what would *you* do, in my shoes?'

'I'm with you,' Bianca said.

Nora hung her head.

Mia sat there with a desolate expression, like a little Cassandra. There was still no trace of her rainbow aura, and it broke my heart. I knew that for Mia it wasn't just about the paintings. I knew she was special, she needed her home and her routines, and she couldn't be thrown unprotected into the outside world. Mia needed looking after, it was clear... it'd been clear since she was little. Her incredible perceptions, her gift, came at a price.

'The Orafi,' she whispered in a low voice.

'Yes.'

'Dad hates them,' Nora said.

'Not any more, because he's dead. And he left all this for Lucrezia to sort,' Bianca said calmly.

The more I got to know my twin again, the more I saw how the frightened little bird who was always desperate to please had grown into a resilient and tenacious woman.

'So,' I continued. 'Yesterday I went to see the Orafi brothers. I believe that it's Lorenzo who makes the decisions. They do want our house, just like you said, Mia. It seems Lorenzo was aware of Father's desperate situation.'

'*Vultures*,' Nora whispered. 'They were always out to destroy Dad.'

'It seems to me that he did a good enough job of destroying himself,' I retorted.

'You know *nothing* about him.'

'I know what he did to me, Nora. And I know what...' I bit my lip, and just at the same time Bianca called me to silence.

'Lulu!'

I said nothing more. I knew it would be disastrous to mention what we suspected about Mum's death to my sisters, without being sure. I'd already gathered that Nora was close to Father and had a certain – misplaced – loyalty towards him. It would just throw oil on the fire.

'Anyway, vultures or not, it beats having it sold for peanuts by the bank. At a bankruptcy auction.' A collective gasp followed my words, and I checked myself. My sisters not only loved Casalta, but they had been sheltered – I had to try and watch my words. 'I'm sorry,' I added.

'I bet they're celebrating,' Nora said. 'The Orafi, I mean.'

'What difference does it make? I mean, I know it's a matter of pride, for us. But sometimes pride must be swallowed,' Bianca said, and I shot her a grateful glance.

'Are we all in agreement?' I looked around. My sisters gave lukewarm nods.

'He didn't do this to punish you,' Mia said.

'You mean leave the mountain of debt in my name? I beg to differ.'

'He did it because he knew that you'd be the one to sort it. The one without ties to Casalta. You were the one who could cut through it all and be pragmatic.'

'Great,' I said sarcastically.

'We're with you,' Bianca asserted again.

Nora murmured something about tending to the horses. 'It's easy for you! You didn't grow up here! You didn't live here! For you it's just a house. We sell and start again, easy. It's just horses. But for us...'

'Which part exactly is easy for me, Nora? Being on my own at boarding school? And then I come back home after twelve years, and I find that my father has lumbered me with debt? Or maybe the part where our father sent me to a clinic for disturbed children for a year, a whole year of being stuck in a hospital with locks on the door and being turned into a zombie with medication, hearing screams day and night? Tell me *which part* was easy for me, Nora!'

Silence fell in the room. I brought a hand to my mouth. I'd never wanted to tell them the truth.

But I just had.

The silence in the room was so vibrant, it was as if another person was sitting there with us.

'I'm sorry. I didn't want you to know. I...'

Bianca and Mia's faces were the colour of ash.

Nora ran from the room. I watched her through the window, running without looking back; on impulse, I followed. She strode across the gardens, with me trying to keep up. I was tall, but she was taller, with longer legs, and I almost ran after her. 'Nora! Nora!'

'Please, leave me alone!'

'I will leave you alone once we talk.'

'No!'

'Eleonora, you're behaving like a child!'

She turned. '*I'm* behaving like a child? You keep badmouthing Dad. I know he was difficult...'

'Badmouthing? *Difficult?*'

'I don't know if he really sent you to that place...'

'You believe I'm lying?'

'Maybe he just wanted to help you. Maybe you needed it!'

She froze, horrified by what she'd just said.

'Let me tell you what that place was like. Then you'll tell me if you think I needed it. If *any* child needs it.'

'I could talk to him.' Nora's voice was low all of a sudden. 'I'm the one who took after the Falconeri the most. I don't even have those weird gifts you say you have. Bianca hearing voices, and Mia being all weird. I just want to be normal! Like everyone around here. *Normal.*'

'You can be whatever you want. And I'm sorry I wasn't there for you. I was too busy surviving; I did my best.'

'I don't want to talk about it any more.' She turned to walk away, and I was left there, somewhere between anger and sadness, and regret: if only I'd stayed closer to Nora. If only I'd stayed closer to them all.

'Nora...' I asked myself if I could tell her. If I could say to her what Father had confessed to Bianca, that he was the one who ended Mum's life, not a fall on the stones.

But it would break her heart.

I stayed quiet.

Once again, she turned around, and the sun at her back gave her dark hair a golden halo – she looked like some ancient Roman goddess, a hunting goddess.

*I know this is not your fault. I'm sorry*, I was hoping she would say. But she didn't.

'I better go,' she said instead, and I was left alone on the golden hill, on this hard, hard morning.

When I returned, Bianca was still ashen.

'I wish you'd told us.'

'There was nothing you could have done.'

Mia's voice was thin. 'We thought it was a school.'

I looked down. 'I didn't want you to know. I didn't want you to be upset.'

Bianca took my hands, and Mia sat at my feet, her head on my knee.

'What happened to you there, Lulu? What happened to you?'

I shook my head. I could have never gone into detail about that place. I didn't even want to remember.

But even there, safe with my sisters, the memories that I'd worked to erase came flooding back.

ISTITUTO LUGANO, 1973 – TWELVE YEARS EARLIER

LUCREZIA

They told me that the Istituto Lugano was a home where children get better. I said my arms were perfectly fine, now all the cuts caused by the glass were healed. They said this was a place where children's *minds* got better, not just their bodies.

A mental hospital, then?

No. I was not allowed to call it that.

I was now sitting in the doctor's office. From the window I could see the black branches of the trees below, and beyond them the other wing of the clinic, under a grey autumn sky. Neon lights illuminated every room; I didn't want to think who was in there or what was happening to them.

'I saw her.'

For months I'd repeated the same statement over and over and again: to the nurses who looked after us, to the doctor who spoke to me three times a week, taking notes, to anyone who would listen. I wrote the words in the condensation on the window, with my spoon in the *pastina* we were given for dinner, in the steam on the shower screen.

*I saw her, I saw her, I saw her.*

It'd become a battle of wills between the world and me.

Dottor Minieri's eyebrows rose to form two perfect 'S's in his high forehead. I had to give it to him: his patience was endless. My umpteenth 'I saw her' must have been grating on his nerves, but he never showed it.

On the desk in between me and the doctor were stacks of drawings I'd made. It was the same scene over and over: a rose bush, a red-haired woman, a little girl with a big 'O' for a mouth. And on every one of the drawings, I'd written in big blue letters: *I saw her.*

'Lucrezia, you're a clever girl; I know by now I can speak to you in direct terms,' the doctor began. He'd told me I was a clever girl countless times, probably to convey the fact that clever girls knew how to get themselves out of situations like the one I was in. He kept trying to give me an out; I kept refusing it. 'Yours was a big loss, a big shock for a child. It's only natural that you... *wished* your mum back into existence.'

Dottor Minieri was kindly, but I was furious with the world, homesick and lonely, and I could only think of one thing: *I would not lie.* I would not say I hadn't seen my mum, when she'd been there, looking at me. And no, she hadn't been a product of my imagination: I was sure. She'd been as real as the doctor there, in front of me, as real as the horrendous painting of a jungle that hung on the wall behind him, as real as the depressing view out of the window.

'Lucrezia?'

'I have nothing else to say. I'm sorry.'

The doctor sighed. A thump came from somewhere, followed by a muffled scream. I sank into myself and raised my shoulders. I don't want to remember the things I saw and heard in that place. Yes, I have memories of a kind hand on my arm and compassionate words when I refused to get out of bed, of warm milk and a stack of books given to me when I broke out in a stress-induced fever. But there are other memories as well, and I'd rather keep them in the recesses of my mind. I was afraid of the other children, afraid of the nurses even when they were kind, afraid of the doctors most of all. I made myself as small as I could, trying to make myself invisible, trying to disappear altogether.

'Lucrezia, tell me. If you and I agree that, yes, you saw your mother that night, then what's going to happen? What would you do with that knowledge?'

'I would tell my father. And he'd get angry. And send me back here again.'

He took off his glasses and began cleaning them with a tissue.

'Because he wouldn't believe you, and he'd think your mind was playing tricks on you, and you needed help. Like the help we're giving you now.'

I thought about it for a moment. 'Maybe he would believe me, though. If I could convince him that I shouldn't be here, because I saw my mum, and she was real.'

'If he believed you, what do you think he'd do?'

'He'd look for my mother! He'd want her back!'

'If there was even the slightest chance of her being alive...'

'He'd look for her!'

'But he's not doing that. Why, do you think? If he believed there was the slightest chance of finding her and bringing her back, wouldn't he look for her?'

*Chip.*

A little sliver came off my wall.

'Yes,' I whispered. At that time, I believed he cared for her.

'He was there, but he didn't see your mother. Your sister and the housekeeper, Matilde, didn't see her either. But all these people loved your mother, and they love you. If they thought she could be brought back, they would try.'

I sniffed. The doctor handed me a tissue. He looked down at my drawings, then up again. His eyes found mine, and I felt a shiver down my spine. I knew what he was about to say, because he'd been saying it for a month, and I never let it seep through my defences, all closed up like the little hedgehog I was.

'If your mum was alive, why would she do this? Appear to you and then run, disappear again, without a word? Would she not be here with you now?'

The words hit me like an icy shower, and this time, they made it through. He'd said that before, but the truth of it had never reached me. I'd never let that simple question get anywhere near my mind and my heart; I never *really* listened.

They'd worn me down.

'But I...' *saw her*, I was about to say. This time, though, I didn't finish the sentence.

For the first time it sank in. She wouldn't have abandoned us.

I *didn't* see her.

She really was gone.

The nurses were all smiles, now. I was called into Dottor Minieri's office one last time, to be told that my recovery had been relatively fast – a year didn't pass quite as fast for me – and complete, that he'd write to my father saying I was ready to face the world again, and normal life. The illusion was shattered now; I could go home whole and sane.

It was like a déjà vu moment, when I stood in the waiting room of the clinic, too excited to sit. I wore the same pink top, my hair longer and held back with an Alice band, jeans instead of shorts. I was smiling – my young heart was ready to move on and start living again.

I didn't know the woman who came to get me in a big, square car that looked like something you'd drive up a mountain, or in the desert. What happened to our family driver, Martino?

'You must be Lucrezia!' the woman said in heavily accented Italian. Only later did I realise that it was a French accent. She wore a matching skirt and blazer, with a brooch at the neck of her shirt – she would have looked severe, had it not been for her kind eyes and an open smile. 'I'm Madame Aubert. It's very nice to meet you.'

My joy was beginning to turn into disquiet. Who was this woman?

'I'll just speak to the doctor a moment, and then we'll get everything sorted in no time.'

Dottor Minieri stood on the doorstep of his visiting room. 'Welcome. Come on in,' he said, and the woman disappeared into his study, leaving a cloud of perfume behind.

I swallowed, my heart beating faster and faster. Whispers could be heard through the door, but I couldn't make out the words.

After what seemed like an eternity I was called inside. By then, my confidence had drained away. 'I'm not going home, am I,' I asked in a small voice. It was more a statement than a question.

Both Minieri's and the woman's faces fell. 'You didn't know?' Madame Aubert said with a half-surprised, half-horrified look to the doctor.

Dottor Minieri was as mystified as she was. 'Your father didn't tell you? In your phone calls?'

'I never speak to my father. Only to Matilde. My father decided I'm not allowed to talk to my sisters in case I... *influence* them.'

'I see.' Minieri's lips became very thin, and a red line, visible to me only, appeared around his head, glowing electric. I blinked – his aura spoke of anger, but it wasn't towards me, I knew that. I gazed from him to the strange woman, and back. I didn't understand what was happening.

Madame Aubert bowed to be level with me. 'Your father enrolled you in my school. It's a small school; we're like a family. You'll be happy, with us.'

My heart sank, and it seemed to me that it made a noise hitting the floor – but it was my little bag, having slipped through my hand.

I'd done what I'd been asked to do; I'd accepted that I hadn't really seen my mother. But I still wasn't allowed home.

I contemplated grabbing something off the doctor's desk and throwing it against the wall, screaming and thumping my feet and disgorging all the anger and disappointment and loneliness I felt at that moment; but that would have just meant more time in the hospital.

Madame Aubert picked my bag up. 'I'll do everything I can to help you feel at home, *chérie*. I promise.'

'Casalta is my home,' I said. I took the bag from her and stepped out, towards the car, with all the dignity a broken girl could muster.

# CHAPTER 19

## CASALTA, 17 APRIL 1985

LUCREZIA

Thankfully, the phone ringing interrupted my memories. It took me a moment to come back to the here and now, before Bianca answered.

'Hello? Vanni. She's here.' Bianca handed me the receiver.

'Hello?'

'Lucrezia?' His voice was unmistakable. Warm, deep – and so very familiar. I felt the corners of my mouth lift in a smile. I was so glad that he was calling me.

'Vanni.'

'You sound...'

'Yes. I know. Just... not the best moment.'

'Look, I was wondering if you wanted a few hours away from everything. What do you say?' I hesitated and looked at my sisters, sitting pale and in shock.

'I don't know. Things here are a little... *heavy*, as you know.'

A sigh. 'I can imagine. It wasn't the right time to ask, I suppose...' I could hear the disappointment in his voice.

'Go! Go have fun!' Mia called out suddenly.

'Who was that?' Vanni asked.

'My sister, Mia. She says we should go and have fun. Maybe just a couple of hours...' I said tentatively.

Bianca was sitting silently, lost in thought; Nora was sulking in the stables; Mia was nodding, her eyebrows raised. 'Fine, then. Yes, I'll come.'

'Great! One condition, though.'

'What's that?'

'That we don't talk about the sale of Casalta, or anything that troubles you. I want to take you away from all that for a little while.'

'That's just what I need, Vanni,' I admitted. 'Thank you.'

'I'll be there in half an hour?'

I couldn't keep the smile out of my voice. 'See you then.'

As soon as I put the receiver back on its cradle, I asked myself if I should stay, try to unknot the many knots, do something practical... But my soul needed my old friend, needed some time to breathe and regroup.

'I won't be long.'

'Have a great time, Lulu,' Mia said, but Bianca was still silent.

Silly, I suppose, that I should feel like smiling and running up the stairs as if I were carefree, and not in the middle of a financial and family crisis. Vanni did that to me: the young girl I was before everything fell apart was tied to his presence – he brought her out of me, and I liked this girl more than my cold, restrained Paris self. I pushed away the guilt of leaving my sisters worrying and wondering about the whole situation: I'd go and breathe some oxygen, and come back ready to face it all.

Guilt about leaving my sisters wasn't the only thing I pushed away. The thought of Claude was also relegated to the back of my mind. He wasn't just far geographically, but emotionally: he was barely there at all, and I knew that for his sake and mine, things needed to change soon.

I was on the doorstep, with Vanni's car there already, waiting for me, when Bianca held me in a tight embrace.

'I wish it'd been me. I wish I could have raised hell and taken you home. I wish...'

'*Shhhhh*,' I soothed. 'I'm here now. It's finished.'

Bianca held both my hands and gazed at me with an intensity that made me hold my breath.

'I love Casalta. But I love you more. And all I want, all I need, is for you to be happy.'

Bianca's words of love, having finally unburdened myself of the truth, walking on Florence's stony streets with Vanni – everything conspired to bring a spring to my step. The change of register, between recalling the dark days of the Istituto Lugano, and being here now, was almost making my head spin. I looked up and around, to the sky and to the tops of Florence's harmonious buildings. Beauty, I reflected, was a balm to the soul.

The day was grey, a little drizzly, but, far from taking away from the city, the weather only added to its allure. We crossed Piazza del Duomo slowly, without rush, without anywhere to be; I gazed all around me in wonder, as if seeing the city for the first time. And in fact, it was the first time I'd seen it as an adult. I caught Vanni's eye, and saw he was looking at me.

'What?' I asked, smiling.

'You're drinking everything in.'

'Yes! I feel like a tourist. I've been here a thousand times, but it's like seeing it all anew.'

'So, I know it's two different places, and you can't compare, and blah blah blah, but... Florence or Paris? Which wins?'

'Florence. Hands down.'

'Right answer!'

We reached the duomo, and my heart skipped a beat as I

stood at its feet, contemplating the striped marble, the domes, the perfect grace of the structure. 'I'd forgotten how the duomo is so huge, and yet so... light. Like it has no weight.'

'*Mmmm.*'

I laughed. 'You don't seem so taken!'

'I'm not into art that much, not like your family. I prefer natural things, not manmade. Fields and trees. They are... pure. You'll think I'm an oaf!'

'Not at all! I understand. So why did you take me here, to the... impure city?' I joked.

'Because it's easier for me to navigate than fields and hills.'

His smile faltered, and for a moment, I was at a loss for words. It was easy to forget his difficulties... Sometimes Vanni's chair struggled a little on the narrow pavements, but even then, I was amazed to see how the chair and him had become a unit, how easily he negotiated any obstacles.

'I know there are places where you can't go right now. But I was just thinking how... well, how it all seems normal. You in this chair, me beside you, walking on. It's just the way things are. Maybe...' I stopped. I didn't know how to finish the sentence. I didn't know if it was a good idea to be so honest, so unguarded.

'*Maybe?*'

'Maybe I've been so happy to see you again that I didn't quite consider anything else.' It was true. The more time I spent with the Vanni of today, the more normal, assumed, his inability to walk seemed to me.

He didn't answer, but his face seemed to tense up. I wasn't sure if those words had pleased him or... hurt him? Why would my words hurt him?

'I mean, of course I *consider* what you went through,' I hastened to add. 'But it doesn't seem important, compared to actually *seeing* you. Not that it's not important...' Ah, I was tripping on my own words. 'I don't know what I'm saying!'

'No, no... I understand. Really, I do.'

'Oh, good.'

The Lucrezia I was in Paris never got herself in a tizzy, but clearly, she wasn't here.

After all, the Lucrezia I was in Paris never got herself anywhere. She safely stayed behind her walls, spoke little, and never offered her side to avoid possible hurt or rejection. I wasn't sure which one of the two I preferred, but in this moment, walking the streets of Florence with my childhood friend, chatting about everything and nothing, no wall would be high enough or mighty enough to shield my heart.

I was always surer and surer, with every step I took, that my life in Paris was crumbling from its very foundations. And I hoped that Claude felt the same; I hoped that the conversation that was on the horizon for us would not cause pain, but freedom.

We stopped to watch the green waters of the Arno flowing by. Vanni rested an elbow on the stone banister, and I bent down to lean on it.

'You're lost in thought,' he observed. 'There must be a lot on your mind, right now.'

I nodded. 'Yes. But you made me promise I wouldn't talk about Casalta...'

'True! That's not allowed.'

'And in fact, I wasn't thinking about that. I was thinking of my partner. Of my job...' I shrugged. 'Of my life. I believed it was settled. I believed *I* was settled. The day I left I thought that the person who went back to Paris would not be the person who left. But I didn't imagine it would be to this extent. Claude feels like a stranger who never knew me. My job... has no connection with my heart. Everything about my old life seems to be slipping between my fingers. Like this water, flowing away... Oh, I bet you're sorry you asked!'

'No, not at all. I like listening to you talk.'

I waited for a moment, hoping he would reciprocate my confidences – but he didn't. We crossed the Ponte Vecchio, the oldest bridge in Florence, passing the jewellery shops that lined it. Here, it was easy to forget modern times: it was like being thrown back to when the Medici ruled the city. My Florence was like a city-wide time machine.

'My mum used to work in one of these, when she arrived. To support herself while she painted. She used to go to the Uffizi almost every day... she used to take us with her too, even when Nora and Mia were babies. The routine was Uffizi first and then ice cream. Just the five of us... Thinking back, how did she manage four small kids in a museum?'

'Your sisters were angels. But you were savage, when you were little!'

'Er, excuse me?' I laughed.

'You were! Like a little girl Tarzan. All composed and calm in public, wild when it was just us children.'

'You're one to talk! You never sat still...'

Oh. I stopped abruptly. I wanted to bite my hand.

'Yeah, well. Anyway. Would you like to go to the Uffizi, then? A trip down memory lane?'

'I'd love to! I'd like to show you something, actually. But... the stairs...'

'There's a lift. A friend of mine, a lady who goes to my same physiotherapist... she visits all the time. There aren't many accessible places, but the Uffizi is one of them.'

'That's good.' It was a different way of seeing the world, I considered: if you couldn't walk, or if you were with someone who couldn't walk, you began to notice steps, stairs, obstacles everywhere. I was in awe of how Vanni negotiated this new world – but I had the feeling he wouldn't have appreciated any praise. I felt he preferred me to behave as if this had always been our reality and nothing had changed. We crossed the bridge again, in the opposite direction, and passed between the wide stone columns of the Uffizi.

I almost held my breath as we made our way into the museum, reaching the upper floor via a lift I'd never been in before. The chill of the thick stone walls, that unique scent I remembered so well – I know it's hard to believe, but I could smell the paint, even if everything was behind glass and long dry.

I took a deep breath, inhaling the fragrance. Maybe I was simply remembering the scent my mum carried with her.

'You look happy,' Vanni observed.

'I am. Come on, there's something I'd like you to see.'

The place was almost empty, on this drizzly day, and we moved through the rooms and corridors with ease, until we arrived at my favourite paintings: those by Bronzino. My name-sake, Lucrezia Panciatichi, met my gaze, sitting with immense dignity and a mysterious, aloof expression, wearing a splendid dress, embroidered in gold.

'My mum chose our names because of these paintings. This is me: Lucrezia.'

Vanni jerked his head from the portrait to me, and back. 'I'm... blown away. The shape of your face... your eyes...'

'I know! Don't ask me how our mum did it, but she did. And this...' We moved forward a little, to the portrait of an exquisitely pretty young girl with creamy skin and pink cheeks.

'This is Bianca. She's not identical to you, but has the same sweet expression as Bianca.'

'You guessed. It's Bianca de' Medici. And this is Maria de' Medici, our Mia...' It was slender, black-eyed girl in a black velvet dress, with a mysterious gaze that seemed to look *through* you – just like Mia.

'She looks like Mia. She really does!'

'I know. And this is Eleonora. Eleonora di Toledo.' She was a strong, solid-looking woman with a little boy beside her.

'Mmmm. Quite matronly, to be Nora.'

I smiled. 'True. Maybe she'll be the one who doesn't look like her portrait. Or maybe she'll grow into it.'

'Maybe. Lucrezia, this is really, really spooky. Your mum seemed to know you before you were born.'

'My mum *was* special. As for being spooky... Maybe just a little.'

'Yes. What colour is my aura now, Lucrezia?'

I smiled and looked down. 'You remembered.'

In the years I was away, I never confided in anyone else. My child's instinct told me not to tell anyone in that horrible hospital, obviously – at boarding school I just wanted to go unnoticed, not to attract any attention to myself, though sometimes my ability to read people's moods was remarked on. I always recoiled – I was terrified that if there was something strange about me, they would send me to the hospital again.

Once in Paris, I hoped I'd left the old Lucrezia behind, like a butterfly out of her chrysalis – I'd built a new, cold identity that certainly didn't involve preternatural talents. The more I ignored the gift, the more atrophied it became. But since I'd come home, it was beginning to bloom again, like a muscle that was being exercised again.

'It'd be impossible to forget. Would you forget, if your best friend told you she could see green all around your head, and looked up at... nothing? Well, not nothing to you, of course. Would you forget if she told you about her sister plucking stories out of thin air?'

I smiled. 'No. I wouldn't forget. But I'm not sure I'd believe her.' I stole a glance of him, as we stood side by side in front of Bronzino's masterpieces.

'I believed you. I still do. And I could see how special Mia is.'

My heart soared. I'd been right, to confide in him. He believed me, and he seemed fascinated instead of daunted.

'Yes. I think Mia is the most magical of us.'

'What about Nora?'

I shrugged. 'Nora is a mystery. You see... our gifts come from Mum, and Nora refuses anything that comes from her. Bianca says she has an affinity to animals, but apart from that, I don't know.'

'So... what do you see around me, now?'

'Wait.' I focused on the space around him, and my eyes were filled with spring green and light yellow... which then morphed into a deep, soothing aqua blue.

I smiled. 'I see... you. Your spirit. It's all beautiful, and... kind.'

'It's not always how I felt, in the last few years,' he said. And then, a thought seemed to hit him.

'Something just came back to me. I saw your mother talking to my dad, once. It wasn't long before you went away. They were over at the warehouse, in our estate. I'm sure it was her. Her hair was impossible to miss.'

'Really? When? We weren't allowed any interaction. Had he known, my father would have...'

I couldn't finish the sentence. We never really knew why our families hated each other so. There were other powerful wine and oil traders around here, other rivals. But with the Orafi, it was always vicious. And it started suddenly... The car accident and its responsibility weighed between us, unmentioned and yet there, hanging in the air, under the gaze of the women in the portraits.

'Hey. I'm sorry I brought this up... Let me see you smile again, please.'

I felt Vanni's hand, warm and strong, find mine. Can something be electrifying and yet comfortable at the same time? The thought of Claude ran through my mind, cold, devoid of any feeling but guilt. And this in itself made me feel even guiltier. I took my hand away, and I could see he was a little startled.

'No, it's fine. Don't worry. Are you hungry? I am,' I said a little too quickly, a little too cheerfully. 'There was a place we used to go to with Mum. Nothing fancy, a tiny restaurant that gave us girls these mini round pizzas... We loved them. It might not be there any more, though.'

'Well, let's see,' Vanni said, and we made our way out of the gallery, under a showery sky. I said a silent goodbye to the women who gave us our names, their beauty forever frozen in time.

'This way.' I led him, but quickly realised that maybe it wasn't the best idea. The alley, enclosed by high stone buildings, was narrow and lined with a slim pavement that made the wheelchair proceed at an angle. The trattoria was still there, but I was dismayed to see how high, how narrow the entrance steps were – the Uffizi had spoiled us with its ramps and its lift, but most other places, in an ancient city like Florence, weren't accessible.

How come I'd never considered such a thing? It had never even occurred to me that simply moving in the world with ease was a privilege.

I crossed my arms. 'We should go and find somewhere a little more welcoming.'

The air around Vanni's head and shoulders coloured crimson – anger. But against who? Me, the steps, the chair?

'No, I don't want to stop you.'

'I don't really care about—'

'*Buongiorno!* Can I help?' A man wearing an apron appeared on the steps. 'Michele! Come here!' he called inside, in a thick Florentine accent.

'It's fine, we don't...' I began, but everyone ignored me. The two men gave Vanni a nod and lifted the chair, with Vanni frowning and glaring at the steps.

'You go first,' he said. The waiters were strong, and careful – but those steps were simply too narrow. Vanni sat powerless while the chair was tipped uncomfortably. Had it not been for one of the waiters grabbing him by the shoulders while the others balanced the chair, he would have fallen.

It was nothing, really, not for those men, not for me, not for the punters inside – but it was for Vanni. The waiter helped him back on the chair, and he was safe on top of the stairs; but the whole restaurant had turned to look, and one of the punters was halfway to us, thinking he might have to help. Vanni's cheeks were flushed, his jaw locked.

He didn't meet my eye while they led us to the table and took our orders. The crimson of his aura had turned blue, not a peaceful sky blue, but a deep and sorrowful blue-black. He took a sip of his wine.

'Are you all right?'

'Totally fine. No problem at all.'

I tilted my head. 'Are you sure?'

'Are *you* okay, Lucrezia?'

'Of course. Why shouldn't I be?'

'Are you not *ashamed*, to be seen with someone who nearly fell flat on his face?'

The bitterness in his words shocked me. There was a blustery sea inside him which I hadn't seen until now, lost as I'd been in all that was happening to me and my sisters.

'I can't believe you're asking me if I felt ashamed to be seen with you. It's absurd!'

'It's not absurd. But anyway. I don't want to spoil our day out...'

'You're not spoiling anything! You *make* our day out. When I saw you again I was too happy to even consider the fact that you can't walk. You were there, in the same room as me. The rest seemed irrelevant. I know it's not and I know your life has changed, but this is the way I felt in that moment: *I didn't care.*'

There was a pause, as both of us digested our conversation. 'Enough about this,' he said then, with a smile that reassured me a little. 'Tell me more about your life in Paris,' he said while one of the waiters laid two plates of fragrant spaghetti with fresh tomatoes in front of us. No fancy French cuisine could beat the simplest of Italian dishes, I considered smugly, and covered my pasta with a generous smattering of parmigiano.

'Well, you know I always was a little bossy...'

'You were,' he said in a serious tone, but with a mischievous light in his eyes.

'You're supposed to say *not at all!*'

'Not at all,' he parroted with a grin.

'Fine, I was! Anyway. I found the perfect job for my bossiness. I'm a personal assistant to a chef. I organise his schedule, deal with the press, make sure everything runs smoothly. He's also... well, like I said, we're together.'

'Oh. That's good.' He rolled some spaghetti around his fork. Quite deliberately, I thought.

'He's not... I mean... It's not a fairy-tale romance. We work well together.'

'That's good,' he repeated.

'So, that's me. Tell me about you.'

I took a sip of wine. An abundant sip.

'Not much to say. I work, as much as Lorenzo allows me... He thinks I could break at any moment. I had a girlfriend... fiancée, actually. Not any more. She couldn't live with this,' he said and patted the armrest of his wheelchair.

I leaned back. The thought of how that must have made him feel was unbearable. I tried not to judge his former girlfriend – we don't all envisage our life the same way, and it was better she left him than both of them living unhappily. But it was hard to imagine what Vanni must have been through. 'That sounds awful.'

He shrugged. 'It taught me a lesson.'

'Not to settle for fair-weather friends? And partners?'

'Not to hope I could have a normal life.'

I couldn't find the words to say that it wasn't true. That it really wasn't true. That he'd become blind to his worth and his talents.

That happiness was within reach, if only he allowed himself to take it. Or at least, try.

Maybe that was something I should have told myself: happiness is possible, if you only try and reach out for it, instead of denying it over and over.

～

I didn't want to go back to it all. I didn't want to say goodbye.

When Maurizio opened the car door for me and it was time to step out, I had to force my body to move in the opposite direction from Vanni, fighting that strange force of gravity that pulled me to him.

The sky weighed heavy on the hills, full of clouds that had only just begun opening. It was darker than it should be at this time of day, with night drawing in almost suddenly, as if it were winter. The first smattering of raindrops hit the car. A storm was brewing.

I turned to him. 'Thank you. Really. Today was...' I couldn't finish the sentence. Every word that came to my mind seemed too sentimental. 'Good.'

I reached the door, and turned around one last time. Vanni raised his hand in a brief goodbye. He was smiling, but the smile died on his lips a moment before I looked away; and he was gone, away into the gathering darkness. The way he'd stopped smiling as soon as he thought I wasn't looking at him worried me: had he not had a good time? I knew that the mishap on the restaurant steps had been upsetting for him, that he'd been affected by that, but I hoped that it hadn't completely spoiled the day for him.

I ran upstairs to get changed, and while I undressed under

the trailing red roses, a thought hit me: there was nothing left of my bond with Claude. Nothing, except goodwill. Maybe the bond had never been there at all. Vanni's eyes, Vanni's smile and the feeling of my hand in his filled my memory, but who knew what was going to happen between us? Everything or nothing.

I had no idea what was going to happen next in my life. The destiny of Casalta was up in the air; the relationship with my sisters was a tapestry in the making, with many hanging threads; everything now revolved around taming this beast my father had unleashed against me, the mountain of debt and the uncertainty of my sisters' future. But what I knew for sure was that my heart was not with Claude, not with my job as his assistant either. The more time I spent in Tuscany, the more my ties to Paris frayed.

*But you know,* I whispered to the roses, *that I'm not telling the whole truth, not even to myself: that I carried Vanni in my heart with me for all these years...*

# CHAPTER 20

## BIANCAMURA, 17 APRIL 1985

VANNI

*I've carried her in my heart for all these years*, I think as I watch her run inside. But I can never have her. As soon as she's out of sight, I let my smile fade.

*Half man. Cripple.* In a fit of self-hatred, I whisper them to my own image in the mirror.

Folded in two, useless, in a chair.

Nobody ever used those cruel words to describe me, but me.

When Lucrezia returned, it was as if the boy I was before the accident had come back with her. I wanted to be myself again. But it wasn't enough. I can delude myself that a clean shave and a little self-respect can change things, but they can't.

Every time Lucrezia had to look down and I had to look up, every time she had to push me on the cobbles, the way we had to sit at the edge of a path instead of climbing the grassy slopes of the Boboli Gardens – having to call the waiters to lift me up the five steps to the restaurant, with the other punters pretending not look... all this meant defeat, humiliation. It stings enough when I am alone; but with Lucrezia there, it was unbearable.

I remember Cristina's tears as if it happened yesterday – I've replayed that day over and over in my mind. Cristina, crying in her hands as she repeated how sorry she was, how ashamed, but she couldn't lie to herself any longer. She couldn't live with me this way.

My brother and I are never short of girls interested in us, or should I say, in the Orafi family; but I refused to see anyone else. I will not go through the humiliation again. I can't give children to my future wife. I can't give her a walk on the beach; we can't stand side by side and kiss. I don't command respect from the men we work with; I can't face a relationship. I can only let life pass me by, maybe with the balm of little moments such as the ones I had today with Lucrezia.

Lorenzo won't allow himself a relationship – women come and go from his life in the space of one night; my father is alone too, as is our estranged mother. We've become a house of bachelors, two of us devoted to the business, one of us – me – in limbo.

I knock at my father's door and make my way in. His room is, as usual, bright and airy, not so much a sickroom but a sanctuary. He's forced to stay in bed most of the time, but whenever he can, he likes to sit in the armchair by the window and look out onto the hills.

'You're back. How did it go?' he says with the smile he's never lost, even if life hasn't been easy on him.

His smile contrasts with the sorry pair we make, two men destroyed in a few minutes, by a falling car.

'I don't know. It was good to see her, but it was awful at the same time. Fosco did his best to crush her spirit.'

'He left quite a few other people crushed in his wake. But he's gone now.'

'He's gone to hell, yes.'

Dad grimaces. Words of hate never sit right with him, even when they have reason to be uttered. 'The Casalta sisters seem in agreement about selling the house to us,' he says. 'The question is, what will happen next?'

'What do you mean?' I pretend not to understand, because I want my father to put into words whatever Lorenzo is planning.

'You do know what I mean, *figlio mio*.'

'Remind me,' I say quietly.

He smiles, his eyes bright and clever and acutely aware of everything that goes on in this house, in the business, in his sons. Whoever dismisses my father as a powerless *invalid* – oh, how I hate that word! – couldn't be more wrong. However, Lorenzo has youth and strength on his side, and a cunning that my father refuses to employ.

'What do you want to happen next, after we buy Casalta? What do you think we should do with the Falconeri house?'

'You're doing it again!' Lorenzo's voice is followed by the scent of his aftershave. He's come in, and is now looking at our father with reproach. 'Vanni can't be burdened with business worries, tasks, whatever! Do you want him to end up like you?'

Here is the real Lorenzo. Smooth and collected with the outside world, vulnerable and highly strung with his family. You'd wonder who's the vulnerable one here, me in my wheelchair, or Lorenzo, standing tall and strong but eternally afraid.

'Your brother is perfectly capable of making decisions for himself, Lorenzo.'

'Er... excuse me? I'm here, in this room, with you. Can you maybe address me directly?' I say without resentment.

'Sorry, Vanni. But you know you shouldn't exert yourself.'

'His legs don't work, but the rest of him does! He can make decisions about business, and so can I,' Dad asserts.

'He needs to concentrate on resting, and physio, and looking after his health!'

'Still here, Lorenzo!' I cry. The back and forth between my

father and my brother doesn't make me feel any more powerless than I usually feel. There's no tug of war for power between my brother and me, because I'm not *really* interested in the family business.

I'm not interested in anything.

My father knows it, and tries to push me to find something to do, something to believe in, anything to feel alive again. 'You both have so much rage inside you. *This* is our life, now. Every day and every night you relive the accident! It was years ago, and yet you never moved on. I'm old and sick and I have more life in me than the two of you!'

'Dad—' Lorenzo begins.

'Don't you dare say I shouldn't get angry because it's *bad* for me!'

'But it is bad for you.' Lorenzo frowns in the exact same way he did when he was little.

'Well. I'll leave you guys to argue it all out, *va bene?*' I say, half annoyed, half touched by their clumsy reciprocal affection.

'Vanni, wait. We haven't finished discussing Casalta. I think we should buy it, as arranged, and give it back to the Falconeri daughters for a token.'

Lorenzo's lips are a thin line, his fists curled by his sides. 'You must be *joking.*'

My father looks at me, and I choose my words carefully. 'I don't know what they want, Lucrezia and her sisters. I don't know that Lucrezia wants to keep Casalta at all.'

'What they want is irrelevant.' Lorenzo sounds calm, but I can feel his voice vibrating with indignation. 'We waited years for this. Fosco Falconeri is dead, and he died bankrupt. Their estate and all it contains will be ours soon; their business will be ours. Why on earth are you even considering giving it back to them?'

'Decency,' my father says. 'Fosco damaged them too.'

'I don't know if you're forgiving, or just a fool.'

Lorenzo has gone too far. The sound of his hard, hard words ripples in the air, in our hearts and minds. He called our father a fool. And to my shock, my strong, resolute father looks aghast, his eyes shiny and his hands open on the blanket.

Fosco Falconeri has broken us once, with the car accident that took my legs. And now, I realise bitterly, he's breaking us again, by turning us into him.

Alone in my room, with a bottle of Chianti for company, I run the scene in my mind over and over and over again: a helpless man, emasculated, almost falling on his face in front of everyone. In front of Lucrezia. The bitterness and self-pity I truly feel are free to flood me, now that I don't have to put on a brave face, smile, to pretend I've accepted the new me – the *cripple*. The word tastes foul in my mouth: Lorenzo and my father would be appalled to hear me use it. But in my mind, I'm free not to be positive, not to be brave, or even fair.

I know that I won't see Lucrezia again. I couldn't bear more humiliation.

I fall asleep when the bottle is empty and the night is at its darkest, with Lucrezia's face dancing behind my closed eyes, and a heart full of grief.

# CHAPTER 21

## CASALTA, 17 APRIL 1985

LUCREZIA

It seemed there was nobody home. I would have liked to sit on the stone stairs for a little while and bask in the day I'd had with Vanni, but the drizzle had turned into rain, fat drops of water bouncing on the ground, on the roof, tapping on the windows. I lit the living room fire, taking advantage of Matilde's absence. Had she been there, she would have insisted on doing it for me. I sat with my legs bent under me and watched the flame.

The Tuscan twilight, framed in the windows, took my breath away. The rain added a dreamy quality to the landscape, and filled the room with a calm blue light.

I thought of Vanni's expression at the restaurant table, his shame and powerlessness after he'd almost fallen... the only dark moment in a day full of light. I longed to take that darkness away for him, to show him that he was not less of a man because of the accident, but *more*. A man who overcame such an ordeal – the fear and pain he must have felt, not to mention the worry for his father. And then adapting to a whole new life, physically and mentally. If anything, I was in awe of him.

Everything about him, his voice, his mannerisms, his expressions, were as familiar as if we'd grown up together. Everything stirred memories in me, snippets of conversations, moments of long ago that had been stored somewhere deep inside me. Free from layers and layers of defences, my heart was so much easier to read, my thoughts so much clearer, that I couldn't live a lie any longer.

I knew that I had to speak to Claude, and it wouldn't be Vanni we discussed, but *us*. Our relationship felt empty, and not because I'd seen my old best friend, and my sisters as well. It was because I'd been reminded that I *could* feel deeply, that life didn't have to be kept in shallow waters so that I would not be hurt. But because here, away from my life in Paris, I could finally see how hollow I'd become, how I'd settled for a loveless relationship and an endless work schedule to distract me from life itself. No, how I'd *searched* for a loveless relationship so that I would never be hurt again the way my father hurt me. But now, I needed more, I *wanted* more.

Claude deserved to know. But... a phone call? I had to tell him in person. When I went back to Paris. When I left Casalta, and Tuscany, and went back to my life.

The idea wasn't as appealing as I had imagined it would be.

I'd dreaded coming back. I'd dreaded seeing my sisters, and facing the toxic mixture of anger and love and regret and sense of abandonment I'd experienced around my family, around this house. Seeing that corridor, the glass doors I'd gone through as a child, the garden where my mother had appeared to me, the place I'd left thinking I would return the day after, and instead I wasn't allowed to go back to.

But the sweet hills outside the window, the lilac sky, the outline of cypresses against the evening light; the stone houses with their terracotta tiles, the scent of this land, made by the unique mixture of our flora, our trees, the castles and churches that spoke of our history... all this went beyond my own story or the story of my family; it went beyond and deeper than the happenings of life. All this was home.

Paris, my flat on that pretty road, in that cream-coloured building dotted by wrought-iron balconies, seemed so far away. Like a dream that never happened. I should have missed Claude at least; I should have been thinking about him and wondering what he was doing – would this not have been normal, for two people in a relationship, two people who loved each other?

But there had been no missing him, or thinking about him before now. It seemed that the entirety of our relationship was enclosed in my work diary, the one where I recorded our business and social commitments. I could even picture it, the thick black book where my whole life was scheduled and blocked off around our engagements. We weren't really a couple. We were a team, a team that was successful, efficient... but loving, not so much. Surely there was more to life than that, at twenty-four years of age?

More to life than a frozen heart, made to work around a schedule.

The dancing flames gave a warm glow to my hands and legs, a halo of light in the room that was getting gloomier and gloomier. Where was everyone? I supposed Nora was at the stables and Mia painting. Matilde had probably gone home, and Bianca was in the village or somewhere in its surroundings, visiting people in need.

'Anyone home? Lulu?' Bianca called out, coming in with her hair damp with rain. 'Oh, I'm still not used to seeing you here! Every time I... I... Oh, *Lulu!*' She ran to me and hugged me tight. 'I still can't believe you're back.'

'Me neither!'

I suppose twins are used to looking at each other's faces and seeing themselves reflected, but after so many years of absence it was a new feeling for me; and from the way Bianca was staring at me, blinking, it was the same for her.

'Coming home and seeing you here, as if all these years haven't passed...' She took her jacket off. She sat on the rug, her legs tucked on one side. My sister always looked graceful, like a china figurine.

I leaned forward and rested my elbows on my knees. 'How was your day?'

Bianca sighed. 'My day was good; you know I love what I do. But the co-op never has funds to pay our wages. Which didn't matter, until now. We all received an allowance from Father, and that was how I kept the service afloat. I pay Renata's wages... she's my colleague... I bought food, medicine, school-books, anything the people we assist need. Now...' She shrugged her shoulders.

'We'll find a way.'

'We? You'll go back to Paris, won't you? I don't even know when I'll see you again... Oh, sorry. I put a dampener on every-thing! Let's not think about that. I don't want to think about that at all. Did you have a good time with Vanni?'

'Yes. It was... good,' I said, trying keep my tone light. But separation or not, she was my twin. She could still read me.

She spoke, looking into the flames. 'I'm so sorry you had to be away from him for so long. Before you left, I saw things were beginning to change between the two of you. You blushed when you talked about him. It was a childhood friendship, but it was turning into something more.'

'I know. That letter you wrote me, the one where you said you saw Vanni at... at our tree.'

'He was so sad, Lulu. His mother is always away, she and Signor Orafi didn't get on at all. I wished I could have helped him.'

I knew this was the right moment. I had to ask.

'Bianca... Do you... Did you have feelings for Vanni?'

Bianca's mouth opened in a little 'O'. 'Do I... What made you think that?'

'I don't know... when you sent me that letter, saying the two of you had met at our treehouse, I became convinced...'

'But that was to talk about you! He needed to know about you! Oh, Lulu, you got it all wrong. All wrong.'

And yet.

'But there's something going on between you and the Orafi brothers. I saw Lorenzo's picture in your room. I'm sorry, I don't mean to put you on the spot. It's just that if you need to talk, well, I'm here. I'm here now.'

'I know. Thank you. But please, Lulu. Let it go.'

She seemed genuinely pained, and I did what she said. I let it go.

For now.

# CHAPTER 22

## CASALTA, 18 APRIL 1985

LUCREZIA

A hesitant sun rose on a new day, soft with rain. Today was the day we would officially let Casalta go.

We took our places around a shiny black table, in the notary's meeting room. Unlike his study, which was full of antiques, this was modern, with abstract posters framed on the wall and brightly coloured chairs. In the centre sat an ominous pile of documents. Cavalli looked smug, the Orafi signet ring shining obnoxiously on his finger.

'Is it only the two of you?' the notary murmured to Bianca.

'Yes. There was no need for my sisters to be here,' she said in a cold tone. 'Therefore, Nora is not here.'

What? What interest did he have in Nora?

'I see. Well, please tell her I was asking after her.'

'She won't know who you are,' Bianca replied, and Cavalli's expression morphed into something between humiliated and piqued. He straightened the papers and the pen in front of him with short, sharp movements.

Across the table was Lorenzo, dressed in a dark suit and silk tie, composed, calm, as if this was just everyday business. Which, for him, I supposed it was.

Vanni wasn't there.

I wanted to turn around and look at the door, hoping he would come in at any moment, or to the windows, where he might come in through the car park. But I didn't move. It'd be so transparent, my desire to see him. And I didn't want it to be, for both my sake and his...

My eyes met Lorenzo's, which were quietly triumphant. I held his gaze; yes, the feud between the Falconeri and the Orafi wasn't mine, but seeing this man lording it over me and my sisters stung. A lot.

Cavalli bumped his pen on the table twice, as if we were children brought to attention. I balked. My nerves were on fire: I couldn't wait to get it all over and done with.

'We all ready?'

'Ready,' Lorenzo said. Bianca nodded, and leaned towards me a little – a gesture imperceptible to others, but comforting to me.

'Good. Let's begin.'

Half an hour of reading and signing documents later, it was done. Casalta was not ours any more.

It was so final.

When I was holding the pen to the very last page, ready to sign and finish it all, something happened. All of a sudden, I saw red roses twirling around my arm as quick as snakes; a thorn pierced my finger, and blood fell on the paper to make my signature.

I jumped and shook my arm, but of course there was nothing there, and everyone stared at me. 'Sorry. A cramp.'

'It's the last one,' Cavalli said. 'We all know what Italian bureaucracy is like, eh?' He attempted a laugh, but nobody joined in. I would have liked to stick the pen in his eye.

I tried again, but again scarlet roses appeared around my

wrist, encircling it – my whole body tensed, waiting for the sting
– my fingers uncurled and the pen fell.

'Lulu?' Bianca whispered.

'I can't sign,' I heard myself saying.

'What?' Lorenzo's voice was icy.

'I can't. I can't give you Casalta.'

I'd like to say that I felt brave and determined, but I was
shaking so much I felt my chair vibrating.

*What did I just say?*

'What did you just say?' Bianca was ashen.

'Excuse me?' Lorenzo was calm and smooth as ever.

'I can't give you Casalta.'

Bianca clasped her hand to her mouth. There was a
moment of silence. Lorenzo's jaw worked, and then he spoke.
He turned to Cavalli as if I wasn't there.

'Please leave us, Cavalli. We have matters to discuss.' He
wasn't asking; he was stating. Never mind that this was the
notary's meeting room.

Our father's lawyer had truly become the Orafi's lackey: he
scurried away and closed the door.

'Look, Lucrezia,' Lorenzo said. 'You don't need to worry
about any of this any more; none of you has to. I'll be more
than happy to take it from here. Settle with the banks, smooth
it all out. We won't let a single worker go. Of course, there will
be a nice payout for each of you. We won't leave you
destitute.'

'I'm not looking for money,' I whispered. I shook my wrist
lightly, expecting to see the roses appear again. Nothing like this
had ever happened to me before.

'Be reasonable. Even if you weren't neck-deep in debt, even
if the business was thriving, with your father gone, there's
nobody to take care of it...'

'Except four perfectly capable women,' I said, with more
determination than I felt. Lorenzo ignored me.

'You can take your time to get settled somewhere else, get back on your feet.'

'We are on our feet, thank you very much,' I said.

Lorenzo laughed.

That laughter of scorn sent me through the roof. Bianca's eyes were wide.

'You find this funny?' I enunciated.

He sighed and leaned back on his chair. And then a smile, slow, knowing, curved his lips. It was the smile of a cat who knows that the mouse will have to come out of its hiding place, sooner or later. 'Of course not. Well, I see your mind is made up. Signorine, I'll speak to you soon, I'm sure.'

He left the room and closed the door behind him, softly. There'd been other signs of annoyance except that working of his jaw.

'What just happened?' Bianca's eyes were even bigger than usual.

'Don't look at me like that; you're freaking me out.'

*'What happened?'*

Cavalli came back inside, with an expression that said: *please, vacate.*

'I'll tell you later,' I said and took her arm. 'I *must* give us a chance,' I whispered so that Cavalli, standing there with his mouth pursed, looking insulted, wouldn't hear us.

'So?' Bianca asked.

'If I told you that a thorn stung me when I was trying to sign, would you believe me? A rose thorn. A rose trailing up my hand,' I said, and mimicked the climbing plant.

'Yes,' she said calmly. 'I would.'

'Well, that's what happened,' I whispered, my heart full and my mind whirling with the consequences.

She nodded and said nothing more until we arrived home, the home that was still our own.

'We didn't sell. Lucrezia didn't sign. Casalta is still ours!' Bianca announced to a mystified Mia, and to Nora, who turned to look at me with a hint of gratitude and respect. Just a hint, mind.

'Lucrezia?' Gabriella's voice was quiet, full of worry.

'I need a moment,' I said, and slipped away down the hall, followed by my sisters' gazes.

I stood in the corridor with the wide glass windows, my father's study at its end. The forbidden room was the place of ultimate terror, for me: the sum of all fears.

The night I saw my mother I'd been called in there to receive judgement, but I never made it inside: I went through the glass, and I was sent away instead.

In my nightmares, the awful dreams that followed me from childhood to adulthood, I made it all the way to the study: but the door would open to a chasm and I'd fall to my death. Other times my father would drag me inside, lock me in, and never let me out again. The dreams were so real I could smell the stale smoke – my father was fond of nausea-inducing cigars – and his aftershave, a fragrance that still caused a reflex of dread and anxiety.

It was time to face this old terror. To exorcise it by looking it in the eye.

Step after step along the corridor, I walked beside my reflection in the black glass. My feet were like lead – I was sure that any moment now my reflection would jump out of the glass and grab me...

I laid a cold, sweaty hand onto the door handle, certain my father would yank the other side, and I'd fall into the abyss...

I lowered the handle and pushed.

I could hear my heart pounding in my ears. I could turn away now; I could choose not to face the blackness inside, and instead return to the light, to my sisters, to life here and now. But I knew that if I did that, the dark would follow me. It would not let me rest.

I stepped inside, and for a moment, between the light-headedness and the pitch dark, I didn't know which was ceiling and which was floor – I felt weightless, falling, falling...

My father's voice resounded in my memory, and his smell, and the noise of broken glass and of my cries... I could have fallen on my knees there and then, my hands over my ears to block that voice, those words.

But I didn't. I fumbled, feeling the walls beside the door for the light switch, until I found it.

Light filled the room, and I blinked as my eyes adjusted. There was no chasm; there were no ghosts to lock me in.

Slowly, as if every step was treacherous, I made my way to my father's desk, and sat on the leather chair. I could hear myself breathing, and I dried a film of cold sweat from my forehead.

I found a block of paper, and a fountain pen. In those folders and papers, piled one on top of the other on the desk and on the shelves around it, were names and contacts. I would list them all, and call them all, until I found a way out for us – someone who'd be crazy enough to help the business, and let my sisters keep Casalta.

I owed my sisters, and Casalta, one last shot.

# CHAPTER 23

## CASALTA, 26 APRIL 1985

LUCREZIA

'Lulu? Lulu, come on. Come upstairs; you need a few hours of proper sleep, at least!'

Bianca's voice woke me, and as sleep faded away, a dull aching filled all my bones. I'd fallen asleep at my father's desk. Again. I followed Bianca in a daze and crawled into my bed.

I'd spent days and nights in that study, trying to find a clue that would help us keep Casalta. I'd made countless calls; I'd gone to see Father's former friends and associates, swallowing my pride in a way I'd never thought possible.

None of them was rude to me – I received condolences and good wishes.

But none of them would help.

When I said that I wasn't asking for a gift, but for a loan, and that my sisters and I would repay them if only we were allowed to keep Casalta – that slowly, our oil and our wine and our individual occupations would make enough to repay such a loan – these businessmen either smiled, or snorted with laughter like Lorenzo had done. They patronised me; they metaphorically patted me on the head, like I was a kitten trying to roar, cute and helpless.

The last name on my list was Gianpaolo Pera, a man larger than he was tall and director of the Florentine bank where my father had one of his accounts. We sat in his office overlooking Piazza Santa Croce, its enchanting view a contrast to the circumstances. Under a sky the colour of pewter and swollen clouds, it was even more beautiful. Pera gave me the missing piece of the jigsaw, the deepest reason why nobody would touch the Falconeri business.

'What exactly are you looking for, Signorina Falconeri?'

'Someone to cover our debts, and let us live in Casalta. They'd be repaid in full with the earnings from the wine and olive business. I know that if it was run properly, it could turn a profit again.'

He shook his head, slowly. '*Mmmm.*'

'Casalta has a huge sentimental value for us. And I'm sure...'

'My apologies, signorina, if I'm mistaken. But I believe you received an offer from Lorenzo Orafi?'

I was taken aback – how did he know? But then, it was the old boys' network, wasn't it? A handful of men controlled pretty much everything.

'We did. But he'd take Casalta,' I said. 'He'd take it all, in exchange for settling our debts.'

'Even if anyone was willing to trust you giving back that amount of money, nobody would go against Lorenzo Orafi. Times have changed. The games have changed. I'm truly sorry. Now that Fosco Falconeri is gone, there's nobody left to handle the business. Lorenzo Orafi is your best bet. If you let him take charge, I'm sure you'll find an agreement that's advantageous for all parties.'

*There's nobody left to handle the business. Let a strong man take charge, you'll be in good hands.*

It was the same message that Lorenzo had given us. I wanted to scream. It was *a strong man* who'd sunk the business, lost everything and dismantled our family. So much for trusting another one of them, believing we'd be in good hands.

To his credit, Pera took a step back. 'You're very brave to be trying this, Signorina Falconeri. I'm not patronising you,' he added, reading my thoughts. 'The problem here is that you're in a financial hole. If you wanted to take charge of the business, and you were starting from nothing, I'm sure you'd succeed. But you'd be starting from ruin.'

'Yes. *Ruin* is the word.'

He leaned over the desk. 'Signorina, please remember this. The word *ruin* might describe the Falconeri empire, but not you and your sisters. You're young; you have everything to live for. Maybe that house of yours is part of the past too, part of the ruin. Something that you must leave behind.'

'I thought so too. But it's not so. My sisters are building something out of Casalta. One is a painter, the youngest. My middle sister has a riding school. And the eldest...'

'Oh, I know Bianca's work. She's a huge help to disadvantaged families all over the province of Florence. I have the utmost respect for her, and for you.'

'You don't know me.'

'I recognise courage and dignity when I see them. You know, I can see some of your father in you.'

*That's not a compliment.*

'I'm nothing like my father.'

Pera stood from his chair and went to perch himself on the desk, beside me. 'You have his determination, and his strength. I knew his dark sides, Lucrezia. But he was very capable, and he had a lot on his shoulders.'

'If he was so capable, then why did he lose everything?'

'It's a good question, and I think I can attempt an answer. He lost everything because he gave up. Something ate him from the inside. After Emmeline's death he was never the same, but in the last few years he truly stopped fighting. I tried to shake him, but I achieved nothing. He wasn't a man to be influenced, for the good or the bad. It was almost as if he let it all fall through his fingers... on purpose. He was tormented.'

*The weight of his sins, I suppose*, I thought, but didn't say. Pera waited a moment, but seeing that I had nothing to comment on the matter, he continued.

'After all is said and done, the fact remains that nobody in their right mind, nobody who wants to keep his business, would stand between Lorenzo Orafi and what he wants. Follow my advice, signorina, let go, move on. I understand it's painful, but you will come out the other side. I wish you the very best of luck. And if there's anything I can help you with, please just call. I mean it.'

A ray of sunshine broke through the clouds and illuminated Piazza Santa Croce and my face, as I looked down onto my hands.

'Thank you.'

As much as I appreciated his kindness, I was deflated. Pera had been my last try.

I sat in Bianca's car and cried furious tears. I banged the steering wheel with my fists and sobbed, away from everyone. Nobody could be allowed to see me like this.

Defeat pervaded every inch of my body. I'd gone from wanting Casalta to be sold, to being indifferent to it, to caring for my sisters' sake... to caring myself. The mysteries of an injured heart, longing to caress the beast that bit you. Or maybe that beast wasn't there any more.

All the yesterdays were gone, and only today remained.

∾

'*More rain over Tuscany! Turns out this is the wettest spring in forty years, so don't put away your umbrellas quite yet...*'

The radio presenter chittered as I drove in between the dryads and onto the gravel, under a grey sky. The rain was like a melody, going from light to heavy and back the same way music rises and falls. Just as I was about to step out of the car the sound of thunder broke the sky, and I jumped. The rain grew even thicker in the short run through the courtyard, a sheet of water between me and the kitchen door.

Matilde ambushed me with towels as if I'd walked miles in the rain instead of a hundred metres, and had boiled water for tea. 'How did it go?'

'Not good. It was our last chance.'

'We'll be fine...' Bianca comforted me.

At that moment Nora appeared, all muddy boots and soaking hair.

'*Lucrezia* will be fine. Us, not so much.'

*Thanks, sister.*

'Nora...' Bianca began, admonishing her.

'Leave it. I'm not even listening,' I said, feeling like I'd reverted to a teenager. We were catching up on sisterly fights, I supposed.

'Well, I'm going. Girls, keep the peace,' Matilde said as if we were children arguing over a favourite toy. Once again, time had done its accordion thing, and years had disappeared like they'd never gone by.

'I'll drive you home,' Nora offered Matilde, and took out her car keys from her pocket.

'Oh, it's not necessary, I have an umbrella. And please don't come inside with those muddy boots...'

'I don't think an umbrella will do much, in this,' I said, gesturing to the storm outside.

'Well, thank you, then.' Matilde gave up, and, after having

wrapped herself in her jacket, zipped up to her neck, she and Nora disappeared into the wind and rain.

'Where's Gabriella?' I asked. 'Somewhere dry, I hope!'

'She's just gone to see her friend in the village; she should be back by tonight. Probably she'll try and wait it out. Tea?'

'Please. Well, we tried,' I said and rubbed my forehead with my fingers.

'I know. Thank you for being here, in all this,' Bianca whispered. 'It's almost been like a trade. I'm about to lose my home, but I got my sister back.'

She found my hand with hers.

'Time to make the call,' I said.

'Time to make the call,' she echoed.

Fat drops of rain were pounding the living room windows as I rested my hand on the receiver, took a deep breath and dialled the number.

A female voice answered, maybe Susanna. 'Orafi residence, who's calling?'

It was like phoning an office, more than a home. 'Lucrezia Falconeri. I'd like to speak to Signor Lorenzo, please.'

'One moment.'

At least there was no holding music, I thought. My heart gave a jump when someone spoke at the other end of the line. 'Lucrezia?'

'Lorenzo.'

'You're ready to sign, I hope.'

'Yes, I am.'

'Good. I think you'll find this was the best decision for everyone. Well—' he began, but I cut him short. I didn't want to speak to him for a minute more than necessary.

'Goodbye, Lorenzo.'

'Goodbye, Lucrezia. I'll have Cavalli phone you when we have a date. Oh... here's Vanni.'

'Of course... Vanni,' I said into the receiver, and the world lost a little bit of its grey.

'Listen... I'm glad you called. I wanted to speak to you.'

'Yes, I—'

'Going to Florence together was a mistake. And I'm not sure your French boyfriend would be happy about it, anyway.'

I was stunned for a moment, then his words sank in. *It's not working out with Claude. I was going to call him, but I wanted to tell him in person...* But none of that came out.

The way his smile had faded just before he disappeared from my sight, after we returned from Florence, and the strange feeling it'd given me, came back to my mind.

'Vanni...'

'After all these years, we don't have much in common. I've changed. I'm not the person you used to know.'

'Understood,' I whispered, while Bianca was searching my face.

'Good. You're better off staying away from someone stuck in a chair. Take care.'

*What?*

I heard the click that told me the conversation was over.

'Lulu?' Bianca was bending towards me. 'You're so pale...'

'I'm fine, I'm fine...'

'You're allowed to be upset, you know? We'll sort it all out. We'll find a home, we'll get jobs – paid jobs – we'll survive.'

I didn't want to tell her what Vanni had just said to me. *You're better off staying away from someone stuck in a chair.*

'Yes. Of course. Things will fall into place.'

'Oh, Lulu. I have to tell you. I can accept all this, losing Casalta, starting again, but... I only have one wish.'

'Tell me.'

'That you won't go,' she blurted out, and then retracted. 'I don't mean to emotionally blackmail you! I know you have a life to go back to. I meant... if you want. If it's what you want... please stay. At least for a while.'

'I'll stay as long as everyone is settled. Doesn't matter how long it'll take. It's a promise.'

Vanni's words took my sleep away. I didn't understand how he could have changed his mind so quickly! Unless the change had happened before I returned, and our connection had just been an illusion. It'd been momentous to me; it had opened my heart in a way I hadn't thought possible any more.

But it hadn't broken his shell.

We'd lost Casalta. My life in Paris made no more sense to me. The memory of Vanni had been shattered, and rejection had taken its place. Everything was in ruin, not just my father's business.

It was barely dawn when I stood at the window and watched the lovely, lovely hills of my home illuminated by the grey-pink light. Humans come and go, but the hills will always be there. And us, the Casalta sisters, were together again; I knew I'd win Nora back too. I'd survive, we'd all survive and there would be a tomorrow.

But I refused to let Vanni get away with despising himself.

I could accept he didn't want me around; I had no right to plonk myself into his life like no time had passed. But I couldn't accept his self-loathing. He'd called himself a *cripple*, and that nasty word kept resounding in my ears.

I remembered once, looking at him when we were in the treehouse – he's only a few months older than me, but all of a sudden he seemed so much stronger and wiser. I would have never told him, of course, but I admired him. I looked up to him. To me, he was... I know it sounds cheesy, but he was the *best*. And this childish awe I had for him was still there.

I'd go from his life, like he asked me: but first, I'd tell him
what I thought of his self-loathing.

Lorenzo didn't waste any time. I tried to negotiate a week's
peace for my sisters, to try and come to terms with the loss of
Casalta, but all I gained was one day. Lorenzo had decided to
come and inspect what he was about to buy. Fair enough, I
suppose, but I suspected he just wanted to rub our faces in it.

He and a few others, some in shirts and ties and some in
working gear, turned up at the house after giving us a few hours'
notice. Vanni wasn't with them, of course – not after what he'd
said to me.

They walked around the house, looking up and around,
following a floor plan that they must have got from Cavalli,
without having asked for permission. After all, the house was to
be theirs: they had the right to any document they wanted.

Nora was at the stables, as usual, and Mia had taken refuge
in her turret; but Bianca and I followed the men every step of
the way.

Their male energy, their careless, proprietary voices rising
to the ceilings – everything about them felt like a violation.
They were stomping around, talking as if we weren't there.

Lorenzo didn't mention any plans, but from what they were
saying, it was clear that Casalta wouldn't be a home any more,
but a guesthouse, a hotel, whatever they'd decide to call it.

'The living room is perfect; it'll make a great hospitality
area,' Lorenzo's associate said, a small, wily man in a stripy suit.
'But the kitchen, for heaven's sake. The kitchen is a cupboard,
really!'

The kitchen where we sat with our mother, where Matilde
prepared countless meals for us, where there was always a pot

on the stove and the copper pots hanging on the walls shone in the sunshine.

'This courtyard is a real asset, though. Guests will *love* it. The fountain might be in the way of the outside dining areas though.'

'Are those steady?' Stripy Suit said, pointing to our dryads. 'Doesn't look like it. We wouldn't want them to fall on people's cars. Or people's heads!'

My heart beat harder, faster, when they followed the corridor and came to the door to my father's study. I stood in front of them. 'No.'

'No? We can't go in there?' Lorenzo said in his calm manner.

'This could be another reception room, I suppose.' Stripy Suit was looking at the floor plan.

'It was Fosco Falconeri's study,' Lorenzo explained, a small, triumphant smile on his lips.

'Many of his things are still in there,' Bianca said.

Lorenzo turned on his heels. 'Make a great big bonfire. I'm saying this for your sake,' he said to me, his back to us.

Stripy Suit had his foot on the stairs when Lorenzo took him by the arm and pulled him down.

'We won't enter your rooms, of course,' he said generously, and Bianca blushed to the tips of her hair.

'I'm touched,' I said.

We certainly weren't in a hurry to show them the way to the oldest part of Casalta, but they followed the floor plan to the garden and to the back of the house, entering Mia's turret from outside. She was like a fluttering bird when they stepped in, small and panicked. Stripy Suit looked up and around. 'Creepy. They close in on you,' he said, talking about Mia's murals.

'I disagree,' Lorenzo said, quite unexpectedly. 'They're beautiful.'

Bianca laid a gentle hand on his arm. 'The frescoes must stay,' she said in her soft voice.

'The frescoes stay, no matter what,' Lorenzo stated. He threw a glance at Bianca as he went, and received one in return.

I'd been right about something tying Bianca to the Orafi brothers, but completely wrong about which one. But whatever there was between them, it seemed so delicate to me, with so much unsaid.

And yet, that one look between them had spoken more than a thousand words – and at that moment, I saw them both shine with a golden halo.

'I didn't dare ask about their plans for the stables,' I said, standing at the main door while the cars left. All my limbs felt heavy, like I'd run a marathon. It was another drizzly day, with a sky full of clouds slowly turning from white to grey. This sun and rain dance, the shifting from grey to shine and back, seemed to reflect my contrasting feelings, as if me and the sky were on a similar quest.

Bianca sighed. 'It'll be awful. Poor Nora will be heartbroken.'

Thinking of Nora's storminess, I steeled myself: she might be furious with me, but I'd try to help her in any way I could. She'd fight me every step of the way, of that I was sure. 'I could do with a coffee,' I said, following Bianca inside.

'I could do with a drink,' Bianca replied, and we both took refuge in the kitchen. She made coffee and poured some marsala liqueur in, making it sweet, warming and with an edge that allowed us to relax.

'At least Mia's paintings will be saved. Lorenzo promised me.'

I observed Bianca's face, and indeed, she did blush a little. I was right, but my twin's heart was so secret, so delicate, that I couldn't ask any questions.

The same way Vanni and I did, I supposed.

'How did this happen?' Bianca cried out in frustration, and for a moment, I thought she'd read my mind.

'What?'

'How did we go from being one of the wealthiest families of the region, to being deep in debt? I don't mind living frugally. But the debt! Our father had many flaws but he was capable, very capable. I don't understand.'

'I asked Pera the same question. He said that after Mum went, Father gave up. That something was eating him inside. I think it was guilt.'

'He kept his feelings so deep inside, none of us truly *saw*. All we knew was that he was always angry, even more than before. If only I'd known about the business. Maybe I could have done something...'

'Father held the reins. What could you have done?'

'Something. Anything. I don't know.'

'We grew up in a man's world. All we could do at that time was obey.'

'Well, not any more. I'll never live in a man's world again...'

The sound of a thunderclap swallowed her words, so loud I almost cowered. Mia ran through into the kitchen, a lick of blue paint on her cheek, just as the wind engulfed the house, howling around the windows. The evening had been swallowed by a full-blown storm in such a short time, it was almost preter-natural.

'Is Nora out in this weather?' she fretted.

'She took Matilde home. She probably stopped by the stables. She'll be in soon, don't worry,' Bianca tried to reassure her. The noise of banging shutters filled the room and made us all jump. I ran up the stairs, and while grabbing the shutters in our bedrooms and working against the wind to get them closed,

I saw thick electrical trees of lightning shoot down from the clouds, into the hills.

I was halfway down the stairs when Nora's voice came from the hall. 'Tuscan tornado! Is everyone okay?'

'Thank goodness you're back...' I began, when a rumble loud enough to shake the walls almost knocked me off my feet. The whole house lit up at once, a white light that blinded me – then, darkness fell.

Lightning had struck very close to us, or maybe the house itself. I could feel the static in my hair, the smell of ozone – the air was the colour of lead with yellow undertones. I heard a thump, then two of the French doors being battered by the wind, and then I came to my senses.

'Blackout! Nobody panic; I have candles and matches,' I heard Bianca call from downstairs. I made my way down slowly, step by step, holding onto the banister, until I finally made it to the living room. I could only guess the silhouettes of Bianca and Mia in the gloom. I felt someone slip beside me; *Gabriella is back*, I thought.

Five faces glowed in the gloom, one by one. Bianca holding the candle holder by the handle with pale-faced Mia beside her – Nora on her way to the door – and a fifth woman, a fifth face gleaming.

It wasn't Gabriella.

It was the woman I'd seen in the crowd in Paris, flaming hair with grey streaks, the features of a painting.

It was the woman I'd seen against the rose bush all those years before, crowned with petals and thorns.

It was my mother.

# CHAPTER 24

## CASALTA, 27 APRIL 1985

LUCREZIA

My chest was rising and falling, and everything was silent: I could hear no thunderclap, no raindrops on the roof – it was like being underwater, deaf and mute and rooted to the spot by an unbearable weight.

Another hallucination. *Or was I seeing a ghost?*

A ghost soaked with rain, in a little puddle of water gathering around her feet.

'Mum!' Bianca called in a strangled voice: she could see her too!

Our mother was alive. In that moment, I knew I had seen her twelve years ago, I had seen her in Paris, I was seeing her now. I hadn't been traumatised by grief, or ill and hallucinating. She'd been somewhere all along, away from us.

*She had abandoned us.*

We were all frozen. Slowly, I came out of my hushed trance, and thunder and rain began to rise and fall again in my ears. The lights came back, flashed once, then returned for good.

My eyes met my mother's gaze, pleading but proud at the

same time; I couldn't speak. It was almost physical, the way I felt the wall around my heart rise up again, the wall that had protected me all those years in exile and that my sisters and Vanni had been chipping away at since I'd returned.

Our mother's gaze untied itself from mine and went on to Bianca, whose mouth was agape, to Nora, who looked away, and finally to Mia, whose face was wet – maybe rain, maybe tears.

It was Mia, the sister who'd known our mother for the shortest time, who threw herself in her arms, her head on Mum's shoulder, with the abandon of a loving child.

Mum spoke for the first time.

'Oh, *my girls*! I missed you so!'

The next few minutes were strange, almost blurred, like a distant memory happening in real time. I stood at a safe distance, apart from everyone else. I stared at my mother, who was sitting at the fireplace with Mia's hands in hers. I studied every little detail, taking her in. She was as I remembered her, hardly changed at all: the long skirt, the dangling earrings, her beautiful hair, now dripping, in a side plait. Night had fallen suddenly, darkness pressing on the windows and the rhythmic thud-thud-thud of the still open shutters.

Yes, a memory come to life, unfolding right in front of me.

So many times I'd seen her sitting right there, with the fire on during the winter and snowy hills behind her, or in a summer dress, sunrays setting her hair on fire. Holding one of my baby sisters, reading Bianca a book, thumbing through a sketchbook...

I wanted to shout at her, to throw her out. I wanted to hold her close and never let her out of my sight again. But I was paralysed. I was frozen in shock, like in one of those nightmares where you try desperately to move, but you can't. The tears behind my eyes, the screams in my throat – everything was stuck inside me, beyond the wall in my heart. I was shaking like a leaf.

All around me, people were springing into action – it seemed that the only one still rooted to the spot was me. How could everyone be so pragmatic? Mia murmured something about making tea and something to eat to warm our mother up, and Bianca disappeared upstairs to get Mum a change of clothes. She almost ran face first into Gabriella.

'Oh, girls, what a fright with the lightning! I ran upstairs to get changed; I was soaked through...'

And then she saw her.

Gabriella recognised my mother at once: not only had she seen her pictures, but it would have been easy to figure out that the red-haired woman was Emmeline, the long-lost mistress of Casalta. She looked like an older carbon copy of us – and not that much older: it seemed to me that our mother was some-where in between a child and a crone, as if her age played by different rules. Gabriella froze, all blood drained from her face. She looked like she was about to faint.

Time seemed to stand still, to contract and expand simulta-neously, so that it seemed an age for us to be standing around her, stunned – but the next moment Bianca peeped from the stairs, holding a dress. 'Mum?' she called, and she seemed to almost have to toil to say that word.

The rain kept drumming on the windows, the wind howling and hissing while our mother followed Bianca upstairs. Panic filled me for a moment – if I let her out of my sight, she might disappear again...

'I need to go check on the horses,' Nora whispered and turned towards the door – I took her hand to hold her back, and she stopped. Her fingers were cold.

'Not now.'

'I can't, Lulu, I can't...'

'You're not alone,' I whispered and squeezed her hand.

We sat in stunned silence until they came back downstairs. Mia had arranged a teapot and cups on the side table. Mum was now dry, wearing a dress of Bianca's with minuscule lavender flowers, a cup of tea in her hands and a blanket over her shoulders. A sodden rucksack lay by her feet. She looked around and took us all in. Only then I noticed that Gabriella had discreetly slipped away.

'My girls...' Mum said.

We all stared back.

'Are you joking?' Nora broke the silence.

'I know I owe you an explanation, Nora...' she began.

'To say the *least*!'

'You were in the garden, that night, weren't you?' I said. For a moment, I was sure I was about to faint. I took a breath. 'When I saw you.'

She nodded. Guilt flooded her face.

'*I went through a window trying to reach you.* Did you see that too?'

'Yes. And it broke my heart. But I wasn't allowed to stay. I always watched over you.' In spite of the guilt painted on her face, in spite of her wet hair and the blanket over her shoulders and her hands red with cold, she looked composed, and calm. Dignified. There was a strength about her, a self-confidence that, at that moment, infuriated me. She should have been ashamed. How could she even show her face?

'You watched *over me*? Father sent me to a mental hospital for children, do you understand? I spent a year in that place; I thought I was mad! I doubted myself for years! How did you ever watch over me, over us?'

A sob escaped my lips. Sorrow and disappointment were choking me.

'I had to do it from afar. If I had come too close, I don't know what he would have done...'

'You could have taken me with you! All of us!'

'I had nothing to offer. I had nobody to go back to in Scotland, no home, nothing to my name. It took me years to get back on my feet. I was barely older than you are now; I knew nothing about the world outside.'

I didn't want to hear. I wanted to put my hands over my ears and block it all out.

'I thought Father killed you!' Bianca said in a low voice. 'He told me he did.'

'You what?' Nora exclaimed. 'How could you have thought that? Of course he didn't! And here's the proof. You thought our father was a murderer?'

'He might as well have killed me, Nora,' my mother said. 'Because he forced me away from you... But I must tell you all that happened, everything, then you'll know why I disappeared. Everything I say now sounds like an excuse.'

'Because it *is* an excuse,' Nora retorted.

Mia drew closer to her. 'It must have been horrible for you, Mum...' Her words came back to me: *I was sure that you'd come back. I'm not sure she will.* Did Mia know she was alive? Did she suspect?

Nora dried her tears of rage. 'For her? Dad was never himself again. We lost Lulu. Bianca was left to carry everything on her shoulders. And everyone worshipped your memory, as if you'd been a heroine, the victim of a cruel fate. But you weren't. You just left.'

I'd never heard Nora utter so many words before. My heart went out to her, to her soft self behind the rough exterior. How little I'd understood her...

'I don't know if I can ever forgive you,' I said. The old sorrow, the loneliness I'd felt as a child when I wasn't allowed to go home, overwhelmed me again. I was a child, being told that her mother was dead, that she'd fallen on the hills, that she would never come back.

My mother blinked many times, quickly, as if I'd thrown a rock at her. I sensed her confidence wavering. 'You of all people know what Fosco was capable of. I wish you had some compassion for me like you want compassion for yourself.'

'I don't want your compassion. I don't want anything from you!' I cried.

And yet, in spite of all our rage, neither Nora nor I left the room. We expressed our rejection, but didn't act on it. I would have liked to. I would have liked to storm out and forget she'd ever come back – but I couldn't. In fact, right at that moment I envisioned myself falling asleep with my head on her lap.

It didn't make sense, and the more confused I was, the more I came undone. I felt Bianca's hand on my back, and we drew closer together.

Mum lifted her hands to the back of her neck and undid a golden chain she wore.

'Look. I always carried it with me. Always.' It was a locket; she opened it and handed it to me. On the left was the tiny photograph of two red-haired toddlers – Bianca and me – and on the right, a toddler and a baby – Nora and Mia. I passed it on to Bianca, and my sisters looked at it. Nobody seemed particularly touched.

'Should we be moved because you carried a photograph of us with you?' I said mercilessly.

'There are things you don't know, but I'll tell you everything...'

'Nothing can change what you've done,' Nora said. 'While she's in this house, I won't be.' She got up, followed by a worried Bianca.

'You can't spend the night at the stables; it's pouring...' I heard Bianca argue, and then the slamming of a door. It didn't look like Nora was concerned about the cold.

Our mother was pale, but she sat with her back straight. 'I'll go...' she began.

'No!' and 'Fine,' Mia and I cried out at the same time.
'Mum is staying,' Bianca said, and her tone was final.

We made Mum's bed in the guest room. Who knew if she slept
– I certainly didn't.

I went into Bianca in the darkness, and sat on her bed.

'Come,' she whispered, and lifted the blankets. I slipped in
beside her like I used to do as a child, curled up together like
two halves of the same person. Laying my head on the same
pillow as my twin, at last, melted some of the soreness I held in
my heart.

'Why did he lie? Why did he tell me he killed her?' Bianca
murmured.

'To intimidate you. It was the perfect way to terrorise you.'

'He hated us, didn't he?'

I thought of what Pera had told me.

'I think that mostly, he hated himself,' I answered.

'I love you, Lulu.'

'I love you, Bianca.'

We held each other tightly, and fell asleep together.

# CHAPTER 25

## CASALTA, 28 APRIL 1985

LUCREZIA

I woke as the sun was rising, the sky half rosy, half the colour of
ash. After the rain, a chilly spring wind had swept the clouds
away and left a smattering of blinking stars...

*My mother has come back.*

Still sleepy, struggling to keep up with all that had
happened, I felt like I was in between worlds: maybe reality and
imagination were mixing in my mind; maybe *she* hadn't
returned at all. Maybe I'd seen her once again, like I had in the
rose garden and in Paris, among the crowd...

*My mother has come back.*

I made my way to the guest room, opened the door as
quietly as I could, and peeped inside. The bed was empty: she
wasn't there. For a moment I thought that yes, I'd dreamed it all:
but the unmade bed, the bag on the floor, the clothes hung in
the wardrobe to dry. It was real.

She'd returned from the dead.

'Lucrezia?'

*My mother.*

*Has.*

*Come back.*

The sweetest voice of all resounded in my ears, the voice I'd dreamed of for so long: my mother's. She was with Bianca; they stood side by side in long nightdresses, holding hands. She looked almost as I remembered her, although there were grey streaks in her hair and her face was a little lined. Typical Mum, not to dye her hair but let it grow long and natural. Her eyes were still that startling blue none of us had inherited. There were freckles on the bridge of her nose and on her arms, and she had northern features: you couldn't have mistaken her for Italian.

I noticed that her hands were stained with paint, and that detail almost made me burst into tears again. That was her. She always had her hands stained with paint... the hands that had stroked my hair, tied my laces, washed me, fed me apple puree with a little spoon. My mum's hands were always a rainbow.

She and Bianca stood close. And it was clear that my twin, with her simple kindness, the gentleness of her nature, had put reconciliation before resentment.

'*Mother?*' I said, with a rancour I knew I couldn't sustain for much longer. I wanted to throw myself in her arms like Mia had done, like Bianca was doing, but I couldn't find my way to forgiveness.

She said nothing, but took my hand with her paint-stained one, and in silent agreement we did what we used to do all those years ago: we climbed out and sat on the ancient stairs, watching dawn break. Nobody could hear us, there, and we could speak in private.

We squeezed ourselves onto one step, our bare feet in a row.

'Why did you leave us?' Bianca asked. Five words, one simple question.

'Because I had no choice,' Mum replied in her accented Italian, and her voice was full of sadness. But she still kept her head high; she didn't grovel for our forgiveness. I didn't need her grovelling, but I certainly needed an explanation.

'You had no choice but running away?' The bitterness was eating me alive, but I had to give her a chance. I had to listen.

Bianca's voice was a whisper. 'How did it come to this, Mum? You leaving us? Pretending you were dead? Why?'

'How did it come to this?' she said, and inhaled deeply, her eyes to the sky. 'I'm going to try and find the words to tell you my story and the story of our family, even though, as you know, drawing is easier than words, for me. I hope I can do justice to everyone involved... However...'

'However?' I snapped.

'However, even if I turn it all round and round in my head, there will always be a missing piece. A transition that I can't quite understand or put in words. I will never be able to understand, and therefore explain, how the man I loved with all my heart, and married, became my tormentor.'

I heard Bianca sucking her breath in. The way Mum spoke those words was so matter-of-fact, so devoid of self-pity, that it seemed even more horrific. I'd been afraid of my father for as long as I could remember, but I didn't consider that for my mother there must have been a *before*. There must have been a time when she'd loved him and trusted him enough to marry him. The picture of their wedding displayed in my father's study said it all, with Mum in her lovely dress and her flaming hair down, crowned with a flower garland. I remembered Matilde's comment one day, while dusting the photograph: how the dress and hairstyle were the subject of gossip, because they were so informal and unusual... like my mum.

'The first time I saw your father, he had a confidence I'd never seen before, in anyone. Like the world was his *birthright*. I think I fell in love with him there and then. If anyone tells you that love at first sight doesn't exist, don't believe them. It does. Oh, God, if it does. Where was my gift, then? How did I not know what would happen? I swear, I didn't see any signs, or feel the shadow of a doubt. Gift or not, millions of women throughout history could tell you the same.'

'Yes,' Bianca whispered. I wondered if she recognised herself in our mother's words.

'Your father came into the shop I was working in to buy a ring. He scoured the most expensive ones, diamonds and yellow gold. I said to him, *I think they are a little...* I tried to say *appariscente*, gaudy, but the word was too difficult for me to pronounce!' She laughed in recollection. How could she laugh? But already I could see how joy and sorrow were mixed up in her story, and she couldn't delete the good memories any more than she could delete the bad ones.

'My Italian was still wonky, and I know he noticed – but he didn't ask any questions about my accent or the way I spoke. I showed him an amethyst mounted on a simple silver band. It was intended for another woman, one his family approved of. You might recognise it, because it turned out to be my engagement ring. We got married six months later. He went against his parents to marry me.'

'I remember how they refused to speak to you,' Bianca said.

'We didn't really know why, though. It was just the way things were,' I intervened. 'Nonno and Nonna didn't want to see Mum; they wanted to see us alone with Father.'

Mum nodded. 'They died when you were little, so no one ever gave you an explanation. Your grandparents hated me. For real. Not just dislike or disapproval, it was proper *hate*. It upset me so much, but I thought they'd come round. They never did, of course. At the time I had no idea what I was marrying into. The Falconeri weren't just wealthy, they were powerful, ingrained in Casalta and these surroundings. They had a whole web of alliances and deals and friendships and business relationships, and Fosco's marriage was supposed to be part of all that.'

Bianca was aghast. 'Did they think you married him for their money?'

'Oh, of course. To them, I was a gold digger through and through. They didn't see... they didn't understand...'

'What?' I asked.

'How much we loved each other, back then. They were so angry. Their precious son broke his engagement, decided by the family, of course, and went and got himself a Scottish girl from who knows where. They forgave him eventually; he was their only son. But they never forgave me. I was all wrong, I had no family, I couldn't offer an alliance or money, I wanted to paint instead of exclusively playing hostess and running the house.'

'I understand,' Bianca whispered.

'I wanted to be loved by them. When I realised it wasn't possible, I tried at least to be liked by them. I failed, obviously.'

'Who was he engaged to? A woman from around here?' I asked.

'Anna Orafi. Gherardo's sister.'

'So that's how the feud began!' Bianca exclaimed.

'Not just that. But I'll get to it.' Mum breathed in again – I could feel the effort it took her to recall some aspects of her story, I could feel her pain on my skin, in my bones... but the question *why did you not take us with you?* burned too hot and painful.

'At the beginning he stood up to his parents, but soon he began resenting me for the rift. It turned out that the Falconeri men had very... efficient ways to get whatever they wanted. I... I don't think I even have the words to describe what happened. One day he adored me, the next day nothing I ever did was good enough for him. In the meanwhile, you two came along, and I was so enthralled with you... He seemed to come round a little. He was proud of you both. He wanted a male child, of course, but he was proud of the new little Falconeri girls. His parents died, and I can't say I was devastated. I received nothing but contempt from them. And then... the reprieve I had when you girls came along ended. There were days of complete silence, days and days. If I spoke to him, he pretended he didn't hear. He looked through me. It was torture.'

'I can't even imagine!' Bianca said. 'You must have felt like a ghost...'

'Yes. I felt like I'd died, but didn't know it. Everyone around me depended on him, of course, so they followed his example. It was like a conspiracy of silence.'

'What about Matilde?' I asked.

'Oh, Matilde was my only friend. She was terrified of your father, but her family had been part of the Falconeri entourage for so long, she couldn't leave. She wouldn't leave anyway, because she loved... she *loves* you girls so much. Matilde had this silent, quiet way of defying your father. She wasn't supposed to talk to me either, but she did, every time we were alone.'

'I can't believe he did that to you...' I whispered. The more I spoke to my mother, the more compassion I felt for her. The more I opened up to my sisters and my family, the more I realised how the whole story had been defined by *my* pain, *my* loneliness, so much so that I'd been blinded to what they'd gone through.

'That was supposed to break me, so I would leave. Divorce was impossible, for a Falconeri, so this was the only solution. Your little sisters were born, but Fosco wasn't as taken by them as he'd been by you. He tolerated them, but that was all. Eleonora was the one who suffered the most about this; she was desperate to be loved by her father... poor little mite. And then there were the other women, of course. I didn't resent them; I was grateful that your father had them, so he left me alone. But the shame... the looks of pity when I went to the village... that was hard. I looked after you girls, I painted, I survived the best I could. I was a shell of a person. I don't even want to remember...' She shivered, and both Bianca and I shimmied closer to her.

'I'm so sorry, Mum,' Bianca whispered.

'And so you left?' I asked.

'Not yet. I had nowhere to go, and four children I couldn't leave behind.'

'You couldn't, but you did,' I said mutinously. I couldn't help it. Mum stopped for a moment to absorb my cruel words, and then began the story again.

'Also, I was afraid for my life. I was sure that if I tried to leave, he'd kill me.'

'I was sure that he did!' Bianca exclaimed.

'I did see you, that night, didn't I? But they convinced me I was crazy. Hallucinating.'

'I was there, yes. Oh, Lulu, please don't make me cry before I finish my story! That was so awful. My heart broke for you...'

'Not enough to stay.' I had to say that, even though I knew it hurt her.

'You'll soon find out why,' she said. I was silent, my eyes on the rising sun and the sweet, golden light illuminating the sky. 'Fosco had tried the silent treatment; he'd tried to make me feel like I didn't exist, like I wasn't worthy of life. He'd humiliated me by taking lovers. But I was still there. Looking after my girls, painting, doing my best. One night he came into my room – because, you know, we'd slept separately for a long time – he stood there and looked at me. He didn't speak, he just looked. There was something in his eyes that terrified me. I knew what he was capable of. In the years I'd spent with him, he didn't really make me part of his business, the family's business... and I'm not talking about the vineyards and the olive trees. But although he didn't speak to me, it would have been impossible not to overhear certain things. I was well aware of how ruthless he could be. Maybe I wasn't even surprised when the first slaps came. Being pushed and shoved...'

I felt ill. That odious man *hit my mother*.

'How come we never knew, Mum?' Bianca asked. She was drying her tears with her fingers. Mum touched Bianca's cheek.

'You were only little. And he was careful. Having lovers wasn't a stain on his reputation, just the opposite. More honour to him.' She laughed bitterly. 'But hitting his wife... You see, he was supposed to be the victim, in our marriage.'

I was outraged. 'The *victim*?'

'Oh, yes. He was supposed to be the man who was trapped by a gold digger inside an unhappy marriage. A foreign seductress who took him away from his fiancée, a good local girl, and his family. I was supposed to be the villain, a stranger who inserted herself in this web of ancient alliances and friendships. And an artist, which for his family and friends was pretty much equivalent to a...'

'A witch!' Bianca finished the sentence.

'Yes,' Mum breathed out. 'I made a huge mistake. *Huge*. I told him about my gift; I told him about knowing I would have the four of you, and why I painted your rooms the way I did. About my premonitory dreams. How this ran in the family, in the women of my family.' She shrugged. 'I never told anyone before. I didn't even talk about it with my father. But I trusted him completely. More fool me, I believed with all my heart and soul he would never, ever leave me, or betray me, or stop loving me. Where was my gift then? I don't know. Of course when things started falling apart he used it all against me. He told me that around here witches would not be burned, but tied up somewhere to die of hunger and thirst.'

'He was mad!' I said. 'Not just evil, but... *mad*!'

'He wasn't either. He was weak, and he tried to make himself bigger. He'd been taught he was meant to have power over everyone – he had to. If someone escaped him, or defied him, there was the proof of his weakness. He couldn't bear it. And he wasn't mad at all. He was calculated. He hit me in a way that left no visible bruises. Only Matilde knew, because we spent so much time together. And then... someone else noticed.'

'A friend?' Bianca asked gently.

Mum nodded. 'A friend. Who became so dear to me.' Her voice broke. 'He tried to set me free. And the four of you with me. But he had feelings for me, and I...'

'You didn't reciprocate?'

'Oh, I did. But he was married. He couldn't allow himself to come too close, and I couldn't be the one to break up his family, even though his marriage was a loveless one. He didn't ask anything of me. He just wanted to help me. To help us. He wanted to spirit us away, and help us so we could get back on our feet.'

'What happened?'

'The plan was discovered. I don't know how. Fosco believed I had a relationship with my friend, he called me a whore and beat me, then he sent me to a hotel in Rome for a few days so that the bruises would heal. Please believe me that nothing happened between my friend and me. We had feelings for each other, but we never acted on them. Your father's insults had no basis.'

'I remember that,' Bianca said in a soft voice. 'Matilde told us you were at an art exhibition. We believed her...'

'Apart from Mia,' I intervened. 'Mia always knew there was something wrong. She knew.'

'My poor baby!' Mum was telling her story so calmly, but with the mention of her youngest daughter, the tears came, and Bianca squeezed her hand. 'I was desperate to leave, but I couldn't go without the four of you. I had nowhere to go, no money of my own, no family I could return to. Even though it was dangerous, even though he knew it would get him into huge trouble, my friend offered to help us and asked for nothing in return. The plan was to take you to Florence, to the Uffizi, as we often did, remember? From there, we'd disappear. He'd set us up somewhere far enough away that your father couldn't find us, and I'd get a job and return every penny to him.'

'But it didn't work.'

'No. I tried and tried to find the courage to do this, but someone, somewhere, must have made your father suspicious: or maybe he simply guessed that something wasn't right. The morning I'd planned to take you to Florence, he stopped me. I remember as if it happened yesterday! He didn't shout or hit me that time, he just said, *No, you're not going anywhere.* I'd waited too long.

'From then on I had his men always watching me. Diego, mainly. He was a boy, not even twenty, but he was ruthless. He sneered at me, he whispered insults, he enjoyed terrorising us. I knew that Fosco wanted me to go and leave you there, but I couldn't! I became sure he'd kill me. I was close to breaking point, but I held on with everything I had.

'By then, I was a shadow of my former self. I was afraid all the time; I'd grown to believe all he said about me, that I was useless, that without him I would end up on the streets. I had to hide all this from you girls; I couldn't have you end up like me... I learned to keep secrets. Your wellbeing depended on it.

'I was allowed to go to the hills to paint, but even then Diego followed me. Not that I would have tried to escape, because I had to stay and protect you. I suppose Fosco figured out that the only way to get rid of me, aside from killing me, was to play on the one thing that I lived for: my daughters. And so he did.

'I went to the hills to paint as usual, and as usual I had Diego at my heels. I didn't notice that Fosco was following too. When we were out of earshot, they ambushed me.' Mum's voice broke. The horror she was describing was almost unspeakable. 'Diego held me still while your father spoke. He said to choose there and then whether I wanted Diego to strangle me and leave me there, or if I'd leave of my own accord. Of my own accord! I couldn't bring myself to say, *Kill me*. I wanted to live. He let an envelope fall at my feet. He said there was money inside, to go away and never come back. And then he said... he said...'

By then both Bianca and I were crying. We couldn't speak, our hands entwined together, holding onto each other as if trying to stop ourselves from falling.

'Mum...'

'He said that if I showed my face anywhere near my daughters, he would punish all of *you* for it. That if I tried to take you with me, you'd pay for it. And if I turned to anyone for help, he would know and he would get them too.'

'You couldn't risk it,' I murmured.

'No. I couldn't. I left. I didn't take that damn envelope, of course. All that I had with me were painting materials and a canvas. I walked away with nothing, not even a change of clothes, nothing. I was desperate. I had nowhere to turn. I was too afraid your father would hurt anyone I asked for help. I walked to Florence, and when I got there I had no idea what to do. I was in shock; I couldn't even cry.

'I wandered around for a while... my feet took me to the Uffizi. They remembered the red-haired woman with the four daughters, so I made up an excuse for not being able to buy a ticket, and they let me in. I went to see our paintings... And just sat there. When closing time came, I hid in a cupboard and came out when everyone was gone. I slept on the floor among the paintings. Lucrezia, Bianca, Eleonora and Maria were there with me...

'I know that if I tell you that they stepped out of the frames and came to lie beside me, you'll believe me. The next morning, I slipped out of the museum and went to the river. I was desperate. I missed you all so much, I couldn't bear to have left you. Jumping in the water seemed a good idea.'

'Oh, Mum! No!' we both cried out.

'Well, I'm here to tell the tale. I didn't jump. But someone saw me looking at the water, an old lady called Maddalena, with an empty house and a warm heart. She took me home with her, she fed me and she let me cry. I was petrified that your father would find me and take it out on Maddalena, but she laughed and said that your father wasn't God and that she wasn't afraid. I tried not to worry, but I couldn't help it. She left me to get washed and changed and went to the shop to do some groceries. I kept asking myself how I could get you back...

'Oh, I'll never forget what happened next! I went to have a shower, and when I came out Diego was there, sitting in the living room as if he were in his own home. I only had a towel around me, I was terrified... I realised at that moment that there was something wrong with Diego. He was enjoying that moment; he enjoyed terrifying me. He played with me like a cat with a mouse. The horror of it... I can't describe it. He said that if I didn't disappear, he'd make me disappear. That he'd hunt me down every step of the way. And that it was just like his master said, your father: you four were better off without their crazy mother.'

'He's a psychopath,' I blurted out in horror, recalling the look in his eyes when we'd met after Father's funeral.

'What did you do?' Bianca said, drying a tear. There were tears on Mum's face, and on mine too... mixing like drops of rain.

'He threw the envelope with money at me again. This time I took it. I bought a change of clothes and a plane ticket to London. I left.' She shrugged her shoulders. 'And never really saw you again. Or should I say, I tried not to see you again. Being away from you was torture. I knew that your father cherished his bloodline...'

'Did he?' I whispered. 'I beg to differ.'

'In his own twisted way. But I was scared of Diego. And my heart was broken, thinking of you growing up without me. I couldn't help it; even if I was terrified of the consequences, I came home to Casalta. And I did more damage than good.'

'It was the night I saw you, wasn't it?'

'Yes. I...' She shook her head. 'I was desperate to just catch a glimpse of my daughters... My poor Lulu...' She took a moment to compose herself. 'Children think their parents are little gods and goddesses, all-powerful and all-knowing. But parents are only human. We don't always know what's best and we certainly aren't all-powerful. I didn't know what was best. I didn't know what the consequences of my choices might be. I left and never came back. I implored the only friend I had left here to watch over you...'

'You *were* in Paris, weren't you? I saw you in the crowd, when we were filming. How did you find me?'

My mother looked down. 'So much time had passed. I paid someone to find you. I knew that you... and all my daughters... thought I was dead. I should have come forward, but I was still afraid of the repercussions. And afraid that... afraid that you'd hate me. I just didn't know what to do. And then I was told that Fosco was dead! There was a battle inside me. I was desperate to see you all again, but how could I show my face when you thought I'd died? When I'd left you alone all these years? But the pull to you was too strong. And here I am.'

'You made the right decision,' Bianca said and wrapped her arms around Mum's waist, laying her head on Mum's chest like she used to when she was a little girl. I held them both, the three of us together in body and in heart.

My poor mother. She'd been through hell and back. It was certainly easier to judge, to condemn her for having left us, when we hadn't known the whole story. The statement that had enraged me so – *There are things you don't know* – was more meaningful now than I could ever have imagined. I didn't know what she'd had to do all that time in order to survive, but she

seemed destitute to me, the way she arrived with that little rucksack and soaking clothes. She'd been battered by life.

'Lucrezia. Can you forgive me? Maybe not now, but...
maybe in the future?'

'Yes, Mum. I forgive you,' I said, and held her to me, and
Bianca too, and the three of us cried together and then laughed
with the joy of having found each other again.

Later that morning, we gathered outside for breakfast, a new,
tentative family tradition we were building, day by day.

Gabriella was there, placid, immaculate in a plaid skirt and
shirt and smelling of soap and lily of the valley. She was confident in her quiet way. 'We haven't met properly,' she said,
calmly, and offered her hand. 'I'm your husband's wife. I'm a
bigamist, it seems.'

The hand that my mum extended to take Gabriella's was
stained with paint. 'I'm sorry. I'm sorry for whatever it was you
had to go through.'

'Well, judging other people's actions is easy, and it has the
pleasant side effect of making one feel smug about one's choices,
don't you think? Sometimes though, wrong choices are the only
right ones.'

Mum's eyes widened a little.

What did that even mean? I looked from one to the other.
Gabriella was talking like a fortune cookie written by someone
who'd run out of ideas, but Mum seemed to be drinking in those
words. She was staring at Gabriella – it was a look of
*recognition*, and I simply could not explain it.

Breakfast was a quick affair, with Nora grabbing a coffee
and going, Mia and Mum disappearing into Mia's studio to
compare notes on painting, and Bianca and me tense about
what lay ahead. Today we'd be back at Cavalli's to sign our

home away, and this time there would be no reprieve. I wondered if Mum knew how dire the situation was.

I caught Bianca in the kitchen, shining copper pans and pots with nervous energy. 'Wrong choices are the right ones, Bianca,' I said solemnly.

'Apparently,' she said, rubbing even harder.

'Is this really the moment to shine pots?'

'I have to do something. I'm too nervous about today... Let's just go. I can't linger around here any longer,' she said, and began taking her gloves off.

'Yes. Let's get it over and done with. And this time, I will sign. I think we should tell Mum.'

'Should we? She'd worry about us... and she's been through so much already. She seems destitute herself. It breaks my heart.'

'No more secrets, Bianca. She should know.'

'Know what?'

Mum's slender figure appeared in the door that opened on the courtyard, the glare of the sun behind her. For a second, I thought back to the day when she disappeared, how we were all staring at the door, hoping to see her, hour after hour, any second now... Maybe we'd gone full circle.

Bianca and I looked at each other.

'It's hard to explain, Mum, we don't want to worry you, and...' Bianca began.

'Father left the estate to me. He's bankrupt. I'm in over my head in debt, and we're selling Casalta to the Orafi. Bianca, Nora and Mia are about to be homeless. But we'll sort it. We'll be fine.'

'*What?*'

Bianca sighed. 'All true.'

'Casalta is going to be sold?'

'Yes. To the Orafi brothers, Lorenzo and Vanni.' I felt a little pang of pain as I pronounced that name.

Mum leaned against the wall. 'Your father lost everything?'

I nodded. 'An old friend of his told me that after you... after all that happened, he wasn't the same. The business fell apart.'

Mum looked from me to Bianca and back. 'I'm so sorry,' she said simply. What else was there to say?

'We have you back.' Bianca smiled. 'And we have Lulu back. Anything else, we can face.'

Later on that day I was at the Orafi's again. This time, I'd managed to avoid Bruno and his ambitions to look like the bodyguard in a film, and I rang the bell like any normal person would. The gate and then the door opened: in front of me was Lorenzo.

'Please no more changing of your mind.' He opened his arms. He wore jeans and a casual shirt, and looked slightly more human and less intimidating than usual.

'I'm here to see Vanni,' I said. I wanted to shake Lorenzo off and make my way to the terrace, but I wanted to avoid being thrown out by wannabe bodyguards.

'I don't think he wants to see *you*,' Lorenzo replied, and I was surprised to see a small flash of concern in his eyes. I was alarmed.

'Is he unwell?'

'He's always unwell, Lucrezia.'

'Can I see him?'

'Like I said, he doesn't want to see you. If you care for him, and I think you do, leave him alone.'

I blinked, trying to process what Lorenzo was saying. I wanted to protest, insist that I should see him – but with what right? Was I owed an explanation, if he'd decided, for whatever reason, that he didn't want me back in his life?

Tears filled my eyes all of a sudden – they almost leaked out of me of their own accord. I was mortified. Not in front of Lorenzo Orafi.

To my surprise, Lorenzo's tone was almost kind. 'He's not the person he used to be. And I'm not going to let him get hurt again.'

'I don't want to hurt him in any way. But the choice is his.'

I turned on my heels and was about to leave, when Vanni's voice filled the hall and called me back.

'Lucrezia?'

'*Vanni!* I...' I didn't finish the sentence because what I saw shocked me. Vanni was unkempt, unshaven and with blue shadows under his eyes. He was wearing a discoloured T-shirt and trousers that could have been a tracksuit or pyjamas.

He looked like someone who'd given up.

'Come,' he said, and turned the wheelchair around.

'Vanni, this is stupid!' Lorenzo almost shouted. He seemed... frightened.

Lorenzo was scared for his brother, just like Bianca had so often been scared for me.

I couldn't quite believe that I did it, but I laid a hand on Lorenzo's arm to calm him before following Vanni outside and to his apartment.

It was dark and stuffy, and the first thing I did was open a window.

'I understand you don't want to see me, but you certainly have no good reason to live like this! What happened to you?' I almost shouted.

Light and air filled the place, illuminating the wooden floor and the empty, dark fireplace.

'You need a shower and a shave. And a change of clothes. For God's sake, Vanni!'

Vanni's face had turned white. 'Who do you think you are, to come and speak to me like this?'

I was bewildered. I let myself fall on one of his buttery

leather sofas, and raked my fingers through my hair. 'You were fine. When you came to my house, and in Florence. We had a great time, and then...'

'We had a great time, and then I humiliated myself. I came home and it hit me again. I'll never be able to walk side by side with my wife. I'll never... I can never have children.'

I took a breath.

'And you came to remind me of all this. I'd made peace with my condition. I wasn't happy, of course, but I was resigned. Then you came. And I wanted more. I wanted to hold you, and kiss you, without you having to bend to me like the invalid that I am! I wanted to—'

'*Shut up!*'

Vanni looked shocked.

'I said, shut up! Oh my God, you're talking so much rubbish. So much rubbish!'

'Easy for you to say! You can walk! You can have a family! You don't need people to take you up and down stairs! I'm not a man any more. I'm not a real man, do you understand?'

'So what do you think you should do? Keep the windows closed and the lights off and not wash and not change and wait to die? Is this what you want?'

'It's better than being reminded every day of what I'm missing.'

'You can't spend the rest of your life regretting what you can't have. You can't spend the rest of your life recriminating...'

'Says the girl who *disappeared*. You couldn't stand looking at your family, at Casalta... at me. Because you were too bitter. And now you tell me not to sit here recriminating. The irony.'

I was stunned. And then, as if I hadn't cried enough since I came back, I burst into tears. I cried and cried, sobs and all.

'Lucrezia! Oh, please, don't cry. Please...'

'My mum is back. She wasn't dead. She abandoned us,' I managed to drag out of myself, in between sobs.

'*What?*'

When I could finally take a hold of myself, I felt lighter.

'It's a long story. But I didn't come here to tell you this. I came to say you must live your life, not throw it away feeling sorry for yourself. I'll go away like you want me to, but embrace life. You must. And yes, that goes for me too.'

I left, without saying another word.

# CHAPTER 26

## CASALTA, 28 APRIL 1985

LUCREZIA

It was another déjà vu moment. Sitting around the pristine table, Cavalli in the place of honour, the arbiter of this money-driven ceremony. The same pile of papers sat in the middle.

I noticed that Bianca was avoiding Lorenzo's eye, and that Lorenzo was a little tenser, his movements a little harsher. We'd probably tested his patience.

*Good*, I thought to myself, recalling his proprietorial attitude when he'd come to our home. He'd behaved as if he owned Casalta already.

Once again, there was no trace of Vanni, and that hurt me more than I could say. He'd been clear about wanting to keep his distance from me, so I shouldn't have been surprised... but it still stung. A part of me was hoping to see him there, smiling again like he had before Florence...

'No more delays?' Lorenzo said, pleasant only on the surface.

'No more delays,' I answered.

Only now Bianca looked at him, a long, even gaze. He held

it, quietly strong as she was. It was a silent battle that neither of them won.

'We have to do all the signatures again,' Cavalli said. 'With the proper date and time, and the witnesses. Wrist at the ready, Signorina Falconeri.'

I grimaced.

I waited to see if the roses would appear again, ready to ignore them this time. But they didn't.

'Last one.'

There was a knock at the door. Cavalli half-closed his eyes, irritated.

'I'm with clients!' he called, but the door opened anyway.

Cavalli's assistant, a nervous-looking, balding man, peeped in. 'I'm so sorry. But the lady here says it can't wait. She's a relative.'

'A relative of who?' Cavalli seemed exasperated.

The woman who'd been waiting outside passed under the assistant's arm, which was extended towards the doorframe. Everyone gasped. It was like a scene from a film.

'Mum?'

Emmeline McCrimmon Falconeri grabbed the documents off the table, and a tug of war with Cavalli followed. Had I not been so profoundly embarrassed, not to mention mystified, I would have found it funny.

'Mum!' Bianca was scarlet.

'Signora!' Cavalli kept pulling.

Lorenzo was too polite to say or do anything to a lady, so he just sat there open-mouthed, like a fish. A fish in a designer suit.

All of a sudden, Cavalli screamed, let go of the papers and began patting himself down. 'What was that!'

'What was what?' Mum said with an innocent expression. I thought back to the roses climbing my arm, the thorn stinging me...

'Something stung me, here, on my arm!'

'Cavalli, maybe you need a glass of water,' Lorenzo said coldly. 'I suppose you're Emmeline Falconeri? I thought you...'

'It's a long story,' I said mechanically just like I'd told Vanni, too surprised by the whole situation to elaborate.

'Emmeline McCrimmon,' Mum said with immense dignity. 'And I'm buying Casalta from Lucrezia, covering the debts and giving everything back to my daughters. Pass me the pen.'

Everyone's jaws slackened.

'Mum, I don't think you understand...' Bianca began in her gentle way.

'Oh, I understand. You explained it to me. Your father lost everything and you are about to be thrown out of Casalta. But not any more.' She grabbed a chair and was about to pull it to sit at the table, when Lorenzo pulled it for her. His manners had the best of him. He looked shell shocked.

'This is the amount Casalta is going for,' Cavalli said, half annoyed, half mocking. He pointed to a number on one of the papers.

'Yes. That's fine.'

'How can you pay for it, Mum?' Bianca was speaking in a slow, soft voice, like you'd speak to a child, or an elderly person who wasn't quite *compos mentis*.

I smiled. 'You're not destitute like we thought, are you?'

'All these years, I had two dreams. To have you back with me, and to become a successful painter. Now I'm with you. As for being a successful painter, I made that come true as well. I have enough set aside to cover the purchase of the house. And to finance anything my daughters decide to do, whether it's rebuilding the business or doing something else.'

Silence fell.

I laughed, a laugh of pure joy. Bianca and I had said we didn't want to live in a man's world any more. That we were tired of having men telling us only they could *save* us, take things in hand, manage the business in lieu of us helpless women.

Turned out, it was a strong, powerful woman who saved Casalta. The one who had been beaten, belittled, intimidated, and ultimately exiled with nothing to her name and nowhere to go.

'Cavalli, please prepare the documents for the Signora.' Everyone turned towards Lorenzo. I was surprised to see him with a half-smile on his lips.

Cavalli shot up like the lackey he was.

'Lorenzo, we—' Bianca began, but Lorenzo shook his head.

'I don't need an explanation, truly,' he said, and offered his hand to my mother, who took it and shook it heartily. 'I don't know how you came back from the dead, Signora Fal— McCrimmon, but well played. Congratulations,' he said and walked out, leaving us all awestruck.

I threw a glance at Bianca – she'd followed Lorenzo with her eyes, and her gaze was still on the door.

'Talk about *deus ex machina!*' On our way out from Cavalli's, I felt like I was walking a metre off the ground. I was so light, I could have flown away. 'Can we walk? I really need to shake off some energy!'

'Yes, please. I'm electric too, right now! Oh, Mum. You came back just at the right time,' Bianca said.

'The right time would have been many years ago,' Mum answered, a shadow of sadness on her face. But the sadness dissolved as she smiled. 'I can't wait to tell Nora and Mia. Oh, and show you the catalogues of my exhibitions... they're in my house in London, but I hope you can all come and see me soon.'

Bianca stopped in her tracks. 'In London?'

'Well... yes,' Mum said. Her expression was expectant: it

was clear that she was holding out for something. For an invitation...

'Are you not staying with us?'

'Do you want me to?'

'More than anything!' Bianca said and held her hands. 'It's a dream come true!'

'I won't be able to be in Casalta all the time; my work is in England. But I'll be here as much as possible. If Nora and Mia agree, though.'

'Mia will be delighted. As for Nora, leave it with us,' Bianca said, beaming.

'What about you, Lucrezia?' Mum asked. 'Will you go back to Paris?'

'I promised I would stay until everything was sorted. And now it is, although not in the way we expected it.'

'So, will you leave, Lulu?' Bianca's voice was shaking a little. The idea of leaving my sisters again, my mum, after all the years of separation, was a stab in the heart.

But would I belong here again?

In my mind's eye, Vanni's face: the hostility, the sorrow. The way he'd looked at me, like I was a painful reminder of what he'd lost, instead of...

Well, a friend.

Although I knew that what I felt for him was not friendship.

'It wasn't the right time to enquire,' Mum said and caressed my back. I decided to change the subject, before more questions had the chance to hit me over something I still wasn't sure about. 'I can't wait to tell Nora and Mia! They're not going to believe it...'

'I hope...' Mum began, but didn't finish.

'What do you hope, Mum?' Bianca asked.

'To have my little Nora back,' she answered, and we were silent.

We decided to walk straight to the stables, looking for Nora to tell her the news – the three of us climbed the hill where Nora's new horse had almost trampled us, and down the gentle slope that'd take us to the outbuildings complex, with the stone warehouses where grapes and olives were processed to be sent to the wine and oil makers. In my memory, they'd been buzzing with activity, but now they were deserted. The period of limbo between my father's death and the next step wasn't finished yet.

Then it struck me: it had nearly ended up with the Orafi taking charge, with all their boasting about strong men looking after the business. It infuriated me, that they'd assumed none of us could do it. It was time to show them we could, and it was exciting, but daunting too. This empty place would have to be filled with activity again. Step by step.

'There's a lot of work to do, now, if we want to try and get the Falconeri firm off the ground again,' I said.

'You don't have to do that. You can create your own business. As long as the workers are looked after, this is your blank sheet,' Mum said.

'You have no idea how relieved I am,' Bianca said, her voice jumpy with every step we took down the slope. 'I can never thank you enough...'

'Lorenzo took it graciously. I certainly didn't expect congratulations from him!' Mum commented.

I threw a glance at Bianca, and saw that her cheeks had grown pink.

'A gallant adversary, I suppose,' I said. I noticed that Mum was looking sideways at Bianca too.

We entered the stables, and a strangely pleasant smell of horses and hay filled my nostrils. The last time I'd been here was before I was sent away – I had a vague memory of small outbuildings with three or four horses that my father and his friends occasionally rode. What I found now was different: the barn that was already there had been extended, and another one added. The place was immaculate, almost licked to perfection: the love that Nora had for her small empire was unmistakable.

Matteo, the man I'd met the first day I was back, was grooming the riotous Ettore, the Maremmano that had almost trampled us, stroking his warm brown neck. Ettore didn't seem riotous today at all: his eyes were semi-closed and he was offering his neck to the grooming.

'Oh hello,' Matteo said cheerfully. 'Are you looking for... *Signora Falconeri*?'

'Yes,' Mum said with a smile. 'It's me. I don't believe you worked here when I lived in Casalta?'

The man was mute for a moment. I was pretty sure what was going through his mind: *She's supposed to be dead.*

'No, but my father did. Vito Campi.'

'Of course! I can see the family resemblance. And your name?'

'Matteo.' He was staring at her like he'd seen a ghost. Which in a way, he had, given that my mother had had a funeral officiated and a casket – empty – buried.

Matteo seemed to give up trying to work out the situation, and gestured towards the back. 'Nora is in the riding barn.'

'Thank you,' Mum said, and he followed us with his eyes, bewildered – he'd seen two long-lost Falconeri women turn up out of the blue in the space of a few weeks. If he hadn't thought that our family was strange before – and I wouldn't have blamed him – he certainly did now.

The riding barn was a light, airy space where Nora gave lessons. She was there, slowly walking alongside a chestnut mare who carried a little girl on her back. We waved, probably more gleefully than she would have expected, considering that we were just back from the supposed sale of the house.

'Just a moment!' Nora called. A couple of circuits later, during which we were almost jumping up and down with excitement, Nora helped the child dismount and took her to her mother, who was waiting by the sidelines.

'Is it done?' she said darkly, walking towards us with strides of her long legs, the girl's helmet in hand.

We looked at each other – in silent agreement, we waited for Mum to give the news. 'Casalta is yours. I'm going to buy it, and give it back to you. This' – she gestured to the barn – 'is all yours still.'

The helmet slipped out of Nora's hand and fell on the dirt with a dull thud.

'But I don't understand.'

'It's *ours*, Nora!' Bianca exclaimed. 'You don't have to rehome your horses; you don't have to sell them or move the school. We can stay in Casalta!'

'How...?'

'It's a long story,' Mum said. 'I suppose the bottom line is that people like my paintings.'

Nora looked at her, long and hard. 'Thank you for doing this,' she said, but there wasn't much feeling in her words. She looked down – and then straight into our mother's face. 'It doesn't change the fact that you abandoned us.'

Mum didn't even blink. 'No. It doesn't.'

'Mum told us what really happened, Nora. You need to know, too.'

'Do I? The end result was that my father's name was covered in mud. That we grew up alone. That you, Lucrezia, never bothered to check on us. You both only thought of yourselves.'

'Nora...' Bianca looked crestfallen. I searched for words, and couldn't find any.

'I'm grateful that you bought Casalta for us. But I can't go any further. Not yet.'

'You need more time,' Mum said. 'I understand...'

'I don't know if I'll ever get there.' Nora's voice was hard, but her expression was one of pain. There was no point in asking myself who suffered the most in all this, who made the most mistakes, who the victim was and who the perpetrator. It didn't matter any more. This wild sister of mine, who was more at ease with horses than with people, who was so beautiful as to turn heads, had built walls as high as mine.

'I promise you, I'll try,' she said. With a last nod of her head, she walked back to the mare and led her out gently.

Mia's reaction was the opposite. She hugged Mum and refused to let her go – not that Mum wanted to be let go. 'I can keep my studio! My frescoes are definitely safe! We don't have to move... I didn't see this coming!'

'What happened to *I know things I'm not supposed to know*?' I teased her.

She raised her shoulders. 'Not this time! I had no idea. And you, Mum... you're a famous painter, now! Is your work in a museum?'

'Not in a museum, no, but art galleries. I do exhibitions a lot. I can't wait for you to see one, to come to England and see the galleries...'

Mia's face fell. 'I can't leave Casalta. I never leave Casalta.'

Bianca was quick to lay a hand on Mia's cheek. 'You don't have to, *tesoro*! You'll only do what you want to do.' Mia looked at Mum, who smiled and nodded, reassuring her.

Mia's enthusiasm was restored. 'Does Nora know?'

'Yes. She's happy, of course.'

Mia studied Mum's face. 'She'll come round. Nora is Nora. I love her, thorns and all.'

Bianca clapped her hands. 'Well, it's time to open a bottle. One of the good ones. Father's *special* ones.'

'The ones he kept for his associates?' Mum asked with glee.

'The very ones! I'll go,' I said, and made my way towards Father's study. It seemed like only yesterday that I couldn't face going inside: now it didn't bother me at all. I stepped in... and I jumped out of my skin, letting out a small cry. There was someone there, sitting at Father's desk, a dark silhouette hunched over the table. I steeled myself and switched on the light, my hand shaking.

It was Gabriella, her face in her hands, crying silently.

My heart was beating hard in my ears – a dark sense of humour made me think, *Thank goodness it's not another parent of mine having come back to life.*

My yelp must have alarmed my sisters and my mum, because they reached me there.

'What happened... Oh, Gabriella!' Bianca ran to her and put her arm around our stepmother's shoulders. We were all shocked by this sudden outburst of emotion. Gabriella had always been on the calm side, and this explosive reaction was out of character, at least as far as I knew. 'I'm so sorry. You must be missing Father so much...'

'That's not why you're crying, Gabriella, is it?' Mum asked gently.

Gabriella shook her head. She was sobbing so hard, she couldn't speak. Something long pushed down had finally erupted.

'The night Fosco died,' Mum said. 'They told me you'd left the room... he was alone, and nobody could have helped.'

My father's wife wiped the tears from her face. It was awful seeing her come undone this way. Why was Mum reminding her of such trauma?

Father's books and folders were watching us from the

shelves. I smelled cigars again – maybe a stale odour left lingering, maybe my imagination.

Mum continued. 'But you were there, weren't you, Gabriella?'

She nodded, still too choked to speak.

I looked from one to the other. 'You were?'

'You didn't give Father his medication,' Bianca said slowly.

Gabriella composed herself a little, and cleared her voice. It came out croaky, full of tears.

'I didn't give it to him. I watched him die. I watched him die, when I could have saved him.'

I think you'd call that *killing someone*.

'What did he do to you?' Mum asked, still in that gentle, compassionate voice.

'To me? Nothing. Nothing at all. He was kind to me, loving. I didn't know there was a *before*. I had no idea that there had been a time when my Fosco was cruel, and he did terrible things. But you see, he wanted to unburden his heart. He wanted a sort of confession, to let it all out. He thought I would understand, I would forgive him. But if he wanted forgiveness, he should have gone to a priest.' That last statement sounded like a sentence, like the announcing of a guilty verdict.

I felt my eyes widen. It was all coming together in my mind, now.

'That night, he told me everything he'd done in the past. Or at least, I want to believe it was everything. How he sent you away, Lucrezia, because you reminded him too much of your mother. He told me what he put you through, Emmeline, what him and Diego did to you.'

'He told you why I was forced to leave...'

'Yes. Which was bad enough. There's something else. Something... unforgivable.'

We waited in silence, while a shiver went down my spine.

'What happened to the Orafi wasn't an accident,' she

continued. 'Fosco sent one of his men to tamper with their car so the brakes would malfunction.'

'Lorenzo was right,' Bianca whispered.

'I never really knew him. I thought I did, but my kind-hearted Fosco never existed. It was never kindness; it was *remorse* that made him be so tender with me. When he told me all those things, he wanted absolution. He expected absolution. But I certainly couldn't absolve him – nobody could, except the people he'd hurt.'

Gabriella swept her hair behind her ears, composed again. Her voice was now a murmur. 'When he saw the horror on my face, he was... surprised. He truly thought I would say it didn't matter, that it was all in the past. When I didn't, I think he couldn't quite believe it. He said he was sorry, that he had night-mares, that he wished he could turn back time... he implored me to understand. But I couldn't. His face turned grey... he couldn't take a breath. His pills were there, within reach, but he couldn't reach them...'

'And you did nothing,' I said.

'I did nothing. *Nothing at all.*'

This quiet, unassuming woman had dismantled my father's house of cards. He had nothing to blackmail her with, no daughters to be staked against her silence, like our mother had; he couldn't terrorise her, or leverage her loyalty, like he'd done with my sisters; he couldn't buy her, like he'd bought Diego and his other lackeys. She wasn't part of the net of misplaced fealty, of reciprocal favours, with Fosco Falconeri at its centre.

'Nobody needs to know!' my mother declared.

'Nobody needs to know,' Bianca, Mia and I repeated at the same time, and it was a little like a ritual, a pact of silence among four women who'd been brought low, but had risen again.

Later, I found Mia in her studio, where she sat on the ground working at her latest painting: she was giving the last touches to Judith's hand, her fingers curled around the knife. Judith was killing Holofernes in an eternal act of justice.

Oh.

She had *known*.

Mia turned around and smiled, her arm raised holding the paintbrush, her head a little tilted. In that moment, she made me think of Artemisia Gentileschi, the woman who'd painted the *Giuditta decapita Oloferne* kept in the Uffizi.

'It's all finished, now,' she said.

# CHAPTER 27

## CASALTA, 29 APRIL 1985

LUCREZIA

Everyone slept late: we were all drained after what had happened the day before. Bianca was already in the living room, phone receiver in hand.

'Morning! Matilde is not here yet, I'm giving her a call, but there's no reply...'

'Good morning, girls!' a voice called from the kitchen. *Matilde!*

We ran through to find her still wrapped in her cardigan, a net bag of plums in her hand. Her face was lined, wan, as if she'd grown ten years older in the space of one night.

'I was just trying to call you,' Bianca said.

'*Tesoro*,' Matilde began and took a step towards Bianca. 'I came to get my things and say goodbye. I can't stay. I can't work for the Orafi.'

Bianca and I looked at each other, smiling, and gave Matilde the news. 'We should have called you yesterday!' I said, guiltily. *But finding out that Gabriella had killed our father kind of distracted us.*

'It's not your fault!' Bianca said at the same time. 'Why don't you sit down? We'll make you breakfast. Please, let us spoil you, for once!'

Matilde didn't move. 'The Signora bought Casalta?'

'Yes!' Bianca exclaimed. 'Please, Matilde, take your cardigan off. Don't leave us. Stay.'

'So, it's all sorted?' she asked in a cautious tone. *Surely it couldn't be*, her eyes said.

'It is all sorted. Only a few signatures to be made at Cavalli's,' Mum said, appearing at the door. She'd had the luggage left at her hotel in Florence sent to Casalta, and she was now dressed in her own clothes, a long blue dress and a purple flowy cardigan, with her red-grey hair in a plait. How distant that first night seemed now, when she'd turned up soaking, with a little bag, like a cat caught in the rain.

'You are staying, aren't you, Matilde?' Bianca said, and Matilde smiled for the first time.

'I'd never leave you, girls. And I'd never work for the Orafi! Oh, signora. You're certainly full of surprises!' she said, and Mum leaned down to give her a hug.

I switched the gas on under the *caffettiera*. 'Honey croissants and coffee for everyone!' I announced.

And so, we sat outside again, all of us, including Gabriella – she was silent and her eyes were puffy, but she was there. Nora too, her hazel eyes sparkling green in the sunshine, wearing a short yellow dress instead of her usual cargo trousers. We stopped Matilde from getting up, and served her hand and foot in spite of her protests.

All the knots were coming loose, one by one. I'd call Claude later today to tell him I wasn't going back – I wasn't looking forward to it, but at the same time I couldn't wait to be truthful, and set him free.

Finally, after Gabriella's unburdening, there were no more secrets to be discovered.

And yet, on this perfect morning, there was an ache in my heart, and it carried the name of Vanni...

When breakfast was finished, Bianca, Mum and I washed the dishes in the kitchen. 'Girls... there's somewhere I need to go, and I'd be so grateful if you could come with me,' Mum said, making sure nobody could overhear.

'Sure, where?'

'Remember I told you about my friend, the man who tried to help me, to help us? I'd like us to go see him.'

'No problem,' I told her. 'What's his name?'

Mum closed her eyes for an instant – all of a sudden, I saw her aura glow white and gold against the early morning light...

'His name is Gherardo Orafi.'

So much for no more secrets to be discovered.

*I should have guessed, I should have guessed, I should have guessed.*

I kept repeating these thoughts with every step that brought us towards the Orafi house. So this was what had started the feud between our families – first Father had called off the engagement with Gherardo's sister, and then... Mum and Gherardo got close and he'd tried to help her; he'd tried to help us.

All the pieces of the jigsaw were now falling into place.

We approached the house from the back – and, just as before, Bruno materialised. His mouth was open to speak, but then he saw Mum, and was silenced.

'*Buongiorno*, signora. I take it you're here to visit Signori Orafi. This way.' If he wondered how it happened that the Signora Falconeri could have returned from the dead, he didn't say.

'What? That's not how you were with me! You were all bodyguard with me!' I protested.

Mum gave me a mischievous look. 'He respects his elders,' she said.

Bruno let us in and the same maid who'd welcomed me, Susanna, came to the door. '*Buongiorno*. Who will I call for?'

We were here to see Gherardo, but I still secretly hoped to see Vanni, of course.

'Signor Gherardo, thank you. You can say it's... it's Emmeline.'

She disappeared and then returned, silent and efficient. 'Please, follow me.'

I threw a longing look to the corridor that led outside and to Vanni's apartment, and followed Susanna.

She took us to a lift – Vanni couldn't have managed the stairs – and we stood silent and immobile for a few seconds, until the door opened to more marble and precious woods. It was like being in a luxurious hotel. The sound of a jazz piano filled the air, a cheerful, sophisticated melody. The maid knocked at a wooden door, and a surprisingly strong voice came from inside.

'Come in.'

The door opened, and in front of us was Lorenzo. He seemed taken aback by our presence, but he recovered quickly, and moved aside.

I made my way slowly inside, gingerly – a sick, invalid man was in here, and I didn't want to upset him... But this wasn't the dark sickroom I'd imagined; it was bright and airy, the windows open and sunrays cutting through it. An old-fashioned record player played the music I'd heard from the hall, and a pile of books sat by the bed... which was empty. I looked around for Signor Orafi and noticed that lovely, colourful paintings decorated every wall. Our vineyards, baskets of grapes, a stormy sky over the hills, the Casalta church, children playing in the square, old women sitting on their doorstep, chatting under a sunny sky, the Casalta fair with its food and wine stands, the graveyard and its sentry cypresses.

I knew that painting style, I was sure.

Either it was Mia's handiwork, or...

'You recognise them, don't you?' a deep, pleasant voice said.

Gherardo Orafi sat in an armchair near the window, a small man so bundled up in blankets, I'd missed him. He seemed frail, with those plaid covers on his legs and thin hands resting on his knees, but lively, benevolent eyes shone from under bushy eyebrows and a grey beard made him look like a small, Mediterranean wizard. He had the same unruly mop of hair that Vanni sported. I was in front of my father's legendary enemy.

'Emmeline!' he said, and his aura rose as gold as my mother's.

'Gherardo!'

She crossed the room and held him in her arms, both crying and laughing at the same time.

'You came back...'

'Finally! I can be with my girls... Oh, Gherardo, it's been so long. Too long.'

'Sit, sit, Emmeline, let me look at you! You haven't changed at all!' His eyes were shiny, and so were Mum's. She sat on a stool beside the armchair, and they held each other's hand.

Lorenzo's face was the picture of shock. In jeans and a black T-shirt, he didn't have the same distant, authoritative air: he seemed younger, and lost. 'You know each other?'

'For many years, yes,' Gherardo said.

'Lorenzo...' Mum began. 'I never meant to bring all this on your family. I'm so sorry...' She turned to Gherardo. 'I was always so afraid to come back and cause more trouble... *This* was my fault,' she said and gestured lightly to the plaid blanket on Gherardo's knees, to the bedside table covered in medicine.

'I knew it. I was sure.' Lorenzo's voice was thin, angry.

'It's done, now, son. Fosco is dead. And you're here, Emmeline!' Gherardo said. Bianca moved closer to Lorenzo, but not too close. There was a wall between them; I could almost *see* it.

'Thank you for all you did for me, back then. I'll be in your debt forever.'

'Oh, but what did I do in the end? I didn't really help. You had to go, and so did Lucrezia... Girls, I can never apologise enough. I always knew what was going on in your home. I tried to protect Emmeline, and you girls, but I failed.'

Lorenzo looked from one to the other. 'You two... had an affair?'

Gherardo shook his head. 'No. Neither of us wanted that. We cared for each other too much...' He squeezed her hand.

'What about Mum? Your *wife*?' Lorenzo spat out.

'Lorenzo, you've always known that the marriage between your mother and me was loveless. She married me because her parents wanted her to; she stayed with me only to save appearances. It's been a long, hard road for both of us. We tried to compensate with friendship, companionship... but it didn't work. She resented me so deeply, she couldn't stand the sight of me. But you always knew that, didn't you?'

Lorenzo looked like a little lost child. 'I tried to fix things. To take care of everyone. That didn't work either.'

'You were the lynchpin of your family, all these years,' Bianca whispered, her face flushed pink.

Mum looked around. 'Fosco Falconeri tried to destroy us all, in different ways. But here we are. Together.'

*Not all of us*, I thought sadly, and looked out of the window to the apartment below, thinking of Vanni.

# CHAPTER 28

## CASALTA, 30 APRIL 1985

LUCREZIA

I sat on Bianca's bed and dialled Claude's number. It rang out, and my heart sank – I was determined to tell him I wasn't going back except to help him and Sophie tie up loose ends so that his work wouldn't be affected by my sudden departure. His work was the most important thing in his life, and it would have been cruel to do any damage to that. I didn't want the situation to drag on, but Claude was often out for work, or socialising. Work, parties, events: that was our life. Maybe I'd call the office and ask Sophie to arrange a call from him, whenever he was free.

I'd make one last try. I dialled again, not holding much hope – if only someone would invent something like Bruno's walkie-talkie, but which could reach people further away... something we could keep in our pockets to be in touch with people at all times.

Oh. Being in touch with people at all times wasn't the best idea, probably...

I jumped when I heard Claude's familiar greeting, efficient and to the point, like him:

'Claude.'

I slipped easily back into my French. 'It's me... hello.'

'*Lucresiah*... I was almost out of the door. Can I call you back? Or even better, you're calling to tell me you're coming back and we'll speak face to face?'

He was so straight to the point, I didn't see the reason for convoluted, emotional explanations. 'Claude... I'm not coming back.'

There was a pause. 'You mean you'll be there a little longer?' I was sure that he understood what I meant, but I played along.

'I'm not coming back *at all*. I'm staying here, with my family. But I'll help tide Sophie over, of course...'

'But... but it's madness! You leave a lucrative job in the best city in the world!'

'Claude.'

'Yes?'

'You didn't mention *us*.'

'What do you mean?'

'You didn't mention me and you. You said I had a lucrative job in a beautiful city. You didn't say "come back to me",' I explained without resentment. 'It was all about that, our relationship, wasn't it? The work, the city, success and fame. Our relationship had no other reason to be.'

'It's the way I am, *Lucresiah*. You always knew... and also... You didn't let it happen. You never let me in. You didn't let anyone in.'

I took a deep breath. He was right. 'I'm sorry.'

'Can we talk about it? Is there anything I can say...?'

'I'm so sorry,' I repeated.

Silence.

'Claude, you'll be fine. You'll find another assistant, and

another girlfriend, maybe one person to cover both roles, like I did. You're a great chef and a committed public figure...'

'Sounds like a *communiqué* for a magazine.'

'It used to be my job, after all.' I smiled.

'And you were good at it. Well, what will you do now?'

'Help run the family estate. There's a lot to do, here,' I answered, and butterflies began dancing in my stomach. The possibilities! I hadn't felt such hope and such joy in so long, I'd forgotten what it was like.

'You will be a great success. Whatever you do.'

'Sounds like a reference letter,' I joked, like he'd done.

'I was your boss, after all.' I could hear the smile in his voice, and it was a relief, but also a vague achy feeling, that after years together neither of us was that distraught about breaking up.

'And you were a good boss. Goodbye, Claude.'

'Goodbye, *Lucresiah*.'

Just as I was putting down the phone, Matilde called me downstairs.

'There's a car for you,' she said.

'A car? I didn't order a taxi...' I peeped from the living room window – Maurizio, the Orafi driver, touched his hat lightly. I went out to speak to him.

It was a windy day, and I had to keep my hair away from my face as I leaned down. Suddenly, I worried that something might have happened to Signor Orafi.

'*Buongiorno*, Maurizio. Is everything okay?'

'Everything good, signorina. Signor Vanni asked me to come get you, if you'd like to come with me.'

'Vanni didn't say anything to me about it...'

'He mentioned that you might decide not to come. Will I go back and tell him?'

'No, of course not. Just give me a moment.'

I ran inside and grabbed my handbag – thankfully I was presentable, wearing the red linen dress and my usual high heels, which had been pretty uncomfortable with all the walking I'd had to do in the last few days, but which I couldn't quite give up.

'Have fun,' Mia and Mum called from the top of the stairs, their hands equally bright with paint.

I didn't know what to answer – I wasn't sure what all this was about. The last time we'd spoken, Vanni had been adamant he didn't want anything to do with me.

I just wanted him to be happy, without or without me.

Maurizio opened the door and I slipped inside, my heart beating hard.

'Are we going to the Orafi house?' I asked.

'No, signorina. He asked me to take you somewhere else. Are you comfortable for me to do that?'

'Of course,' I said, and tried to relax for the rest of the journey. We drove towards the outskirts of Florence, until we arrived at a squat, red-roofed building with a ramp in the front. A blue-lettered sign said, '*Centro Medico*'. A clinic?

Maurizio parked the car and opened my door. 'Thank you. Here?' I asked.

'Yes. Signor Vanni is waiting inside,' he said, and I followed him to the reception. A blonde woman in a white and blue uniform shirt welcomed us.

'Signorina Falconeri, for Vanni Orafi.'

'Oh, yes. He let us know. Please, come in,' she said. I thanked Maurizio and followed the rubber-shoed lady down a corridor that smelled of disinfectant. The environment was clean, bordering on sterile, but colourful children's pictures decorated the walls and plants in vases brightened the space.

'Is this... a clinic?'

'It's a rehabilitation clinic for people with spine and brain injuries,' she said. 'Did Vanni not tell you?'

Why had he asked me to come here?

'Rehabilitation? But his accident happened years ago...'

'He still needs physio. It's nice he wanted to share this aspect of his life with you. You're such a good-looking couple!' she gushed.

'We're not...'

Vanni had come out of a side door, and a woman in a maroon tracksuit was behind him. Vanni too was wearing a tracksuit, grey with a black stripe on the side, and he looked very different from the last time I'd seen him. He'd kept the beard, but he'd had his hair cut; but the biggest difference was in his eyes. They were still dark, still full of a certain sadness, but resolute.

'Lucrezia. Thank you for agreeing to come here.'

'Of course.'

'I wanted to show you what my life is like. What the life of a paraplegic is like,' he said. His gaze was serious, almost solemn.

I nodded.

'This is Carla, my physiotherapist. She's been helping me since I ended up in this.'

'And it's been a pleasure,' Carla said as she shook my hand. Her cheerful smile contrasted with Vanni's gravity. She was so tiny, I wondered how she managed patients as tall as Vanni. 'Well, shall we begin with arms and shoulders? Ease our way in?'

'Sure,' Vanni said, and, using his arms, he made the transition to a wide metal chair, painted bright yellow.

After ten minutes, I was in awe of both my friend, and Carla. The exercises were gruelling. Vanni's skin was covered in sweat that he dried with a bandana he kept tied to his wrist. Carla was simultaneously sweet, almost tender, and unrelenting

– her job, it seemed to me, went beyond the physical to also include motivating him and keeping him strong.

Carla helped him onto a mat on the ground, and now the hard bit began.

'This is to avoid the muscles becoming rigid and seizing up,' she explained. She began to move and stretch his legs, in a way that made it look as if she was doing all the work – but Vanni was holding onto the ground on both sides, grimacing in pain.

'Too much?' Carla asked.

'I'm fine,' he murmured. He wasn't fine. I don't know how it could be that he was in pain, if he couldn't feel his legs – but somehow the muscles that Carla's exercises were stimulating could still hurt, and they did. I felt my nails sinking into my palms as I saw Vanni squeeze his eyes closed...

'You did well! So well!' Carla said. She looked across the room and met my eyes.

A gentle breeze blew on us as we sat on the terracotta terrace of a trattoria, waiting for our meal. The sun shone higher and warmer than it had since I'd arrived: spring was coming into its own.

'You look different,' I told Vanni. 'I can't put my finger on it, but something about you is... different.'

'I could say the same thing. You look lighter. Maybe it's the whole Casalta thing being resolved...'

'And being out of a relationship that wasn't working.'

'Your French boyfriend...'

'Claude. We're not together any more.'

'I suppose I should bring myself to say that I'm sorry...'

I laughed. 'Don't worry. I'm not sorry, and neither is he. I'm glad to say I didn't break his heart in the slightest.'

Vanni refilled my glass. 'Your mum has been incredible! Even Lorenzo had to admit it.'

'I know. Who would have thought? She's been through so much, Vanni. One day I'll tell you what my father did to her.'

Vanni shook his head. 'I want us to put this all behind us. All the evil things that your father did. He's dead and gone...' *Thanks to Gabriella*, I thought but obviously didn't say. '...and we're learning to overcome the consequences. Yes, I am different. After what you told me when you came to visit me. I was feeling sorry for myself. Self-pity is the worst poison, isn't it? Worse than anger.'

'I should know. I felt sorry for myself for years.'

He took my hand, and his touch made me smile again. I laid my other hand on his and drank in the feeling. I wanted to kiss those hands, to kiss him, to be with him and never part again.

'Maybe we can come out of it together?'

'Absolutely, completely yes. Yes.'

It was really us. The boy and girl sitting side by side in the treehouse, the man and woman separated and almost broken. Now we were together, and whole.

'But I need you to see what my life is really like. To see what it's like being with someone who has so many limitations. So many challenges. What you saw today is just the beginning. There are medical appointments, and it takes hours to do anything, and there are so many places where I can't go, and—'

'Wait. I thought we were going to come out of self-pity together?' I smiled.

'This is not self-pity. This is my reality. I couldn't face you telling me what Cristina told me, and...'

'Hey. Hey. Don't be afraid. I lost you for twelve years; I have no intention of losing you again.'

'But does it not scare you, Lucrezia?'

'Being with you doesn't scare me. You know what does?'

'What?'

'Being *without* you.'

'Matteo?'

'Signorina Lucrezia. Hello. Are you looking for your sister?'

'No, I was looking for you. But please, call me Lucrezia.'

'Lucrezia, then. What can I help you with?'

'A favour. I'm sorry to ask, and please feel free to say no... It'd be a few hours' work, and it's not really in your job description...'

'I'm sure Nora can spare me for a bit. These guys here are all clean and fed and have enjoyed plenty of fresh air and exercise. Haven't we?' The chestnut horse Matteo was beside rubbed its muzzle against his face.

'In that case, thank you! Can I show you...'

'Sure.'

He followed me to the small, sparse pine wood at the back of the house. It was kept simply, grass on the ground covered in pine needles and ferns along the slope of the hill. Among the pines, there was one with a low branch that extended out as if wanting to give passers-by a hug. A bit further on, the little door to Mia's studio opened in the stone wall.

I considered for a moment if I should give Matteo the bare bones of the project, but then I decided to tell him what I had in mind. I felt that if I did, he would embrace the spirit of what I was trying to do.

'You know Vanni Orafi, don't you?'

'Everyone knows the Orafi around here. I used to play with Vanni when we were children.'

'So did I, in a treehouse. You see, he built that treehouse; he loved it. But he had an accident...'

'I heard. Bad luck. I'm so sorry.' It wasn't really bad luck, but never mind.

'Now he can't climb trees any more. So, I thought...' I gestured to the pine and its low-hanging branch, and Matteo didn't let me finish the sentence.

'To make a ground-level treehouse,' he said matter-of-factly, as if it was the most obvious idea in the world.

'Exactly!'

I considered this man's warm, kind eyes and his steady manner – he exuded calm, and he had a solid, rugged hand-someness. I wondered if he and Nora were just co-workers, or friends – or more than friends. They would make a lovely couple.

'Do you have a project in mind?'

'I do! This is my project,' I said and took out a piece of paper from the folds of my skirt. 'Please ignore the fact that I absolutely can't draw.' I laughed.

'No, it's good. Well, leave it with me...'

'Leave what with me?' Nora appeared behind me and made me jump.

'Are all my sisters silent as cats?' I said, thinking of Mia, who could pretty much make herself invisible.

'I'm used to moving quietly so I don't startle the horses.'

'Lucrezia asked me to help her with a project,' Matteo said.

Nora shrugged. 'Sure, no problem. Can I see?'

After all that had been said between Nora and me I was a little wary, but I showed her my piece of paper. 'It's for Vanni,' I specified. I expected her to balk, but she didn't.

'Mmmm.'

She turned the paper round and round in her hand. I was sure she was about to say something about the Orafi being our father's sworn enemies, and then storm off...

'Well, all these bits with picnic baskets and blankets and cute things are Bianca's domain, but I can help with the struc-ture. Matteo and I can have it done in a few hours.'

I stared at her.

'What?' she snapped.

'Nothing. Nothing. Well, thank you.'

Nora shrugged. I had the feeling she wanted to say something else, but she didn't. She walked away. Matteo lingered for a moment more.

'You might have just tamed her,' Matteo whispered in my ear.

# CHAPTER 29

## CASALTA, 1 MAY 1985

### LUCREZIA

Matteo and I were admiring our masterpiece, when I heard the phone ringing from inside the house.

'Thank you, thank you, thank you, Matteo! This is amazing!' I gave him a peck on the cheek. 'Sorry, must run!'

A peck on the cheek? The old Lucrezia wouldn't even have *touched* another human. I'd changed, or maybe I'd become the person I was always meant to be.

'It's been a pleasure,' he said and patted one of the smooth, soft wood planks while I turned around and ran.

'Hello?' I answered, out of breath. It was Gherardo.

'Lucrezia, my dear! I hope I'm not interrupting anything. I need your help, if I might ask.'

'Of course.'

'I have a nice lady here who's helping us redesign the house. And I need both your advice and Bianca's,' Gherardo said. 'We really want everything spruced up. A new beginning.'

I laughed. Was he for real? This was not a request I would

have expected from my father's former archenemy. 'Signor Orafi?'

'Gherardo!'

'Gherardo. I don't know anything about interior design. And if you listen to Bianca your whole house will be pink and frilly.'

'Excuse me!' Bianca, who'd just come down, elbowed me. I signalled to her to come and listen, and we sat cheek to cheek with the receiver between us.

'Wouldn't it be better to ask Mum and Mia?'

'I did, but they're busy, and the designer can only come today.'

'Gherardo,' Bianca said.

'Yes.'

'Since when were you so into decorating?'

'I've always been, my dear. Can I send you the car?'

'It's okay, we'll drive there.'

'Does this make sense to you?' I asked Bianca as we stepped out in the sunshine.

'Nope. It sounds strange. But he asked for our help, so let's go.'

The following two hours were spent looking at fabric swatches with Gherardo and a woman with talon-like scarlet nails and enormous hair, named Annasara. 'Forest green. Very *manly*,' she gushed.

Signor Gherardo looked like he was somewhere between losing the will to live and falling asleep. I could relate.

'Can I take you signorine for a visionary stroll around the estate?' Annasara offered.

I gave Gherardo a pleading look. 'Sure,' Bianca said wearily, always helpful.

At that moment, the phone on Gherardo's bedside table rang, and he lifted the receiver.

'A-ha. A-ha. A-ha. Girls, you're needed back home,' he said.

Bianca and I exchanged a look. It was all too strange.

'Well, I'm sorry we couldn't be much help, but I'm sure that Vanni and Lorenzo...' Bianca began.

'Sì, sì, they'll do it.' Gherardo waved her off. 'It's time you go.'

'Oh, sure.' He was almost throwing us out of the house.

'You're probably tired,' Bianca said, considerate as always.

'Exhausted!' Gherardo adjusted his position on the armchair, and I saw that under his house jacket he wore steel-grey linen trousers and a white shirt. A very stylish outfit. Probably a little too stylish for the house, even by Gherardo's standard?

'Can we get you anything before we go?' Bianca asked.

'I'm perfectly fine, thank you. Susanna will see you out.' He rang a bell and Susanna arrived, ready to take us and Annasara to the door.

'What was all that about?' I said, once inside the car.

Bianca shrugged. 'Maybe he's a little confused?'

'Bianca, he's unwell physically, but his mind is perfectly sound.'

'Well, we'll ask Mum. Poor Gherardo.'

'*Forest green is so manly,*' I imitated the designer, and we both dissolved in fits of laughter.

'Shame we missed the *visionary stroll,*' Bianca said drily.

'We have visitors,' I said as soon as we arrived at the house. Cars were lined up outside the courtyard, under the dryads' watchful eye.

'That's Gherardo's car? What...'

Mum stood in front of the kitchen door, preventing us from getting inside. 'To the gardens, girls!' she commanded us. She wore a bright flowery dress down to her ankles and a rose behind her ear. The penny was beginning to drop.

'Oh, Lulu! I think...' Bianca began, taking my arm. 'It's the first of May, our birthday. With all that happened, we forgot all about it!'

The rose garden was decorated with red and pink ribbons, and a table laden with food and wine had been set up. Nora and Mia were there, and Gabriella. Vanni, Lorenzo, even Gherardo! How had he made it here so fast? Matilde stood beside Gabriella, and I spotted Matteo, Pera, even... was that Cavalli? Everyone began intoning 'Happy Birthday', and to my shame I started to cry. Thankfully Bianca was crying too...

So did Cavalli. For some reason. 'He begged me to come,' Mum said, following my gaze. 'Didn't have the heart to say no.'

'I can't believe you did all this for us! You're right, Bianca, with all that happened I forgot about our birthday!'

'I never forgot. Every first of May, I celebrated you,' Mum said quietly.

Next thing I knew, Vanni was beside me. The look we exchanged said everything – and although we were in a crowd, I had to bend over and kiss him.

The party was in full swing. There was way more food than we could eat, as is the case in every Italian celebration. The wine was flowing, and old-fashioned music played in the background, with Nora and Matteo dancing, and Matilde twirling around with Pera. Mia was dancing too, on her own, in Mia's style. Bianca and Lorenzo, instead, sat at opposite ends of the table, Bianca beside Mum, Lorenzo beside Gherardo.

When the party was folding and people beginning to leave, I took Vanni's hand and led him behind the house, where his surprise was waiting for him.

Matteo and Nora had done a wonderful job. Planks of wood made a sort of open box with the tree branch for a roof and pine needles for a floor, and blankets decorated and softened the walls. It was almost identical to our old treehouse, except it was on the ground. I'd threaded fairy lights in the branches, like fireflies in the twilight gloom.

'Oh, Lucrezia!'

'Do you like it?'

'It's amazing! How did you...?'

'My sister and a friend helped. Come,' I said, and helped him on the ground. He settled under the branch-roof, and I sat beside him. From under a blanket I revealed a basket with a bottle of wine and two glasses. 'Ta-da!'

He laughed. 'Ta-da indeed!'

'To us.' We clinked the glasses together.

'To us. I didn't think it was possible,' he whispered. His face looked so perfect, so beloved, in the half-gloom and twinkling lights.

'To be together again?'

'To come to life again,' he said, and kissed me, and there was no more reason to speak.

# EPILOGUE

LUCREZIA

Bianca, Nora, Mia and I walked up the hill, barefoot and with jumpers thrown over our dresses, as the sun was rising.

The four of us stood together, overlooking Casalta, with the breeze in our hair and dew on our feet and on the hems of our dresses.

The Falconeri sisters were reunited, at last. And I knew, I knew as sure as the sky above us and the ground below us, that we'd never be torn apart again.

# A LETTER FROM DANIELA

Dear readers,

Thank you once again for following me in another adventure! If you'd like to keep up to date with all my latest releases, you can sign up at the following link. Your email address will never be shared, and you can unsubscribe at any time.

*www.bookouture.com/daniela-sacerdoti*

This time we're going to Tuscany, to a village by the name of Casalta, not far from Florence. I think I can safely say that the Tuscan countryside is one of the loveliest places in the world and has inspired writers and artists for hundreds of years. To get in the mood, I reread *A Room With a View* by E.M. Forster and I was once again blown away by his soul-stirring descriptions of Florence, and reminded how beauty can truly change the course of our life.

*The Tuscan Sister* is the first of four books, each telling the story of a Falconeri sister: Lucrezia, Bianca, Eleonora and Maria. Their mother named them after four portraits by the painter Bronzino, kept in the Galleria degli Uffizi, the famous museum in Florence. If you happen to be there, go say hello to my girls, it's worth it!

In this novel, I'm delving into the depths of family constellations: love and resentment, guilt and loyalty, and all the complicated feelings that go with family ties. I fell in love with the idea of telling the stories of four sisters, painting their world one novel at a time – and in each one, hinting at themes that will be explored in the following one. So if while reading about Lucrezia in this book you feel that there's more to unravel about the other sisters – fear not, each of them will have the spotlight in the following three novels.

Dear readers, as always, I appreciate you more than I can say. There are so many distractions now, so many claims to our time, that choosing one story and focusing on it has become a feat of concentration. So thank you for choosing my Casalta sisters, whether this is your first tale of mine or you are a veteran of my worlds.

Talking about my worlds – I've buried a little Easter egg within *The Tuscan Sister*, for long-time fans: a connection to my Scottish novels, starting from the Glen Avich quartet down to my Seal Island stories. A family link. If you find it, I'd love for you to let me know in a review.

No writer writes in a vacuum – writer and reader are both sides of a story which, otherwise, would be a monologue. So thank you for giving my characters a face in your imagination, for relating them to your lives, for letting them take you somewhere else, sometime else, for a little while.

Daniela Sacerdoti

Caravino, Italy, 21 February 2024

## ACKNOWLEDGEMENTS

My heartfelt thanks to:

Simona Sanfilippo: you truly are seed, root and leaf to this windswept writer.

Jessie Botterill, my former editor, with endless gratitude.

Jess Whitlum-Cooper, my current editor, and everyone on the publishing team – Imogen, Peta, Saidah, Richard, thank you!

Francesca Meinardi and Irene Zaino, as always in the eons of time we've known each other.

Elisabetta, my mind-clearing walks partner.

Lucrezia Riberi, colleague and inspiration.

My beloved neighbours and community in our little village – only we know its preciousness.

Ivana Fornera and Edoardo Sacerdoti, my constellation.

But most of all, thank you to the earth, the sky and the sun: Ross, Sorley and Luca. You are everything to me.

# PUBLISHING TEAM

**Turning a manuscript into a book requires the efforts of many people. The publishing team at Bookouture would like to acknowledge everyone who contributed to this publication.**

## Commercial
Lauren Morrissette
Hannah Richmond
Imogen Allport

## Cover design
Sarah Whittaker

## Data and analysis
Mark Alder
Mohamed Bussuri

## Editorial
Jess Whitlum-Cooper
Imogen Allport

## Copyeditor
Rhian McKay

## Proofreader
Becca Allen

Printed in Great Britain
by Amazon

47115433R00158